There were only five candidates now. The idol had moved. Its raised foot had fallen, crushing one of the heads. Its other foot had risen. The body of the man who had been two to my left lay beneath it. His head, held by the hair, dangled from one of the idol's hands. Before the lights had gone out that hand had clutched a bunch of bones. Another hand that had clutched a sword still did so, but now that blade glistened. There was blood on the idol's lips and chin and fangs. Its eyes gleamed.

How had they managed it? Was there some mechanical engine inside the idol? Had the priest and his assistant done the murder? They would have had to move fast.

The priests seemed startled, too.

TOR BOOKS BY GLEN COOK

AN ILL FATE MARSHALLING
REAP THE EAST WIND
THE SWORDBEARER*
THE TOWER OF FEAR

THE BLACK COMPANY:

The First Chronicle of the Black Company:
  THE BLACK COMPANY

The Second Chronicle of the Black Company:
  SHADOWS LINGER

The Third Chronicle of the Black Company:
  THE WHITE ROSE

The Fourth Chronicle of the Black Company:
  SHADOW GAMES: First Book of the South

THE SILVER SPIKE

The Fifth Chronicle of the Black Company:
  DREAMS OF STEEL: Second Book of the South

*forthcoming

GLEN COOK
DREAMS OF STEEL

SECOND BOOK OF THE SOUTH

**THE FIFTH
CHRONICLE
OF THE
BLACK
COMPANY**

TOR
fantasy

A TOM DOHERTY ASSOCIATES BOOK
NEW YORK

DREAMS OF STEEL

Copyright © 1990 by Glen Cook

A Tor Book
Published by Tom Doherty Associates, Inc.
49 West 24th Street
New York, N.Y. 10010

Cover art by Keith Berdak

ISBN: 0-812-50210-8

First edition: April 1990

Printed in the United States of America

0 9 8 7 6 5 4 3 2 1

For Keith, because I like his style

Chapter One

Many months have passed. Much has happened and much has slipped from my memory. Insignificant details have stuck with me while important things have gotten away. Some things I know only from third parties and more I can only guess. How often have my witnesses perjured themselves?

It did not occur to me, till this time of enforced inactivity befell me, that an important tradition was being overlooked, that no one was recording the deeds of the Company. I dithered then. It seemed a presumption for me to take up the pen. I have no training. I am no historian nor even much of a writer. Certainly I don't have Croaker's eye or ear or wit.

So I shall confine myself to reporting facts as I recall them. I hope the tale is not too much colored by my own presence within it, nor by what it has done to me.

With that apologia, herewith, this addition to the Annals of the Black Company, in the tradition of Annalists before me, the Book of Lady.

—Lady, Annalist, Captain

Chapter Two

The elevation was not good. The distance was extreme. But Willow Swan knew what he was seeing. "They're getting their butts kicked."

Armies contended before the city Dejagore, at the center of a circular, hill-encompassed plain. Swan and three companions watched.

Blade grunted agreement. Cordy Mather, Swan's oldest friend, said nothing. He just tried to kick the stuffing out of a rock.

The army they favored was losing.

Swan and Mather were whites, blond and brunette, hailing from Roses, a city seven thousand miles north of the killing ground. Blade was a black giant of uncertain origins, a dangerous man with little to say. Swan and Mather had rescued him from crocodiles a few years earlier. He had stuck. The three were a team.

Swan cursed softly, steadily, as the battle situation worsened.

The fourth man did not belong. The team would

not have had him if he volunteered. People called him Smoke. Officially, he was the fire marshall of Taglios, the city-nation whose army was losing. In reality he was the Taglian court wizard. He was a nut-brown little man whose very existence annoyed Swan.

"That's your army out there, Smoke," Willow growled. "It goes down, you go down. Bet the Shadowmasters would love to lay hands on you." Sorceries yowled and barked on the battlefield. "Maybe make marmalade out of you. Unless you've cut a deal already."

"Ease up, Willow," Mather said. "He's doing something."

Swan looked at the butternut-colored runt. "Sure enough. But what?"

Smoke had his eyes closed. He mumbled and muttered. Sometimes his voice crackled and sizzled like bacon in an overheated pan.

"He ain't doing nothing to help the Black Company. You quit talking to yourself, you old buzzard. We got a problem. Our guys are getting whipped. You want to try to turn that around? Before I turn you over my knee?"

The old man opened his eyes. He stared across the plain. His expression was not pleasant. Swan doubted that the little geek's eyes were good enough to make out details. But you never knew with Smoke. With him everything was mask and pretense.

"Don't be a moron, Swan. I'm one man, too little and too old. There are Shadowmasters down there. They can stomp me like a roach."

Swan fussed and grumbled. People he knew were dying.

Smoke snapped, "All I can do—all any of us can do—is attract attention. Do you really want the Shadowmasters to notice you?"

"They're just the Black Company, eh? They took their pay, they take their chances? Even if forty thousand Taglians go down with them?"

Smoke's lips shrank into a mean little prune.

On the plain a human tide washed around a mound where the Black Company standard had been planted for a last stand. The tide swept on toward the hills.

"You wouldn't be happy about the way things are going, would you?" Swan's voice was dangerous, no longer carping. Smoke was a political animal, worse than a crocodile. Crocs might eat their young but their treacheries were predictable.

Though irked, Smoke replied in a voice almost tender. "They *have* accomplished more than we dreamed."

The plain was dense with the dead and dying, man and beast. Mad war elephants careened around, respecting no allegiance. Only one Taglian legion had maintained its integrity. It had fought its way to a city gate and was covering the flight of other Taglians. Flames rose beyond the city from a military encampment. The Company had scored that much success against the apparent victors.

Smoke said, "They've lost a battle but they saved Taglios. They slew one of the Shadowmasters. They've made it impossible for the others to attack Taglios. Those will spend their remaining troops recapturing Dejagore."

Swan sneered. "Just pardon me if I don't dance for joy. I liked those guys. I didn't like the way you planned to shaft them."

Smoke's temper was strained. "They weren't fighting for Taglios, Swan. They wanted to use us to hammer through the Shadowlands to Khatovar. Which could be worse than a Shadowmasters' conquest."

Swan knew rationalization when he stepped in it. "And because they wouldn't lick your boots, even if they were willing to save your asses from the Shadowmasters, you figure it's handy, them getting caught here. A pity, say I. Would've been some swell show, watching your footwork if they'd come up winners and you had to deliver your end of the bargain."

"Ease up, Willow," Mather said.

Swan ignored him. "Call me a cynic, Smoke. But I'd bet about anything you and the Radisha had it scoped out to screw them from the start. Eh? Wouldn't do to have them slice through the Shadowlands. But why the hell not? I never did get that part."

"It ain't over yet, Swan," Blade said. "Wait. Smoke going to get his turn to cry."

The others gawked at Blade. He spoke so seldom that when he did they knew it meant something. What did he know?

Swan asked, "You see something I missed?"

Cordy snapped, "Damn it, will you calm down?"

"Why the hell should I? The whole damned world is swamped by conniving old farts like Smoke. They been screwing the rest of us since the gods started keeping time. Look at this little poof. Keeps whining about how he's got to lay low and not let the Shadowmasters find out about him. *I* think that means he's got no balls. That Lady . . . You know who *she* used to be? *She* had balls enough to face them. You give that half a think you'll realize how she laid more on the line than this old freak ever could."

"Calm down, Willow."

"Calm down, hell. It ain't right. Somebody's got to tell old farts like this to go suck rocks."

Blade grunted agreement. But Blade didn't like anyone in authority.

Swan, not as upset as he put on, noted that Blade was in position to whack the wizard if he got obnoxious.

Smoke smiled. "Swan, once upon a time all us old farts were young loudmouths like you."

Mather stepped between them. "Enough! Instead of squabbling, how about we get out of here before that mess catches up with us?" Remnants of the battle swirled around the toes of the foothills. "We can gather the garrisons from the towns north of here and collect everybody at Ghoja."

Swan agreed. Sourly. "Yeah. Maybe some of the Company made it." He glowered at Smoke.

The old man shrugged. "If some get out they can train a real army. They'd have time enough now."

"Yeah. And if the Prahbrindrah Drah and the Radisha was to get off their butts they might even line up a few real allies. Maybe come up with a wizard with a hair on his ass. One who wouldn't spend his whole life hiding out in the weeds."

Mather started down the back of the hill. "Come on, Blade. Let them bicker."

After several seconds Smoke confessed, "He's right, Swan. Let's get on with it."

Willow tossed his long golden hair, looked at Blade. Blade jerked his head toward the horses below the hill. "All right." Swan took a last look at the city and plain where the Black Company had died. "But what's right is right and what's wrong is wrong."

"And what's practical is practical and what's needful is necessary. Let's go."

Swan walked. He would remember that remark. He was determined to have the last word. "Bullshit, Smoke. That's bullshit. I seen a new side of you today. I don't like it and I don't trust it. I'm going to watch you like your conscience."

They mounted up and headed north.

Chapter Three

In those days the Company was in service to the Prahbrindrah Drah of Taglios. That prince was too easygoing to master a numerous, factious people like the Taglians. But his natural optimism and forgiving nature were offset by his sister, the Radisha Drah. A small, dark, hard woman, the Radisha had a will of sword steel and the conscience of a hurtling stone.

While the Black Company and the Shadowmasters contested possession of Dejagore, or Stormgard, the Prahbrindrah Drah held an audience three hundred miles to the north.

The prince stood five and a half feet tall. Though dark, his features were caucasic. He glowered at the priests and engineers before him. He wanted to throw them out. But in god-ridden Taglios no one offended the priesthoods.

He spied his sister signalling from the shadowed rear of the chamber. "Excuse me." He walked out. Bad manners they would tolerate. He joined the Radisha. "What is it?"

"Not here."

"Bad news?"

"Not now." The Radisha strode off. "Majarindi looked unhappy."

"He got his hand caught in a monkey trap. He insisted we build a wall because Shaza has been having holy visions. But once the others demanded a share he sang a different song. I asked if Shaza had begun having un-visions. He wasn't amused."

"Good."

The Radisha led her brother through tortuous passages. The palace was ancient. Additions were cobbled on during every reign. No one knew the labyrinth whole except Smoke.

The Radisha went to one of the wizard's secret places, a room sheltered from eavesdroppers by the old man's finest spells. The Prahbrindrah Drah shut the door. "Well?"

"A pigeon brought a message. From Smoke."

"Bad news?"

"Our mercenaries have been defeated at Stormgard." The Shadowmasters called Dejagore Stormgard.

"Badly?"

"Is there any other . . . ?"

"Yes." Before the appearance of the Shadowmasters Taglios had been a pacifist state. But when that danger first beckoned the Prahbrindrah had exhumed the ancient strategikons. "Were they annihilated? Routed? How badly did they hurt the Shadowmasters? Is Taglios in danger?"

"They shouldn't have crossed the Main."

"They had to harry the survivors from Ghoja ford. They're the professionals, Sis. We said we wouldn't second-guess or interfere. We didn't believe they could win at Ghoja, so we're way ahead. Give me details."

"A pigeon isn't a condor." The Radisha made a face. "They marched down with a mob of liberated slaves, took Dejagore by stealth, destroyed Storm-

shadow and wounded Shadowspinner. But today
Moonshadow appeared with a fresh army. Casualties were heavy on both sides. Moonshadow may
have been killed. But we lost. Some of the troops
retreated into the city. The rest scattered. Most of
the mercenaries, including the captain and his
woman, were killed."

"Lady is dead? That's a pity. She was exquisite."

"You're a lustful ape."

"I am, aren't I? But she did stop hearts wherever
she went."

"And never noticed. The only man she saw was her
captain. That Croaker character."

"Are you miffed because he only had eyes for her?"
She gave him a savage look.

"What's Smoke doing?"

"Fleeing north. Blade, Swan, and Mather will try
to rally the survivors at Ghoja."

"I don't like that. Smoke should've stayed down
there. Rallied them there, to support the men in the
city. You don't give away ground you've gained."

"Smoke is scared the Shadowmasters will find out
about him."

"They don't know? That would surprise me." The
Prahbrindrah shrugged. "What's he saving himself
for? I'm going down there."

She laughed.

"What?"

"You can't. Those idiot priests would steal everything but your eyes. Stay. Keep them occupied with
their idiot wall. I'll go. And I'll kick Smoke's butt till
he gets off it and does something."

The prince sighed. "You're right. But go quietly.
They behave better when they think you're watching."

"They didn't miss me last time."

"Don't leave me twisting in the wind. They're hard
to deal with when they know more than I do."

"I'll keep them off balance." She patted his arm.
"Go shock them with your turnaround. Work them

into a wall-building frenzy. Get benevolent toward whichever cult shows the most productivity. Get them cutting each other's throats."

The Prahbrindrah grinned boyishly. That was the game he loved. That was the way to accumulate power. Get the priests to disarm themselves.

Chapter Four

It was a bizarre little parade. At its head was a black thing that could not decide if it was a tree stump or someone weirdly built carrying a box under one arm. Behind that a man floated a yard off the ground, feet foremost, inelegantly sprawled. An arrow had pierced his chest. It still protruded from his back. He was alive, but barely.

Behind the floating man was another with a lance through him. He drifted a dozen feet up, alive and in pain, sometimes writhing like an animal with a broken spine. Two riderless horses followed him, both black stallions bigger than any war charger.

Crows by the hundred circled above, coming and going like scouts.

The parade climbed the hills east of Stormgard, moving in twilight. Once it paused, remained motionless twenty minutes while a scatter of Taglian fugitives passed. They saw nothing. There was magic at work there.

The column continued moving by night. The crows

continued flying, formed a rearguard, watched for
something. Several times they cawed at shifting
shadows, but settled down quickly. False alarms?

The party halted ten miles from the beleaguered
city. The thing leading spent hours collecting brush
and deadwood, piled it in a deep crack in a granitic
hillside. Then it seized the floating lance, dragged its
victim off, stripped him down.

A bitter, remote, whispering voice exclaimed,
"This isn't one of the Taken!" when the man's mask
came off.

The crows became raucous. Discussing? Arguing?
The leader asked, "Who are you? What are you?
Where did you come from?"

The injured man did not respond. Maybe he was
beyond communication. Maybe he did not speak that
language. Maybe he was stubborn.

Torture produced no answers.

The inquisitor tossed the man into the woodpile,
waved a hand. The pile burst into flame. The stump
thing used the lance to keep its victim from escap-
ing. The burning man had a bottomless well of energy.

There was sorcery at work here.

The burning man was the Shadowmaster Moonshadow. His army had triumphed outside Stormgard but his own fortune had been inglorious.

The party did not move on till the Shadowmaster
was consumed, the fire burned to ashes and the ashes
cooled. The stump thing gathered the ashes. As it
travelled it disposed of those pinch by pinch.

The man with the arrow in him bobbed in the
stump thing's wake. The stallions brought up the
rear.

The crows maintained their patrols. Once a large
catlike thing came too near and they went into par-
oxysms. The stump did something mystical. The
black leopard wandered away, absent of mind.

Chapter Five

A slight figure in ornate black armor strained savagely. A corpse toppled off the heap of corpses piled upon the figure. The shift in weight made it possible to wriggle out of the heap. Free, the figure lay motionless for several minutes, panting inside a grotesque helmet. Then it pulled itself into a sitting position.

After another minute the figure struggled out of its gauntlets, revealed delicate hands. Slim fingers plucked at the fastenings holding its helmet. That came away, too.

Long black hair fell free around a face to stun a man. Inside all that ugly black steel was a woman.

I have to report those moments that way because I don't recall them at all. I remember a dark dream. A nightmare featuring a black woman with fangs like a vampire. Nothing else. My first clear recollection is of sitting beside the heap of corpses with my helmet in my lap. I was panting, only vaguely aware that I had gotten out of the pile somehow.

The stench of a thousand cruel gut wounds filled the air like the stink of the largest, rawest sewer in the world. It was the smell of battlefields. How many times had I smelled it? A thousand. And still I wasn't used to it.

I gagged. Nothing came up. I had emptied my stomach into my helmet while I was under the pile. I had a vague recollection of being terrified that I would drown in my own vomit.

I started shaking. Tears rolled, stinging, hot tears of relief. I had survived! I had lived ages beyond the measure of most mortals but I had lost none of my desire for life.

As I caught my breath I tried to put together where I was, what I was doing there. Besides surviving.

My last clear memories weren't pleasant. I remembered *knowing* that I was about to die.

I couldn't see much in the dark but I didn't need to see to know we had lost. Had the Company turned the tide Croaker would have found me long ago.

Why hadn't the victors?

There *were* men moving on the battlefield. I heard low voices arguing. Moving my way slowly. I had to get out of there.

I got up, managed to stumble four steps before I fell on my face, too weak to move another inch. Thirst was a demon devouring me from the inside out. My throat was so dry I couldn't whine.

I'd made noise. The looters were quiet now.

They were sneaking toward me, after one more victim. Where was my sword?

I was going to die now. No weapon and no strength to use one if I found one before they found me.

I could see them now, three men backlighted by a faint glow from Dejagore. Small men, like most of the Shadowmasters' soldiers. Neither strong nor particularly skilled, but in my case they needed neither strength nor skill.

Could I play dead? No. They wouldn't be deceived. Corpses would be cool now.

Damn them!

Before they killed me they would do more than just rob me.

They wouldn't kill me. They would recognize the armor. The Shadowmasters weren't fools. They knew who I'd been. They knew what I carried inside my head, treasures they dreamed about getting out. There would be rewards for my capture.

Maybe there are gods. A racket broke out behind the looters. Sounded like a sally from Dejagore, some kind of spoiling raid. Mogaba wasn't sitting on his hands waiting for the Shadowmasters to come to him.

One of the looters said something in a normal voice. Someone told him to shut up. The third man entered his opinion. An argument ensued. The first man didn't want to investigate the uproar. He'd had enough fighting.

The others overruled him.

The fates were kind. Two responsible soldiers handed me a life.

I lay where I'd fallen, resting for several minutes before I got onto hands and knees and crawled back to the mound of bodies. I found my sword, an ancient and consecrated blade created by Carqui in the younger days of the Domination. A storied blade, but no one, not even Croaker, had heard its tale.

I crawled toward the hummock where, when I'd seen him last, my love had been making his final stand, just him and Murgen and the Company standard, trying to stem the rout. It seemed an all-night trek. I found a dead soldier with water in his canteen. I drained it and went on. My strength grew as I crept. By the time I reached the hummock I could totter along upright.

I found nothing there. Just dead men. Croaker was not among them. The Company standard was gone. I felt hollow. Had the Shadowmasters taken him?

They would want him badly for crushing their army at Ghoja, for taking Dejagore, for killing Stormshadow.

I could not believe they had him. It had taken me too long to find him. No god, no fate, could be so cruel.

I cried.

The night grew quiet. The sortie had withdrawn. The looters would return now.

I started moving, stumbled into a dead elephant and almost shrieked, thinking I had walked right into a monster.

The elephants had carried all kinds of clutter. Some might be useful. I scrounged a few pounds of dried food, a skin of water, a small jar of poison for arrowheads, a few coins, whatever caught my fancy. Then I walked northward, determined to reach the hills before sunrise. I discarded half my plunder before I got there.

I hurried. Enemy patrols would be out looking for important bodies come first light.

What could I do now, besides survive? I was the last of the Black Company. There was nothing left. . . . Something came into me like a lost memory resurfacing. I could turn back time. I could become what I had been.

Trying not to think did not help. I remembered. And the more I remembered the more angry I became. Anger shaped me till all my thoughts were of revenge.

As I started into the hills I surrendered. Those monsters who had raped my dreams had written their own decrees of doom. I would do whatever it took to requite them.

Chapter Six

Longshadow paced a room ablaze with light so brilliant he seemed a dark spirit trapped in the mouth of the sun. He clung to that one crystal-walled, mirrored chamber where no shadow ever formed unless called forth by dire exigency. His fear of shadows was pathological.

The chamber was the highest in the tallest tower of the fortress Overlook, south of Shadowcatch, a city on the southern edge of the world. South of Overlook lay a plateau of glittering stone where isolated pillars stood like forgotten supports for the sky. Though construction had been underway for seventeen years, Overlook was incomplete. If Longshadow did finish it, no force material or supernatural would be able to penetrate it.

Strange, deadly, terrifying things hungered for him, lusted for freedom from the plain of glittering stone. They were shadow things that could catch up with a man as suddenly as death if he didn't cling to the light.

Longshadow's sorcery had shown him the battle at Stormgard, four hundred miles north of Shadowcatch. He was pleased. His rivals Moonshadow and Stormshadow had perished. Shadowspinner had been injured. A touch here, a touch there, subtly, would keep Shadowspinner weak.

But he couldn't be killed. Oh, no. Not yet. Dangerous forces were at work. Shadowspinner would have to be the breakwater against which the storm spent its energies.

Those mercenaries in Stormgard should be given every chance to sap Spinner's troop strength. He was far too strong now that he had possession of all three northern Shadow armies.

Subtlety. Subtlety. Each move had to be made with care. Spinner wasn't stupid. He knew who his most dangerous enemy was. If he rid himself of the Taglians and their Free Company leaders he'd turn on Overlook immediately.

And *she* was out there somewhere, shuffling counters in her own game, not in the ripeness of her power but deadly as a krite even so. And there was the woman whose knowledge could be invaluable, alone, a treasure to be harvested by any adventurer.

He needed a catspaw. He couldn't leave Overlook. The shadows were out there waiting, infinitely patient.

He caught a flicker of darkness from the corner of his eye. He squealed and flung himself away.

It was a crow, just a damned curious crow fluttering around outside.

A catspaw. There was a power in the swamps north of that miserable Taglios. It festered with grievances real and imagined. It could be seduced.

It was time he lured that power into the game.

But how, without leaving Overlook?

Something stirred on the plain of glittering stone.

The shadows were watching, waiting. They sensed the rising intensity of the game.

Chapter Seven

I slept in a tangle of brush in a hollow. I'd fled through olive groves and precariously perched hillside paddies, running out of hope, till I'd stumbled onto that pocket wilderness in a ravine. I was so far gone I'd just crawled in, hoping fate would be kind.

A crow's call wakened me from another terrible dream. I opened my eyes. The sun reached in through the brush. It dappled me with spots of light. I'd hoped nobody could see me in there but that proved a false hope.

Someone was moving around the edge of the bushes. I glimpsed one, then another. Damn! The Shadowmasters' men. They moved back a little and whispered.

I saw them for just a moment but they seemed troubled, less like hunters than the hunted. Curious.

They'd spotted me, I knew. Otherwise they wouldn't be back there behind me, murmuring too low for me to catch what they said.

I couldn't turn toward them without showing them

I knew they were there. I didn't want to startle them. They might do something I'd regret. The crow called again. I started turning my head slowly.

I froze.

There was another player here, a dirty little brown man in a filthy loincloth and tattered turban. He squatted behind the brush. He looked like one of the slaves Croaker had freed after our victory at Ghoja. Did the soldiers know he was there?

Did it matter? He wasn't likely to be any help.

I was lying on my right side, on my arm. My fingers tingled. My arm was asleep but the sensation reminded me that my talent had shown signs of freshening since we'd come down past the waist of the world. I hadn't had a chance to test it for weeks.

I had to do something. Or they would. My sword lay inches from my hand. . . .

Golden Hammer.

It was a child's spell, an exercise, not a weapon at all, just as a butcher knife isn't. Once it would have been no more work than dropping a rock. Now it was as hard as plain speech for a stroke victim. I tried shaping the spell in my mind. The frustration! The screaming frustration of knowing what to do and being unable to do it.

But it clicked. Almost the way it had back when. Amazed, pleased, I whispered the words of power, moved my fingers. The muscles remembered!

The Golden Hammer formed in my left hand.

I jumped up, flipped it, raised my sword. The glowing hammer flew true. The soldier made a stabbed-pig sound and tried to fend it off. It branded its shape on his chest.

It was an ecstatic moment. Success with that silly child's spell was a major triumph over my handicap.

My body wouldn't respond to my will. Too stiff, too battered and bruised for flight, I tried to charge the second soldier. Mostly I stumbled toward him. He gaped, then he ran. I was astonished.

I heard a sound like the cough of a tiger behind me.

A man came out of nowhere down the ravine. He threw something. The fleeing soldier pitched onto his face and didn't move.

I got out of the brush and placed myself so I could watch the killer and the dirty slave who had made the tiger cough. The killer was a huge man. He wore tatters of Taglian legionnaire's garb.

The little man came around the brush slowly, considered my victim. He was impressed. He said something apologetic in Taglian, then something excited, rapidly in dialect I found unfamiliar, to the big man, who had begun searching his victim. I caught a phrase here and there, all with a cultish sound but uncertain in this context. I couldn't tell if he was talking about me or praising one of his gods. I heard "the Foretold" and "Daughter of Night" and "the Bride" and "Year of the Skulls." I'd heard a "Daughter of Shadow" and a "Year of the Skulls" before somewhere, in the religious chatter of god-ridden Taglians, but I didn't know their significance.

The big man grunted. He wasn't impressed. He just cursed the dead soldier, kicked him. "Nothing."

The little man fawned. "Your pardon, Lady. We've been killing these dogs all morning, trying to raise a stake. But they're poorer than I was as a slave."

"You know me?"

"Oh, yes, Mistress. The Captain's Lady." He emphasized those last two words, separately and heavily. He bowed three times. Each time his right thumb and forefinger brushed a triangle of black cloth that peeped over the top of his loincloth. "We stood guard while you slept. We should have realized *you* would need no protection. Forgive us our presumption."

Gods, did he smell. "Have you seen anyone else?"

"Yes, Mistress. A few, from afar. Running, most of them."

"And the Shadowmasters' soldiers?"

"They search, but with no enthusiasm. Their mas-

ters didn't send many. A thousand like these pigs."
He indicated the man I had dropped. His partner
was searching the body. "And a few hundred horsemen. They must be busy with the city."

"Mogaba will give them hell if he can, buying time
for others to get clear."

The big man said, "Nothing on this toad either,
jamadar."

The little man grunted.

Jamadar? It's the Taglian word for captain. The
little man had used it earlier, with a different into-
nation, when he'd called me the Captain's Lady.

I asked, "Have you seen the Captain?"

The pair exchanged looks. The little man stared at
the ground. "The Captain is dead, Mistress. He died
trying to rally the men to the standard. Ram saw it.
An arrow through the heart."

I sat down on the ground. There was nothing to
say. I'd known it. I'd seen it happen, too. But I hadn't
wanted to believe it. Till that instant, I realized, I'd
been carrying some small hope that I'd been wrong.

Impossible that I could feel such loss and pain.
Damn him, Croaker was just a man! How did I get
so involved? I never meant it to get complicated.

This wasn't accomplishing anything. I got up. "We
lost a battle but the war goes on. The Shadowmasters will rue the day they decided to bully Taglios.
What are your names?"

The little man said, "I'm Narayan, Lady." He
grinned. I'd get thoroughly sick of that grin. "A joke
on me. It's a Shadar name." He was Gunni, obviously. "Do I look it?" He jerked his head at the other
man, who was Shadar. Shadar men tend to be tall
and massive and hairy. This one had a head like a
ball of kinky wire with eyes peering out. "I was a
vegetable peddler till the Shadowmasters came to
Gondowar and enslaved everyone who survived the
fight for the town."

That would have been before we'd come to Taglios, last year, when Swan and Mather had been doing their inept best to stem the first invasion.

"My friend is Ram. Ram was a carter in Taglios before he joined the legions."

"Why did he call you jamadar?"

Narayan glanced at Ram, flashed a grin filled with bad teeth, leaned close to me, whispered, "Ram isn't very bright. Strong as an ox he is, and tireless, but slow."

I nodded but wasn't satisfied. They were two odd birds. Shadar and Gunni didn't run together. Shadar consider themselves superior to everyone. Hanging around with a Gunni would constitute a defilement of spirit. And Narayan was low-caste Gunni. Yet Ram showed him deference.

Neither harbored any obviously wicked designs toward me. At the moment any companion was an improvement on travelling alone. I told them, "We ought to get moving. More of them could show up. . . . *What* is he doing?"

Ram had a ten-pound rock. He was smashing the leg bones of the man he'd killed. Narayan said, "Ram. That's enough. We're leaving."

Ram looked puzzled. He thought. Then he shrugged and discarded the rock. Narayan didn't explain his actions. He told me, "We saw one fair-sized group this morning, maybe twenty men. Maybe we can catch up."

"That would be a start." I realized I was starving. I hadn't eaten since before the battle. I shared out what I'd taken off the dead elephant. It didn't help much. Ram went at it like it was a feast, now completely indifferent to the dead.

Narayan grinned. "You see? An ox. Come. Ram, carry her armor."

Two hours later we found twenty-three fugitives on a hilltop. They were beaten men, apathetic, so down they didn't care if they got away. Few still had their weapons. I didn't recognize any of them. Not surprising. We'd gone into battle with forty thousand.

They knew me. Their manners and attitude improved instantly. It pleased me to see hope blossom among them. They rose and lowered their heads respectfully.

I could see the city and plain from that hilltop. The Shadowmasters' troops were leaving the hills, evidently recalled. Good. We'd have a little time before they picked it up again.

I looked at the men more closely.

They had accepted me already. Good again.

Narayan had begun speaking to them individually. Some seemed frightened of him. Why? What was it? Something was odd about that little man.

"Ram, build us a fire. I want a lot of smoke."

He grunted, drafted four men, headed downhill to collect firewood.

Narayan trotted over, grinning that grin, followed by a man of amazing width. Most Taglians are lean to the point of emaciation. This one had no fat on him. He was built like a bear. "This is Sindhu, Mistress, that I know by reputation." Sindhu bowed slightly. He looked a humorless sort. Narayan added, "He'll be a good man to help out."

I noted a red cloth triangle at Sindhu's waist. He was Gunni. "Your help will be appreciated, Sindhu. You two get this bunch sorted out. See what resources we have."

Narayan grinned, made a small bow, hustled off with his new friend.

I settled crosslegged, separate from the rest, faced the city, closed out the world. The Golden Hammer had come easily. I'd try again.

I opened to what little talent I retained. A peppercorn of fire formed in the bowl of my hands. It *was* coming back.

There is no way to express my pleasure.

I concentrated on horses.

Half an hour later a giant black stallion appeared, trotted straight to me. The men were impressed.

I was impressed. I hadn't expected success. And that beast was only the first of four to respond. By the time the fourth arrived so had another hundred men. The hilltop was crowded.

I assembled them. "We've lost a battle, men. Some of you have lost heart, too. That's understandable. You weren't raised in a warrior tradition. But this war hasn't been lost. And it won't end while one Shadowmaster lives. If you don't have the stomach to stick it out, stay away from me. You'd better go now. I won't let you go later."

They exchanged worried glances but nobody volunteered to travel alone.

"We're going to head north. We'll gather food, weapons, and men. We'll train. We're coming back someday. When we do, the Shadowmasters will think the gates of hell have opened." Still nobody deserted. "We march at first light tomorrow. If you're with me then, you're with me forever." I tried to project a certainty that we could terrify the world.

When I settled for the night Ram posted himself nearby, my bodyguard whether or not I wanted one.

I drifted off wondering what had become of four black stallions that had not responded. We had brought eight south. They had been specially bred in the early days of the empire I had abandoned. One could be more valuable than a hundred men.

I listened to whispers, heard repeats of the terms Narayan had used. They troubled most of the men.

I noticed that Ram had his bit of folded cloth, too. His was saffron. He didn't keep it as fastidiously as did Narayan or Sindhu. Three men from two religions, each with a colored cloth. What was the significance?

Narayan kept the fire burning. He posted sentries. He imposed a modest discipline. He seemed altogether too organized for a vegetable dealer and former slave.

The dark dream, the same as those before, was particularly vivid, though when day came I retained only an impression of a voice calling my name. Unsettling, but I thought it just a trick of my mind.

Somewhere, somehow, the night rewarded Narayan with bounty enough to provide everyone a meager breakfast.

I led the mob out at first light, as promised, amidst reports that enemy cavalry were approaching the hills. Discipline was a pleasant surprise, considering.

Chapter Eight

Dejagore is surrounded by a ring of hills. The plain is lower than the land beyond the hills. Only a dry climate keeps that basin from becoming a lake. Portions of two rivers have been diverted to supply irrigation to the hill farms and water for the city. I kept the band near one of the canals.

The Shadowmasters were preoccupied with Dejagore. While they weren't pressing me I wasn't interested in covering a lot of ground. The future I'd chosen would be no easy conquest. The chance that the enemy might appear encouraged discipline. I hoped to keep that possibility alive till I instilled a few positive habits.

"Narayan, I need your advice."

"Mistress?"

"We'll have trouble holding them together once they feel safe." I always talked as though he, Ram, and Sindhu were extensions of myself. They never protested.

"I know, Mistress. They want to go home. The adventure is over." He grinned his grin. I was sick of it already. "We're trying to convince them they're part of something fated. But they have a lot to unlearn."

That they did. Taglian culture was a religious confusion I hadn't begun to fathom, tangled in caste systems which made no sense. I asked questions but no one understood. Things were as they were. It was the way they'd always been. I was tempted to declare the mess obsolete. But I didn't have the power. I hadn't had that much power in the north. Some things can't be swept away by dictate.

I continued asking questions. If I understood it even a little I could manipulate the system.

"I need a reliable cadre, Narayan. Men I can count on no matter what. I want you to find those men."

"As you say, Mistress, so shall it be." He grinned. That might have been a defensive reflex learned as a slave. Still . . . The more I saw of Narayan the more sinister he seemed.

Yet why? He was essentially Taglian, low caste. A vegetable vendor with a wife and children and a couple of grandchildren already, last he had heard. One of those backbone of the nation sorts, quiet, who just kept plugging away at life. Half the time he acted like I was his favorite daughter. What was sinister in that?

Ram had more to recommend him as strange. He was twenty-three and a widower. His marriage had been a love match, rare in Taglios where marriages are always arranged. His wife had died in childbirth, bearing a stillborn infant. That had left him bitter and depressed. I suspect he joined the legions looking for death.

I didn't find out anything about Sindhu. He wouldn't talk until you forced him and he was creepier than Narayan. Still, he did what he was told, did it well, and asked no questions.

I've spent my entire life in the company of sinister characters. For centuries I was wed to the Domina-

tor, the most sinister ever. I could cope with these
small men.

None of the three were particularly religious, which
was curious. Religion pervades Taglios. Every minute
of every day of every life is a part of the religious experience, is ruled by religion and its obligations. I was
troubled till I noted a generally reduced level of religious fervor. I picked a man and quizzed him.

His answer was elementary. "There ain't no priests
here."

That made sense. No society consists entirely of
committed true believers. And what these men had
seen had been enough to displace the foundations of
faith. They'd been pulled out of their safe, familiar
ruts and had been thrown hard against facts the traditional answers didn't explain. They'd never be the
same. Once they took their experiences home Taglios wouldn't be the same.

The band trebled in size. I had better than six hundred followers hailing from all three major religions
and a few splinter cults. I had more than a hundred
former slaves who weren't Taglian at all. They could
make good soldiers once they gained some confidence. They had no homes to run to. The band would
be their home.

The problem with the mix was that every day was
a holy day for somebody. If we'd had priests along
there would have been trouble.

They began to feel safe. That left them free to indulge old prejudices, to grow lax in discipline, to forget the war and, most irritating, to remember that I
was a woman.

In law and custom Taglian women are less favored
than cattle. Cattle are less easily replaced. Women
who gain status or power do so in the shadows,
through men they can influence or manipulate.

One more hurdle I'd have to leap. Maybe the biggest.

I summoned Narayan one morning. "We're a hun-

dred miles from Dejagore." I wasn't in a good mood.
I'd had the dream again. It had left my nerves raw.
"We're safe for the moment." The confidence of the
men in their safety showed as they started their day.
"I'm going to make some major changes. How many
men are reliable?"

He preened. Smug little rat. "A third. Maybe more
if put to the test."

"That many? Really?" I was surprised. It wasn't
evident to me.

"You see only the other sort. Some men learned
discipline and tolerance in the legions. The slaves
came out of bondage filled with hatred. They want
revenge. They know no Taglian can lead them against
the Shadowmasters. Some even sincerely believe in
you for yourself."

Thank you for that, little man. "But most will have
trouble following me?"

"Maybe." That fawning grin. Hint of cunning. "We
Taglians don't deal well with upheavals in the natural order."

"The natural order is that the strong rule and the
rest follow. I'm strong, Narayan. I'm like nothing
Taglios has ever seen. I haven't yet shown myself to
Taglios. I hope Taglios never sees me angry. I'd
rather spend my wrath on the Shadowmasters."

He bowed several times, suddenly frightened.

"Our ultimate destination remains Ghoja. You may
pass that word. We'll collect survivors there, win-
now them and rebuild. But I don't intend to get there
till we have this force whipped into shape."

"Yes, Mistress."

"Collect whatever weapons are available. Take no
arguments. Redistribute them to the men you think
reliable. Assign those men to march in the lefthand
file. The men to their right are to be religiously
mixed. They are to be separated from those they
knew before Dejagore."

"That may cause trouble."

"Good. I want to pinpoint its sources. I'll give it back

with interest. Go on. Get them disarmed before they understand what's happening. Ram. Give him a hand."

"But . . ."

"I can look out for myself, Ram." His protection was a nuisance.

Narayan did move fast. Only a few men had to be separated from their weapons by force.

Organized according to my orders, we marched all day, till they were too exhausted to complain. I halted them in the evening and had Narayan form them for review, with the reliables in the rear. I donned my armor, mounted one of the black stallions, rode out to review them with little witchfires prancing about me. There wasn't much to those. I hadn't made large strides recapturing my talent.

The armor, horse, and fires formed the visible aspect of a character called Lifetaker, whom I had created before the Company moved to the Main to face the Shadowmasters at Ghoja. In concert with Croaker's Widowmaker she was supposed to intimidate the enemy by being something larger than life, archetypally deadly. My own men could use a little intimidation now. In a land where sorcery was little more than a rumor the witchfires could be enough.

I passed the formation slowly, studying the soldiers. They understood the situation. I was looking for that which I would not tolerate, the man disinclined to do things my way.

I rode past again. After centuries of watching people it wasn't difficult to spot potential troublemakers. "Ram." I pointed out six men. "Send them away. With the nothing they had when they joined us." I spoke so my voice carried. "Next winnowing, those chosen will taste the lash. And the third winnowing will be a celebration of death."

A stir passed through the ranks. They heard the message.

The chosen six went sullenly. I shouted at the others, "Soldiers! Look at the man to your right! Now look at the man to your left! Look at me! You see soldiers, not Gunni, not Shadar, not Vehdna. Soldiers! We're fighting a war against an implacable and united enemy. In the line of battle it won't be your gods at your left and your right, it will be men like those standing there now. Serve your gods in your heart if you must, but in this world, in the camp, on the march, on the field of battle, you won't set your gods before me. You'll own no higher master. Till the last Shadowmaster falls, no reward or retribution of god or prince will find you more swiftly or surely than mine."

I suspected that was maybe pushing too hard too soon. But there wasn't much time to create my cadre.

I rode off while they digested it. I dismounted, told Ram, "Dismiss them. Make camp. Send me Narayan."

I unsaddled my mount, settled on the saddle. A crow landed nearby, cocked its head. Several more circled above. Those black devils were everywhere. You couldn't get away.

Croaker had been paranoid about them. He'd believed they were following him, spying on him, even talking to him. I thought it was the pressure. But their omnipresence did get irritating.

No time for Croaker. He was gone. I was walking a sword's edge. Neither tears nor self-pity would bring him back.

During the journey north I'd realized that I'd done more than lose my talent at the Barrowland. I'd given up. So I'd lost my edge during the year-plus since.

Croaker's fault. His weakness. He'd been too understanding, too tolerant, too willing to give second chances. He'd been too optimistic about people. He couldn't believe there is an essential darkness shadowing the human soul. For all his cynicism about motives he'd believed that in every evil person there was good trying to surface.

I owe my life to his belief but that doesn't validate it.

Narayan came, sneaky as a cat. He gave me his grin.

"We've gained ground, Narayan. They took that well enough. But we have a long way to go."

"The religion problem, Mistress?"

"Some. But that's not the worst hurdle. I've overcome such before." I smiled at his surprise. "I see doubts. But you don't know me. You know only what you've heard. A woman who abandoned a throne to follow the Captain? Eh? But I wasn't the spoiled, heartless child you imagine. Not a brat with a pinch of talent who fell heir to some petty crown she didn't want. Not a dunce who ran off with the first adventurer who'd have her."

"Little is known except that you were the Captain's Lady," he admitted. "Some think as you suggest. Your companions scarcely hinted at your antecedents. I think you're much more, but how much more I dare not guess."

"I'll give you a hint." I was amused. For all Narayan seemed to want me to be something untraditional he was startled whenever I didn't behave like a Taglian woman. "Sit, Narayan. It's time you understood where you're placing your bets."

He looked me askance but settled. The crow watched him. His fingers teased at that fold of black cloth.

"Narayan, the throne I gave up was the seat of an empire so broad you couldn't have walked it east to west in a year. It spanned two thousand miles from north to south. I built it from a beginning as humble as this. I started before your grandfather's grandfather was born. And it wasn't the first empire I created."

He grinned uneasily. He thought I was lying.

"Narayan, the Shadowmasters were my slaves. Powerful as they are. They disappeared during a great battle twenty years ago. I believed them dead till we unmasked the one we killed in Dejagore.

"I'm weakened now. Two years ago there was a great battle in the northernmost region of my empire. The Captain and I put down a wakening evil left over from the first empire I created. To succeed, to prevent that evil from breaking loose, I had to allow my powers to be neutralized. Now I'm winning them back, slowly and painfully."

Narayan couldn't believe. He was the son of his

culture. I was a woman. But he wanted to believe. He said, "But you're so young."

"In some ways. I never loved before the Captain. This shell is a mask, Narayan. I entered this world before the Black Company passed this way the first time. I'm old, Narayan. Old and wicked. I've done things no one would believe. I know evil, intrigue, and war like they're my children. I nurtured them for centuries.

"Even as the Captain's lover I was more than a paramour. I was the Lieutenant, his chief of staff.

"I'm the Captain now, Narayan. While I survive the Company survives. And goes on. And finds new life. I'm going to rebuild, Narayan. It may wear another name for a while but behind the domino it will *be* the Black Company. *And* it will be the instrument of my will."

Narayan grinned that grin. "You may be Her indeed."

"I may be who?"

"Soon, Mistress. Soon. It's not yet time. Suffice it to say that not everyone greeted the return of the Black Company with despair." His eyes went shifty.

"Say that, then." I decided not to press him. I needed him pliable. "For the moment. We're building an army. We're woefully beggared of an army's most precious resource, veteran sergeants. We have no one who can teach.

"Tonight, before they eat, sort the men by religion. Organize them in squads of ten, three from each cult plus one non-Taglian. Assign each squad a permanent place in the camp and the order of march. I want no intercourse between squads till each can elect a leader and his second. They'd better work out how to get along. They'll be stuck in those squads."

Another risk. The men were not in the best temper. But they were isolated from the priesthoods and culture which reinforced their prejudices. Their priests had done their thinking for them all their lives. Out here they had nobody but me to tell them what to do.

"I won't approach Ghoja before the squads pick leaders. Fighting amongst squad members should be punished. Set up whipping posts before you make the assignments. Send the squads to supper as you form them. Learning to cook together will help." I waved him away.

He rose. "If they can eat together they can do anything together, Mistress."

"I know." Each cult sustained an absurd tangle of dietary laws. Thus, this approach. It should undermine prejudice at its most basic level.

These men would not rid themselves of ingrained hatred but would set it aside around those with whom they served. It's easier to hate those you don't know than those you do. When you march with someone and have to trust him with your life it's hard to keep hating irrationally.

I tried to keep the band preoccupied with training. Those who had been through it with the hastily raised legions helped, mainly by getting the others to march in straight lines. Sometimes I despaired. There was just so much I could do. There was only one of me.

I needed a firm power base before I dared the political lists.

Fugitives joined us. Some went away again. Some didn't survive the disciplinary demands. The rest strove to become soldiers.

I was free with punishments and freer with rewards. I tried to nurture pride and, subtly, the conviction that they were better men than any who didn't belong to the band, the conviction that they could trust no one who wasn't of the band.

I didn't spare myself. I slept so little I had no time to dream, or didn't remember that I'd dreamed. Every free moment I spent nagging my talent. I'd need it soon.

It *was* coming back slowly. Too slowly.

It was like having to learn to walk again after a prolonged illness.

Chapter Nine

Though I wasn't trying to move quickly I outdistanced most of the survivors. For loners and small groups, foraging outweighed speed. Once I slowed to avoid reaching Ghoja, though, more and more caught up. Not many decided to enlist.

Already the band was recognizably alien. It scared outsiders.

I guessed maybe ten thousand men had escaped the debacle. How many would survive to reach Ghoja? If Taglios was fortunate, maybe half. The land had turned hostile.

Forty miles from Ghoja and the Main, just inside territory historically Taglian, I ordered a real camp built with a surrounding ditch. I chose a meadow on the north bank of a clean brook. The south bank was forested. The site was pleasant. I planned to stay, rest, train, till my foragers exhausted the countryside.

For days incoming fugitives had reported enemy light cavalry hunting behind them. An hour after we began making camp I got a report of smoke south of the wood. I walked the mile to the far side, saw a cloud rising from a village six miles down the road. They were that close.

Trouble? It had to be considered.

An opportunity? Unlikely at this stage.

Narayan came running through the dusk. "Mistress. The Shadowmasters' men. They're making camp on the south side of the woods. They'll catch us tomorrow." His optimism had deserted him.

I thought about it. "Do the men know?"

"The news is spreading."

"Damn. All right. Station reliable men along the ditch. Kill anybody who tries to leave. Put Ram in charge, then come back."

"Yes, Mistress." Narayan scampered off. At times he seemed a mouse. He returned. "They're grumbling."

"Let them. As long as they don't run. Do the Shadowmasters' men know we're this close?"

Narayan shrugged.

"I want to *know*. Put out a picket line a quarter mile into the wood. Twenty good men. They're not to interfere with scouts coming north but they're to ambush them headed back." They wouldn't be expecting trouble going away. "Use men who aren't good for anything else to raise an embankment along the creek. Drive stakes into its face. Sharpen them. Find vines. Sink them in the water. There's no room to maneuver on the south bank. They'll have to come straight at us, hard. Once you've got that started, come back." Best get everybody busy and distract them from their fears. I snapped, "Narayan, wait! Find out if any of the men can handle horses."

Other than my mounts there were just a half dozen animals with the band, all strays we'd captured. I'd had to teach Ram to care for mine. Riding amongst Taglians was restricted to high-caste Gunni and rich

Shadar. Bullock and buffalo were the native work animals.

It was the tenth hour when Narayan returned. In the interim I prowled. I was pleased. I saw no panic, no outright terror, just a healthy ration of fear tempered by the certainty that chances of surviving were better here than on the run. They feared my displeasure more than they feared an enemy not yet seen. Perfect.

I made a suggestion about the angle of the stakes on the face of the embankment, then went to talk with Narayan.

I told him, "We'll scout their camp now."

"Just us?" His grin was forced.

"You and me."

"Yes, Mistress. Though I'd feel more comfortable if Sindhu accompanied us."

"Can he move quietly?" I couldn't picture that bulk sneaking anywhere.

"Like a mouse, Mistress."

"Get him. Don't waste time. We'll need all the darkness we've got."

Narayan gave me an odd look, took off.

We left a password, crossed the creek. Narayan and Sindhu stole through the woods as though to stealth born. Quieter than mice. They took our pickets by surprise. Those had seen nothing of the enemy.

"Awfully sure of themselves," Sindhu grumbled, the first I'd heard him volunteer an opinion.

"Maybe they're plain stupid." The Shadowmasters' soldiers hadn't impressed me with anything but their numbers.

We spied their campfires before I expected them. They'd camped among the trees. I hadn't foreseen that possibility. Damned inconsiderate of them.

Narayan touched my arm diffidently. Mouth to ear, he breathed, "Sentries. Wait here." He stole forward like a ghost, returned like one. "Two of them. Sound asleep. Walk carefully."

So we just strolled in to where I could see what I wanted. I studied the layout for several minutes. Satisfied, I said, "Let's go."

One of the sentries had wakened. He started up as Sindhu drifted past, firelight glistening off his broad, naked back.

Narayan's hand darted to his waist. His arm whipped, his wrist snapped, a serpent of black cloth looped around the sentry's neck. Narayan strangled him so efficiently his companion didn't waken.

Sindhu took the other with a strip of scarlet cloth. Now I knew what peeked from their loincloths. Their weapons.

They rearranged their victims so they looked like they were sleeping with their tongues out, all the while whispering cant that sounded ritualistic. I said, "Sindhu, stay and keep watch. Warn us if they discover the bodies. Narayan. Come with me."

I hurried as much as darkness allowed. Once we reached camp I told Narayan, "That was neatly done. I want to learn that trick with the cloth."

The notion surprised him. He didn't say anything.

"Collect the ten best squads. Arm them. Also the twenty men you think best able to handle horses. Ram!"

Ram arrived as I began readying my armor. He grew troubled. "What's the matter now?" Then I saw what he'd done to my helmet. "What the hell is this? I told you clean it, not destroy it."

He was like a shy boy as he said, "This apes one aspect of the goddess Kina, Mistress. One of her names is Lifetaker. You see? In that avatar her aspect is very like this armor."

"Next time, ask. Help me into this."

Ten minutes later I stood at the center of the group I'd had Narayan assemble. "We're going to attack them. The point isn't glory or victory. We just want to discourage them from attacking us. We're going in, we're doing a little damage, then we're getting out."

I described the encampment, gave assignments, drawing in the dirt beside a fire. "In and out. Don't waste time trying to kill them. Just hurt somebody. A dead man can be left where he falls but a wounded man becomes a burden to his comrades. Whatever happens, don't go beyond the far edge of their camp. We'll retreat when they start getting organized. Grab any weapon you can. Ram, capture every horse you can. Everybody. If you can't grab weapons grab food or tools. Nobody risk anybody's life trying to grab just one more thing. And, lastly, be quiet. We're all dead if they hear us coming."

Narayan reported the dead sentries still undiscovered. I sent him forward to eliminate as many more as he and Sindhu could manage. I had the main party cover the last two hundred yards in driblets. A hundred twenty men moving at once, no matter how they try, make noise.

I looked into the camp. Men were stirring. Looked like it was near time to change the guard.

Ram's bunch joined us. I donned my helmet, turned my back on my men, walked toward the only shelter in the camp. It would belong to the commander. I set the witchfires playing over me, unsheathed my sword.

Fires ran out its blade.

It *was* coming back.

The few southerners awake gawked.

The men poured into the camp, stabbed the sleeping, overwhelmed those who were awake. I struck a man down, reached the tent, hacked it apart as the man within reacted to the uproar. I wound up two-handed and struck off his head, grabbed it by the hair, held it high, turned to check the progress of the raid.

The southerners were making no effort to defend themselves. Two hundred must have died already. The rest were trying to get away. Could I have routed them so easily?

Sindhu and Narayan came running, prostrated themselves, banged their heads on the ground and gobbled at me in that cant they used. Crows fluttered through the trees, raucous. My men hurtled around hacking and slashing, spending the wealth of fear they'd carried through the night.

"Narayan. See what the survivors are doing. Quickly. Before they mount a counterattack. Sindhu. Help me control these men."

Narayan ran off. He came back in a few minutes. "They've started gathering a quarter mile down the road. They think a demon attacked them. They don't want to come back. Their officers are telling them they can't survive if they don't recover their camp and animals."

That was true. Maybe another glimpse of the demon would encourage them to stay away.

I got the men into a ragged line, advanced to the edge of the wood. Narayan and Sindhu sneaked ahead. I wanted warning if the southerners were inclined to fight. I'd back off.

They fled again. Narayan said they killed those officers who tried to rally them.

"Fortune smiles," I recall murmuring. I'd have to take a closer look at this demon Kina. She must have some reputation. I wondered why I'd never heard of her.

I withdrew to the captured encampment. We'd come into a lot of useful material. "Ram, get the rest of the band. Have them bring the stakes from the embankment. Narayan, think about which men are least deserving of receiving arms." There would be enough to go around now, almost.

Arms would be a trust and honor to be earned.

The change was dramatic. You'd have thought it was another Ghoja triumph. Even those who hadn't participated gained confidence. I saw it everywhere. These men had a new feeling of self-worth. They were proud to be part of a desperate enterprise and they gave me my due place in it. I walked through the camp dropping hints that soon they would be part of something with power.

That had to be nurtured, and continually fertilized with suspicion and distrust of everyone outside the band.

It takes time to forge a hammer. More time than I would get, probably. It takes years, even decades, to create a force like the Black Company, which had been carried forward on the crest of a wave of tradition.

Here I was trying to magic up a Golden Hammer, something gaudy but with no real substance, deadly only to the ignorant and unprepared.

It was time for a ceremony alienating them from the rest of the world. Time for a blood rite that would bind them to one another and me.

I had the stakes from the embankment planted along the road south of the wood. Then I had all the dead southerners decapitated and their heads placed atop the stakes, facing southward, ostensibly warning travellers who shared their ambitions.

Narayan and Sindhu were delighted. They hacked off heads with great enthusiasm. No horror touched them.

None touched me, either. I'd seen everything in my time.

Chapter Ten

Swan lay in the shade on the bank of the Main, lazily watching his bobber float on a still, deep pool. The air was warm, the shade was cool, the bugs were too lazy to bother him. He was half asleep. What more could a man ask?

Blade sat down. "Catch anything?"

"Nope. Don't know what I'd do if I did. What's up?"

"The Woman wants us." He meant the Radisha, whom they had found waiting when they'd reached Ghoja—much to Smoke's dismay. "She's got a job for us."

"Don't she always? You tell her to stick it in her ear?"

"Thought I'd save you that pleasure."

"I'd rather you'd saved me the walk. I'm comfortable."

"She wants us to drag Smoke somewhere he don't want to go."

"Why didn't you say so?" Swan pulled his line out

of the water. There was no bait on his hook. "And I thought there weren't any fish in that crick." He left his pole against a tree, a statement of sorts. "Where's Cordy?"

"Probably there waiting. He was watching Jah. I told him already."

Swan looked across the river. "I'd kill for a pint of beer." They'd been in the brewery business in Taglios before the excitement swept them up.

Blade snorted, headed for the fortress overlooking Ghoja ford.

The fort stood on the south bank of the Main. It had been built by the Shadowmasters after their invasion of Taglios had been repulsed, to defend their conquests south of the river. The fortress had been overwhelmed by the Black Company after the victory north of the river. Taglian artisans were reinforcing it and beginning a companion fortress on the north bank.

Swan scanned the scabrous encampment west of the fortress. Eight hundred men lived there. Some were construction workers. Most were fugitives from the south. One large group particularly irked him. "Think Jah has figured out that the Woman is here?"

Jahamaraj Jah was a power-hungry Shadar priest. He had commanded the mounted auxiliaries during the southern expedition. His flight north had been so precipitous he'd beaten Swan's party to the ford by several days.

"I think he's guessed. He tried to sneak a messenger across last night." The Radisha, through Swan, had forbidden anyone to cross the river. She didn't want news of the disaster reaching Taglios before its dimensions were known.

"Uhm?"

"Messenger drowned. Cordy says Jah thinks he made it." Blade chuckled wickedly. He hated priests. Baiting them was his favorite sport. All priests, of whatever faith.

"Good. That'll keep him out of our hair till we figure out what to do with him."

"I know what to do."

"Political consequences," Swam cautioned. "That your solution to everything? Cut somebody's throat?"

"Always slows them down."

The guards at the fortress gate saluted. They were favorites of the Radisha and, though neither Blade nor Swan nor Mather wanted it, they commanded Taglios' defenses now.

Swan said, "I got to learn to think in the long term, Blade. Never thought we'd be back at this after the Black Company showed."

"You got a lot to learn, Willow."

Cordy and Smoke waited outside the room where the Radisha holed up. Smoke looked like he had a bad stomach. Like he'd make a run for it if he got a chance.

Swan said, "You're looking grim, Cordy."

"Just tired. Mostly of playing with the runt."

Swan raised an eyebrow. Cordy was the calm one, the patient guy, the one who poured oil on the waters. Smoke must have provoked him good. "She ready?"

"Whenever."

"Let's do it. I got a river full of fish waiting."

"Better figure on them getting grey hair before you get back." Mather knocked, pushed the wizard ahead of him.

The Radisha entered the room from the side as Swan closed the door. Here, in private, with men not from her own culture, she didn't pretend to a traditional sex role. "Did you tell them, Cordy?"

Willow exchanged glances with Blade. Their old buddy on a nickname basis with the Woman? Interesting. What did he call her? She didn't look like a Cuddles.

"Not yet."

"What's up?" Swan asked.

The Radisha said, "I've had my men mixing with the soldiers. They've heard rumors that the woman who was the Lieutenant of the Black Company survived. She's trying to pull the survivors together south of here."

"Best news I've heard in a while," Swan said. He winked at Blade.

"Is it?"

"I thought it was a crying shame to lose such a resource."

"I'll bet. You have a low mind, Swan."

"Guilty. Hard not to once you've had a gander at her. So she made it. Great. Gets us three off the hook. Gives you a professional to carry on."

"That remains to be seen. There'll be difficulties. Cordy. Tell them."

"Twenty-some men from the Second just came in. They'd stayed off the road to avoid the Shadowmasters' patrols. About seventy miles south of here they took a couple prisoners. The night before our guys grabbed them Kina and a ghost army supposedly attacked their camp and killed most of them."

Swan looked at Blade, at the Radisha, at Cordy again. "I missed something. Who's Kina? And what's got into Smoke?" The wizard was shaking like somebody had dunked him in icewater.

Mather and Blade shrugged. They didn't know.

The Radisha sat down. "Get comfortable." She chewed her lip. "This will be difficult to tell."

"Then just go straight at it," Swan said.

"Yes. I suppose." The Radisha collected herself. "Kina is the fourth side of the Taglian religious triangle. She belongs to none of the pantheons but terrifies everybody. She isn't named lest naming invoke her. She's very unpleasant. Fortunately, her cult is small. And proscribed. Membership is punishable by death. The penalty is deserved. The cult's rites always involve torture and murder. Even so, it persists, its members awaiting someone called the Foretold and the Year of the Skulls. It's an old, dark religion that knows no national or ethnic bounds. Its members hide behind masks of respectability. They sometimes call themselves the Deceivers. They live normal lives among the rest of the community. Anyone could belong. Few of the common people know they exist anymore."

Swan didn't get it and said so. "Don't sound much different from the Shadar Hada or Khadi avatars."

The Radisha smiled grimly. "Those are ghosts of the reality." Hada and Khadi were two aspects of the Shadar death god. "Jah could show you a thousand ways Khadi is a kitten compared to Kina." Jahamaraj Jah was a devotee of Khadi.

Swan shrugged, doubting he could tell the difference if they drew pictures. He'd given up trying to understand the welter of Taglian gods, each with his or her ten or twenty different aspects and avatars. He indicated Smoke. "What's with him? He shakes any more we'll have to change his diaper."

"Smoke predicted a Year of Skulls—a time of chaos and bloodshed—if we employed the Black Company. He didn't believe it would come. He just wanted to scare my brother out of doing something that scared him. But he's on record as having predicted it. Now there's a chance it might come."

"Sure. Come on." Swan frowned, still lost. "Let me get this straight. There's a death cult around that makes Jah and his Khadi freaks look like a bunch of nancy boys? That scares the guano out of anybody who knows who they are?"

"Yes."

"And they worship a goddess named Kina?"

"That is the most common of many names."

"Why aren't I surprised? Is there any god down here without more aliases than a two-hundred-year-old con man?"

"Kina is the name given her by the Gunni. She has been called Patwa, Kompara, Bhomahna, and other names. The Gunni, the Shadar, the Vehdna, all find ways to accept her into their belief systems. Many

Shadar who become her followers, for example, take her to be the true form of Hada or Khadi, who is just one of her Deceits."

"Gah. All right. I'll bite. There's a bad-ass in the weeds called Kina. So how come me and Cordy and Blade never heard of her before?"

The Radisha appeared mildly embarrassed. "You were shielded. You're outsiders. From the north."

"Maybe so." What did the north have to do with it? "But why the panic? One garbled thing about this Kina from a prisoner who's got no reason to tell the truth? And Smoke goes to wetting his pants? And you start foaming at the mouth? I got a little trouble taking you serious."

"Point taken. You shouldn't have been shielded. I'm sending you to check out the story."

Swan grinned. He had a lever. "Not without you stop jacking us around. Tell us the whole story. Bad enough you messed with the Black Company. You think you're going to mess us around because we weren't born in Taglios. . . ."

"Enough, Swan." The Radisha wasn't pleased.

Smoke made a whining noise. He shook his head.

"What's with him?" Willow demanded. Much more of that weirdness and he was going to strangle the old guy.

"Smoke sees a ghost in every shadow. In your case he's afraid you're spies sent ahead by the Black Company."

"Sure. Moron! That's another thing. How come everybody is so damned twitchy about those guys? They maybe kicked ass around here heading north but that was back at the dawn of time, practically. Four hundred years ago."

The Radisha ignored that. "Kina's antecedents are uncertain. She's a foreign goddess. The legends say a prince of Shadow tricked the most handsome of the Lords of Light out of his physical aspect for a year. While he wore that he seduced Mahi, Goddess of Love, and sired Kina on her. Kina grew up more beautiful than her mother but empty, without a soul, without love or compassion, but hungry to possess them. Her hunger couldn't be satisfied. She preyed upon men and gods alike, Shadow and Light. Among her names are Eater of Souls and Vampire Goddess. She so weakened the Lords of Light that the Shadows thought to conquer them and sent a horde of demons against them. The Lords of Light were so pressed they begged Kina for help. She did help, though *why* she did isn't explained. She met the demons in battle, overthrew them, and devoured them and all their wickedness."

The Radisha paused a moment. Then, "Kina became much worse than she had been, gaining the names Devourer, Destroyer, Destructor. She became a force beyond the gods, outside the balance of Light and Shadow, enemy of all. She became a terror so great Light and Shadow joined forces against her. Her father himself tricked her into falling into an enchanted sleep."

Blade muttered, "Makes as much sense as the story of any other god. Meaning it don't."

Squeaking, Smoke said, "Kina is a personification of that force some call entropy." To the Radisha, "Correct me if I'm wrong."

The Radisha ignored him. "Before Kina fell asleep she realized she'd been tricked. She took a huge breath, exhaled a minute fraction of her soul-essence, no more than a ghost of a ghost. That specter wanders the world in search of living vessels it can possess and use to bring on the Year of the Skulls. If that avatar can free enough souls and cause enough pain, Kina can be wakened."

Swan chuckled like an old woman scolding. "You believe any of that stuff?"

"What I believe doesn't matter, Swan. The Deceivers believe. If the rumor spreads that Kina has been seen, and there's *any* evidence to support it, they'll preach a crusade of murder and torture. Wait!" She raised a hand. "The Taglian people are ripe for an outburst of violence. By damming the normal discharge for generations they've created a reservoir of potential violence. The Deceivers would like that to explode, to bring on the Year of the Skulls. My brother and I would prefer to harness and direct that ferocity."

Blade grumbled about the absurdities of the theological imagination and why didn't people have sense enough to smother would-be priests in their cradles?

The Radisha said, "We don't think the Deceivers have a formal, hierarchical priesthood. They seem to form loose bands, or companies, under an elected captain. The captain appoints a priest, an omen reader, and so forth. His authority is limited. He has little influence outside his band unless he's done something to gain a reputation."

Blade said, "They don't sound so bad to me."

The Radisha scowled. "The main qualification of a priest seems to be education and probity toward his own kind. The bands indulge in crimes of all sorts. Once a year they share out their spoils according to the priest's estimation of the members' contributions toward the glory of Kina. To support his decisions, in the event of dispute, the priest keeps a detailed chronicle of the band's activities."

"Fine and dandy," Swan said. "But how about we get to what you want us to do? We supposed to drag Smoke around to see if we can sniff out what really happened to the Shadowmasters' soldiers?"

"Yes."

"Why bother?"

"I thought I just explained . . ." The Radisha controlled herself. "If that was a true apparition of Kina we have bigger troubles than we thought. The Shadowmasters may be the lesser half."

"I warned you!" Smoke squealed. "I warned you a hundred times. But you wouldn't listen. You had to bargain with devils."

"Shut up." The Radisha glared. "I'm as tired of

you as Swan is. Go find out what happened. And learn what you can about the woman Lady, too."

"I can handle that," Swan said, grinning. "Come on, old buddy." He grabbed Smoke's shoulder. He asked the Radisha, "Think you can manage Jahamaraj Jah without us?"

"I can manage him."

Mounted, ready to ride, waiting for Blade and Smoke, Swan asked, "Cordy, you get the feeling you're out in the woods in the middle of the night and everybody's doing their damnedest to hide the light?"

"Uhm." Mather was more the thinker than Willow or Blade. "They're afraid if we know the whole story we'll desert. They're desperate. They've lost the Black Company. We're all that's left."

"Like the old days."

"Uhm."

The old days. Before the coming of the professionals. When their adopted homeland had made them reluctant captains because the feuding cults couldn't tolerate taking orders from native nonbelievers. A year in the field, playing blind lead the blind, overcoming political shenanigans daily, had convinced Swan that Blade had a point, that it wouldn't hurt the world a bit if you rid it of a few hundred thousand selected priests.

"You buy that Kina stuff?"

"I don't think she told any lies. She just forgot to tell the whole truth."

"Maybe when we get Smoke out there forty miles from nowhere we can squeeze it out of him."

"Maybe. As long as we don't forget what he is. We scare him too much and he's liable to show us what kind of wizard he is. Button it. They're coming."

Smoke looked like he was headed for the gallows. Blade looked as unhappy as ever. But Swan knew he was pleased. Blade figured he was going to get a chance to kick some deserving asses.

Chapter Eleven

The wounded man thought he was trapped in a drug dream. He'd been a physician. He knew drugs did strange things to the mind. Dreams were strange enough. . . . He couldn't wake up.

Some fractured shard of rationality lodged in a corner of his brain watched, sensed, wondered vaguely as he drifted eternally a few feet above a landscape he seldom saw. Sometimes branches passed overhead. Sometimes there were hills in the corners of his eyes. Once he wakened while drifting through tall grass. Once he felt he was passing over a broad expanse of water.

Occasionally a huge black horse looked down at him. He thought he knew the beast but couldn't assemble the pieces in his mind.

Sometimes a figure in shapeless robing bestrode the beast, stared down out of an empty cowl.

These things were all real, he suspected. But they fell into no meaningful pattern. Only the horse seemed familiar.

Hell. He couldn't recall who *he* was. His thoughts wouldn't sequence. Probable pasts kept intruding on the apparent now, often as real.

Those intrusions were shards of battle, uncertain on the jagged edges, bright as blood in the center. Great slaughters, all. Sometimes names attached themselves. Lords. Charm. Beryl. Roses. Horse. Dejagore. Juniper. The Barrowland. Queen's Bridge. Dejagore again. Dejagore often.

Infrequently he recalled a face. The woman had marvellous blue eyes, long black hair, and always wore black. She must have been important to him. Yes. The only woman . . . Whenever she appeared she vanished again in moments, replaced by the faces of men. Unlike the bloodlettings, he could put no names to them. Yet he had known them. He felt they were ghosts, waiting to welcome him among them.

Occasionally pain consumed his chest. He was his most alert when it was most intense. The world almost made sense then. But the creature in black would come and he would tumble back amongst the dreams.

Was the black companion Death? Was this his passage to the nether realm? His mind wouldn't function well enough to examine the proposition.

He hadn't been religious. He'd believed that death was it. When you died you were dead, like a squished bug or drowned rat, and your immortality was in the minds of those you left behind.

He slept far more than he was awake. Thus time eluded him.

He experienced a moment of profound *déjà vu* as he passed beneath a solitary half-dead tree, shortly before entering a dark wood. That tree had been important somehow, sometime.

He drifted through the wood, out, across a clearing, in through the entrance of a building. It was dark inside.

A lamp found life at the edge of his vision. He descended. A flat surface pressed against his back.

The figure in black came, bent over him. A hand concealed in a black glove touched him. Consciousness fled.

He awakened ravenous. A lance of agony bored through his chest, throbbed. He was drenched in his own sweat. His head ached, felt as though it was stuffed with sodden cotton. He was running a fever. His mind worked well enough to catalog symptoms and conclude that he had been wounded and was suffering from a severe cold. That could be a lethal combination.

Memories came tumbling back like a rowdy litter of kittens, all over one another, not making much sense.

He'd led forty thousand men into battle outside Dejagore. It hadn't gone well. He'd been trying to rally the troops. An arrow out of nowhere had driven through his breastplate and chest, miraculously finding nothing vital. He'd fallen. His standard-bearer had donned his armor, trying to turn the tide with a valiant fiction.

Obviously Murgen had failed.

He made a strangling sound through a desert throat.

The figure in black appeared.

Now he remembered. It had dogged the Black Company down the length of the world, accompanied by a horde of crows. He tried to sit up.

The pain was too much for him. He was too weak.

He knew this dread thing!

It came out of nowhere, a lightning bolt, but it was conviction.

Soulcatcher!

The impossible. The dead walking . . .

Soulcatcher. One-time mentor. One-time mistress of the Black Company. More recently a deadly enemy, but still long ago. Supposedly dead for a decade and a half.

He'd been there. He'd seen her slain. He'd helped hunt her down. . . .

He tried to rise again, some vague force driving him to fight the unfightable.

A gloved hand stayed him. A gentle voice told him, "Don't strain yourself. You aren't healing well. You haven't been eating or taking enough fluids. Are you awake? Are you sensible?"

He managed a feeble nod.

"Good. I'm going to prop you up in a slightly elevated position. I'm going to feed you broth. Don't waste energy. Let your strength come back."

She propped him, had him sip through a reed. He downed a pint of broth. And kept it down. Soon a glimmer of strength trickled through his flesh.

"That's enough for now. Now we'll get you cleaned up."

He was a disgusting mess. "How long?" he croaked.

She placed a pot of water in his hands, inserted another reed. "Sip. Don't talk." She started cutting his clothing off him.

"It's been seven days since you were hit, Croaker." Her voice had become another voice entirely. It changed every time she paused. This voice was masculine, mocking, though he wasn't the mockery's object. "Your comrades still control Dejagore, to the embarrassment of the Shadowmasters. Your Mogaba is in command. He's stubborn but he could be embarrassed himself. And however stubborn he is, he can't hold out forever. The powers ranged against him are too great."

He tried to ask a question. She forestalled him. The mocking voice asked, "Her?" Wicked chuckle. "Yes. She survived. There'd be no point to this if she hadn't."

A new voice, female but as hard as a diamond arrowpoint, snarled, "She tried to kill me! Ha-ha! Yes. You were there, my love. You helped. But I don't hold a grudge. You were under her spell. You didn't know what you were doing. You'll redeem yourself by helping me take my revenge."

The man didn't respond.

She bathed him. She was free with the water.

He'd been diminished by his wound but he was still a big man, four inches over six feet tall. He was about forty-five years old. His hair was an average, unnoteworthy brown. He'd begun to go bald in front. His eyes were hard, humorless, icy blue, narrow and deeply set. He had a ragged, greying beard surrounding a thin-lipped mouth that seldom smiled. His face bore scattered reminders of a childhood pox and more than a few memories of acne. He might have been moderately good-looking once. Time had been unkind. Even in repose his face looked hard and a little off center.

He didn't look like what he had been all his adult life, the Black Company's historian and physician. His appearance was more suited to the role he had inherited, that of Captain.

He'd described himself as looking like a child molester waiting for a chance to strike. He wasn't comfortable with his appearance.

Soulcatcher scrubbed him with a vigor that recalled his mother's. "Don't take the skin off."

"Your wound is healing slowly. You'll have to tell me what I did wrong." She'd never been a healer. She was a destroyer.

Croaker was puzzled by her interest. He wasn't valuable. What was he? Just a dinged-up old mercenary, alive well beyond the expectations of his kind. He squeaked a question.

She laughed, voice filled with childlike delight. "Vengeance, dear. A simple, gentle, guileful vengeance. And I won't lay a hand on her. I'll let her do it to herself." She patted his cheek, drew a finger along the line of his jaw.

"It took a while but I knew the moment was inevitable. Fated. The consummation, the exchange of the magic, deadly three words. Fated. I sensed it before you met." Again the childlike laughter. "She was an age finding something so precious. My vengeance will be to take it away."

Croaker closed his eyes. He could not yet reason closely. He understood only that he was in no immediate danger. The plot was easily voided. He would become a tool of no value, broken.

He put it out of mind. First he had to heal. Time enough later to do what had to be done.

More laughter. This from a woman adult and knowing. "Remember when we campaigned together, Croaker? The trick we played on Raker? The fun we had tormenting Limper?"

He grunted. He remembered. Everything but the fun.

"Remember how you always thought I could read your mind?"

He remembered that. And the terror it had inspired. That old fear crept back.

"You *do* remember." She laughed again. "I'm so glad. We're going to have such fun. The whole world thinks we're dead. You can get away with anything when you're dead." Her laugh gained an edge of madness. "We'll haunt them, Croaker. That's what we'll do."

He'd regained enough strength to walk. With help. His captor made him walk, forced him to gain strength. But still he slept most of the time. And dreamed terrible dreams when he did.

The place anchored the dreams. He didn't know that. His dreams told him it wasn't a good place, that the very trees and earth and stone remembered evils done there.

He felt they were true dreams but found no supporting evidence while he was awake. Unless he counted the ominous crows. Always there were the crows, tens and hundreds and thousands of crows.

Standing in the doorway to their shelter—a half-ruined stone structure, buried in vegetation, in the heart of a dark wood—he asked, "What is this place? The wood where I chased you a few months ago?"

"Yes. It's the holy grove of those who worship Kina. If we cleared the creepers you could see carved representations. Once it was important to the Black Company, who took it from the Shadar. The ground is filled with bones."

He turned slowly, looked into her empty cowl. He wouldn't look at the box she carried. He knew what must be in it. "The Black Company?"

"They made sacrifices here. One hundred thousand prisoners of war."

Croaker blanched. That wasn't something he wanted to hear. He had a long romance with the history of the Company. There was no place in that for a wicked past. "Truth?"

"Truth, my love. I've seen the books the wizard Smoke concealed from you in Taglios. They include the missing volumes of your Annals. Your forebears were cruel men. Their mission required the sacrifice of a million souls."

His stomach knotted. "To what? To whom? Why?"

She hesitated. He knew she wasn't being honest when she said, "That wasn't clear. Your lieutenant Mogaba might know, though."

It wasn't what she said but the way she said it, the voice she used. He shuddered. And he believed. Mogaba had been strange and secretive throughout his association with the Company. What was he doing to the Company's traditions now?

"Kina's disciples come here twice a year. Their Festival of Lights comes in a month. We have to finish before then."

Troubled, Croaker asked, "Why *are* we here?"

"We're recovering our health." She laughed. "Where we won't be bothered. Everyone shuns this place. Once I've nursed you back you're going to help me." Still amused, she pushed back her cowl.

She had no head.

She lifted that box she always carried, a battered

thing a foot to a side, opened a little door. A face looked out. It was a beautiful face, like the face of his lover, though less careworn and lacking life's animation.

Impossible.

His stomach knotted again. He recalled the day that head had been struck from its body, to lie in the dust staring up at him and Lady. Her sister. It had been a blow well-earned. Soulcatcher had betrayed the Lady. Soulcatcher had meant to supplant her sister as ruler of the empire.

"I can't do anything like that."

"Of course you can. And you will. Because it will keep both of you alive. We all want to live, don't we? I want her to live because I want her to hurt. I want to live because I want to watch her hurt. You want to live because of her, because you revere the Company, because . . ." Gentle laughter. "Because where there's life there's hope."

Chapter Twelve

Thunder stampeded. Silver lightning lashed the wine-dark clouds, cracked the umber sky. A mold-grey horde howled across a basalt plain, toward the golden chariots of the gods.

A figure stepped from the line, ten feet tall, polished ebony, naked, lifting each foot knee-high to the side, then swinging the leg forward and stamping down. The earth shook.

The figure was female, perfection but hairless, wore a girdle of children's skulls. Her face was protean, one moment radiant dark beauty, the next a nightmare of burning eyes and vampire fangs.

The figure seized a demon and devoured him, rending, tearing, flinging entrails. Demon blood spurted and sprayed. It burned holes in the face of the plain. The figure's jaws distended. She swallowed the demon's head whole. A lump ran down her neck like a mouse bulging a snake's throat.

The horde beset her. And could do her no harm. She devoured another screaming devil, then another

*and another. With each she grew and waxed more
terrible.*

*"I am here, Daughter. Open to me. I am your
dream. I am power."*

*The voice floated like gossamer in golden caverns
where old men sat beside the way, frozen in time,
immortal, unable to move an eyelid. Mad, some covered by fairy webs of ice, as though a thousand spiders had spun with threads of frozen water. Above,
an enchanted forest of icicles hung from the cavern
roof.*

"Come. I am what you seek. You are my child."

*But the footing was treacherous, making it impos-
sible to advance or retreat.*

*The voice called, summoned, with infinite pa-
tience.*

This time I remembered both dreams when I wakened. I still shivered with the chill of those caverns.
The dream was different every time, I thought, and
yet was the same. A summoning.

I'm not stupid. I've seen enough incredibilities to
know the dreams were more than nightmares. Something had singled me out. Something was trying to
recruit me, to what cause I couldn't yet guess. The
method was ancient. I've used it a thousand times.
Offer power, wealth, whatever the desire is, dangling
the lure till the fish bites, never revealing the cost.

Did this thing know me? Unlikely. I was receptive
so it was trying to pull me.

I wouldn't accept it as a god, though it might want
to be thought one. I've met only one god, Old Father
Tree, master of the Plain of Fear. And he's no god in
the accepted sense, only a being of immense longev-
ity and power.

This world has shown me just two beings stronger
than I. My husband, the Dominator, whom I cast into
oblivion. In a thousand years he may be remembered
as a dark god.

And Father Tree, greater than ever I could have been, who has roots anchoring him. He can project his power outside the Plain of Fear only through his servants.

Croaker told me about a third power that lies buried under Father Tree, imprisoned while the tree survives. The tree is immortal by human standards.

Where there are three great powers there could be more. The world is old. Yesterday is shrouded. Those who become great in one age often do so by mining the secrets of ages past. Who knows how many great evils lie beneath this haunted earth?

Who knows but what the gods of all men in all ages are but echoes of those who followed a path like mine and have, nevertheless, fallen victim to implacable time?

Not a thought to soothe the soul. Time is the enemy whose patience can't be exhausted.

"Mistress? Are you troubled?" Narayan's grin was absent. He showed genuine concern.

"Oh." He'd come up quietly. "No. A bad dream that lingered. Nightmares are the coin we pay for doing what we have to do."

He looked at me oddly.

"Do you have nightmares, Narayan?" I'd begun to press him quietly, to weigh his answers to questions probing his flanks.

"Never, Mistress. I sleep like a baby." He turned slowly, surveyed the camp. The countryside was shrouded in mist. "What's the agenda today?"

"Do we have practice weapons enough for a mock combat? One battalion against the other?" I had enough men to field two battalions of four hundred men, with a few hundred left to carry out camp duties and provide one inept cavalry troop.

"Barely. You want that?"

"I'd like to. But how can we reward the victors?" Training involved competitions now, with rewards for winning and for effort. Superior effort, even in losing, deserves recognition. Recognition encourages soldiers to give their best.

"There's relief from fatigues, foraging, and sentry duty."

"That's a possibility." I was also considering letting individuals send for their wives after we moved to Ghoja.

Ram brought me a breakfast bowl. We weren't eating well but we were getting bulk enough, so far. Narayan asked, "How much longer can you stall here?"

"Not long." Time was turning against us. The existence of the band had to be known up north. Potential political enemies would be digging in.

"Instead of mock combat we'll have a review. Spread a rumor that I'm thinking of moving out if what I see pleases me." That ought to motivate them.

"Yes, Mistress." Narayan retreated. He gathered his cronies, a dozen men who showed snips of colored cloth at their waists.

An interesting group. They sprang from all three major religions, two minor cults, and from among the liberated foreign slaves. They pretty much ran the camp though only Narayan and Ram had official standing. They kept the peace. The men weren't quite sure how to take them, but responded seriously because of that aura of the sinister that I'd noted myself.

Narayan admitted nothing. He handled my probes deftly. There was no doubt he directed the dozen, though several sprang from higher castes.

I kept an eye on him. Time would betray him—if he didn't open up, as he hinted he might.

For the moment he was too useful to press.

I nodded approval. "They almost look like soldiers." We'd have to get them uniform dress.

Narayan nodded. He seemed smug, as though his genius had produced our triumph and sparked a renascent spirit.

"How're the riding lessons coming?" Just making talk. I knew. Abysmally. None of these clowns belonged to a caste that got closer to a horse than to trail along behind cleaning up. But, damn, it would be a sin to waste those mounts.

"Poorly. Though a few men show promise. Not including myself or Ram. We were born to walk."

"Show promise" had become his favorite expression. In reference to everything. As he taught me to use the strangler's kerchief, or *rumel*, at my insistence, he said I showed promise.

I suspected he was surprised at how easily I picked it up. Its manipulation came as naturally as breathing, as though it was a skill I'd had all along. Maybe it came of centuries of practice at the quick, subtle gestures needed to manipulate sorceries.

"You were saying you were going to move?" Narayan asked. "Mistress." The honorific was becoming an afterthought. Narayan remained Taglian. He was beginning to take me for granted.

"Our foragers are having to range pretty far."

Narayan didn't reply but seemed reluctant to go.

I had a feeling I was being watched. At first I credited it to the crows. They kept me uncomfortable. Now I understood Croaker's reaction better. They didn't behave the way crows ought. I'd mentioned them to Narayan. He'd grinned and called them a good omen.

Meaning they were a bad omen for someone else.

I scanned our surroundings. The crows were there, in their scores, but . . . "Narayan, collect the dozen best horsemen. I'm taking a patrol out."

"But . . . Do you think . . . ?"

How could I get through? "I'm no garden rose. I'm taking a patrol out."

"As you command, Mistress, so shall it be."

It had better, Narayan. It had better.

Chapter Thirteen

Swan glanced at Blade. The black man's attitude toward Smoke had grown from disdain into contempt. The wizard had no more spine than a worm. He shook like a leaf.

Cordy said, "That's her."

Swan nodded. He grinned but kept his thoughts to himself. "She's putting something together. That gang is more organized than any I've seen down here."

They backed off the knoll from which they'd been watching the camp. Blade said, "We going to drop in?" He had hold of the wizard's sleeve like he expected the runt to run.

"Not yet. I want to circle around, check it out down south. Shouldn't be that far to where they hit the Shadowmasters' men. I want to see the place. If we can find it."

Cordy asked, "Think they know we're here?"

"What?" The idea startled Swan.

"You said they're organized. Nobody ever accused

the Lady of not being efficient. She should have pickets out."

Swan thought. No one had entered or left the camp, but Mather had a point. If they wanted to remain unnoticed they'd better move on. "You're right. Let's go. Blade, you were down here before. Know how to cross that creek somewhere that's not too far out of the way?"

Blade nodded. In those desperate days before the Black Company picked up the reins he'd led guerrillas behind the Shadowmasters' main forces.

"Lead on. Smoke, old buddy, I wish I could get a peek inside your head. I never seen anybody so ready to drizzle down his leg."

The wizard said nothing.

Blade found a game ford three miles east of the south road, led the way through woods narrower than Swan expected. When they reached the southern side, Blade said, "Road's two miles that way."

"I figured." The sky was dark with buzzards. "That's where we'll find our dead men."

That was the place.

The air was still. The stench hung like a poisonous miasma. Neither Swan nor Mather had a stomach strong enough to let them take a close look. Blade, though, seemed to have no sense of smell.

He returned. Swan said, "You look green around the gills."

"Not much but bones left. Been a while. Two hundred, three hundred men. Hard to tell now. Animals been at them. One thing. No heads."

"Eh?"

"No heads. Somebody cut them off."

Smoke moaned, then chucked his breakfast. His mount shied.

"No heads?" Swan asked. "I don't get it."

Mather said, "I've got an idea. Come on." He rode south, toward where crows circled, dipped, and squabbled.

They found the heads.

Blade asked, "Want to get a count?" He chuckled.

"No. Let's drop in on our friends."

Smoke made protesting noises.

Cordy asked, "You still hot to trot with your proud beauty?"

Swan couldn't think of a flip answer. "Maybe I'm starting to see Smoke's viewpoint. Don't let me get on her bad side."

Blade said, "Only a mile to their camp straight up the road."

Swan snorted. "We'll go around, thank you."

After they crossed the game ford, Mather suggested, "Suppose we go up the road a ways and come down like we don't know nothing about back there? See what they say if they think we just rode in."

"Stop whining, Smoke," Swan said. "Go with it. You got no choice. You're right, Cordy. It'll give us a clue if she's going to play games."

They rode north till they were behind a rise, turned west to the road, then turned south. They were almost back to the crest when Mather, in the lead, yelled, "Yo! Look out!"

Chapter Fourteen

We crossed the creek into the wood, walking our mounts behind Sindhu, who had scouted till he knew every leaf and twig of the surrounding terrain. He led us along a meandering game trail which paralleled the creek going westward. I wondered what had become of the game. We hadn't seen anything bigger than a squirrel. A few native deer might have eased the food problem, though neither Gunni nor Shadar touch meat.

It was a long walk. My companions grumbled and bickered.

The watching presence centered on a grove on a knoll whence it would be possible to observe events in our camp. I'd lapsed. I'd been thinking too far ahead. If I'd had the sense of a goose I'd have had a squad posted there. The outlying pickets were too scattered to spot everything moving in the area, even if people weren't sneaking around. Fugitives slipped through all the time. They left their traces.

I had a good idea what I'd find on that knoll. Somebody from up north who'd heard rumors and had gotten worried that I might be trouble. I meant to be a lot, for the Shadowmasters and anybody who got between us.

We crossed the creek a few miles downstream, out of sight of the knoll, moved back to the east, and discovered that there was no way to approach the grove unseen the last third of a mile. I told the men, "All we can do is ride straight at it. Let's do it without getting in a hurry. Maybe they won't run till we're so close they can't get away."

I didn't know if they could control themselves. The excitement had them again. They were pumped up, scared and eager.

"Let's go."

We'd covered half the open ground when the watchers flushed like quail. "Shadar," somebody noted.

Yes. Mounted Shadar, in uniform, cavalry equipped. "Jahamaraj Jah's men!" I snapped.

The men cursed. Even those who were Shadar.

Jah was the leading Shadar priest in Taglios. Croaker's doing. Jah's concession to his debt hadn't lasted through the fighting at Dejagore. He and his cavalry had abandoned the field while the outcome was in question. Most of the men had seen them run, or had heard. I'd been pushing the idea that the battle would've been ours had Jah stood his ground.

It could be true. Jah had contributed nothing when a feather's weight might have tilted the balance.

I thought he'd run because he'd suffered an opportunistic flash. He'd intuited that the battle would go poorly and had decided to beat everybody home. He'd play a strong hand there because he'd be the only man with a military force—however inept—to back him up.

He deserved some special thought now.

I didn't have to order a chase. There were five Shadar. Their flight was proof they were blackhearts. The men rode with blood in their eyes. Unfortunately, the Shadar were better riders.

I did want to talk to them. I urged my stallion to his best pace and closed up fast.

No everyday mount stood a chance against him.

The Shadar hit the north road. As I nosed up on the most laggardly the leaders swept over the crest. And collided with riders headed south.

Horses shied. Men yelled. Riders came unhorsed. I circled a Shadar who regained his feet and tried to run. He'd lost his helmet. I grabbed him by the hair, ran him fifty yards before turning to examine the victims of the collision.

Well. Swan, Mather, and Blade. And that sneaking twit of a hedge wizard, Smoke. What now?

Mather, Smoke, and Blade had kept their seats. Swan was on the ground, groaning and swearing. He got up, swore some more, kicked a fallen Shadar, looked around for his horse.

Smoke was rattled right down to his ankles. He had no color left, was whispering some sort of prayer.

Mather and Blade ignored Swan's histrionics. I presumed that meant he wasn't hurt.

My captive tried to get away. I ran him a few yards, let him loose when the horse was moving faster than he could keep up. He flung forward, slid on his face, stopped at Swan's feet. Swan sat down on him. I asked Mather, "What are you doing here?" He was the only one of the bunch who made straight sense.

"The Radisha sent us. Wants to know what's happening down here. There have been rumors. Some say you're alive, some say dead."

"I'm not yet. Not quite."

My men arrived. "Ghopal. Hakim. Take these two somewhere and ask them why they were snooping." They were Narayan's cronies, the only two who could ride. He'd probably sent them along to keep an eye on things.

Swan got up and leaned against Mather's leg. "You

don't have to twist no arms to find that out. Been some wild rumors lately. You've got Jah jumpy as a cat in a kennel.''

"Oh?"

"Things were going his way. He got back from Dejagore before anybody else. Only bad luck put the Radisha at Ghoja before him. She closed the ford. He still figured he had the world by the oysters, then here comes word somebody's kicked the feathers off a gang of the Shadowmasters' boys. Right behind comes a rumor that it was you. You not being dead don't look so good for Jah's ambitions. The Company picked up a lot of respect putting it together so fast. Made all those priests look like conniving, selfish jerks.''

Blade chuckled.

Mather said, "You collected some of that respect, being a woman and having everybody know how much you had to do with it falling together.'' He looked me in the eye. "But being a woman is going to be a handicap now."

"I've been on my own before, Mather." And I hadn't been happy a moment. But happiness is a fleeting creature. It's no birthright. Not anything I expect but something I accept when I stumble into it. Meantime, power will do nicely. "And Jah has liabilities. He's vulnerable. I have a thousand men over there. Every one will tell you Jah ran out on us at Dejagore. We would've won if it wasn't for him.''

Swan surprised me. "We watched the battle. We saw. So did a lot of men who've come in. Even some of Jah's own men admit it.''

"A liability," Mather said. "But it's not going to undo him.''

Ghopal reminded me that three Shadar had escaped. True. And they would fly straight to their master, who was sure to make a move. But I doubted he'd do it right away. He was a vacillator. He'd worry a while before committing himself.

"Back to camp. Swan. Come. Ghopal. Bring the

prisoners." I rode ahead as hard as the stallion could carry me.

"Sound the alarm and the recall," I told the soldiers at the north gate. "Narayan! Ram!"

They came running. Narayan gasped, "What is it, Mistress?"

"We're pulling out. Right now. Forced march. Get the men ready. Let the horses carry most of the load. Make sure each man carries food. We won't stop for meals. Move."

They scooted.

It was midafternoon. Ghoja was forty miles away, a ten-hour jaunt if everyone kept the pace. If the night wasn't too dark. It shouldn't be if the sky stayed clear. There'd be a quarter moon rising an hour after sunset. Not a lot of light, but maybe enough.

The horns that we'd taken from the Shadowmasters' cavalry kept sounding recall. The pickets came running. The gang I'd left up the road arrived. Swan and Mather were impressed by the chaos.

Mather said, "You've taught well."

"I think so."

"What're you fixing to do?" Swan asked.

"Take charge at Ghoja before Jah can react."

He groaned.

"You have a problem with that?"

"Only that we just got finished riding down here. Forty more miles and I won't have a spine left."

"So walk. Sindhu! Come here." I took the wide man aside, gave him instructions. He left smiling, gathered two dozen men with strong stomachs, mostly his cronies, and crossed the creek. I sent another man to round up the poles we used for practice pikes and spears.

Swan asked, "You mind if we get something to eat?"

"Help yourself. Then find me. I want to talk to you."

Idiot. He gave me a big, nervous smile. I didn't

need to be a mind-reader to get what was going on in the back of his head.

The troops got it together faster than I expected. They had the word. Ghoja. Straight through.

I still had a serious problem, lack of a command structure. I had solid squads and the squad leaders by tens had picked company commanders, but none of those had had more than a few days' practice. And neither of my formally organized battalions had anyone in charge.

"Mather."

He set his food aside. "Ma'am?"

"You strike me as a responsible man. Also, you have field experience and a reputation. I have two battalions of four hundred men but no commanders. My man Narayan can muddle through with one if I keep him out of trouble. I need somebody to handle the other. A known hero would be perfect—if I thought he wouldn't work against me."

Mather looked me in the eye for several seconds. "I work for the Radisha. I couldn't."

"I could."

I turned. That was Blade.

Smoke had a squeaking fit.

Blade grinned, the first I'd seen him do so. "I don't owe you anything, little man." He turned to Swan. "What did I say? Ain't over yet."

Something flickered across Swan's face. He wasn't happy. "You're putting us in a bad spot, Blade."

"You putting yourself there, Swan. You said it, what kind of people they are. Soon as they got what they want they going to stick it in you. That right, wizard? Like you done the Black Company?"

Smoke staggered. He would've been dead if he'd had a bad heart. He looked like he expected me to roast him. I smiled. I'd let him stew a little first. "I'll accept your offer, Blade. Come meet your hundred-leaders."

Once we were out of earshot of the others I asked, "What did you mean by that remark?"

"Less than it sounded. The wizard, the Radisha, the

Prahbrindrah, they hurt you more by deceit than treachery. They withheld information. I can't tell you what. I don't know. They thought we were spies you sent ahead. But I can tell you they never meant to keep their agreement. For some reason they don't want you to get to Khatovar."

Khatovar. Croaker's mystery destination, the place the Black Company had originated. For four hundred years the Company moved northward slowly, in the service of various princes, till it came into mine, then of my enemies, and was reduced to a handful of men. After the battle in the Barrowland, Croaker turned back south with fewer followers than my squad leaders had today.

We'd gathered a man here, a man there, and when we'd reached Taglios we'd discovered we couldn't cross the last four hundred miles because the principalities of the Shadowmasters lay between us and Khatovar. There was only one way to cover those final miles. Take Taglios, already pressed by the Shadowmasters, with its pacifist history, and win an impossible war.

The agreement with the Prahbrindrah had been that the Company would train and lead a Taglian army. Once the war had been won that army would support the Company's quest for Khatovar.

"Interesting," I told Blade. "But not a surprise. Sindhu!" He was back. He'd moved fast. Whatever he was, he could do a job. I told him, "I want you to stick to our guests." I indicated Swan, Mather, and Smoke. "Show the little one your rumel if they abuse our hospitality."

He nodded.

"They're to walk like everyone else."

He nodded again, went back to mounting skulls on poles.

Blade watched for a moment but said nothing, though I'm sure he had thoughts.

We marched out an hour after I decided to move. I was pleased.

Chapter Fifteen

We didn't reach Ghoja in ten hours but I hadn't expected to make four miles an hour in the dark. We did get in before dawn and, with Blade's connivance, we chose a campsite which both shouldered the road and almost nudged Jahamaraj Jah's encampment. We were there an hour before anyone noticed. Sloppy. Deadly sloppy. If we'd been the Shadowmasters' cavalry we could have cleaned the area.

We used the skulls and poles to mark the bounds of the camp. I had the interior laid out in a checkerboard cross with the center square for the headquarters group, the four squares on its points for four battalions with the squares between as drill grounds. The men grumbled about having to set up for twice their number—especially since certain favored individuals, who had been performing well, only had to stand around holding poles with skulls atop them.

Croaker had been fond of showmanship. He'd said you should adjust the minds of observers to think what you wanted them to think. That was never my style, but in the past I'd had brute force to waste. Here, let everyone think I believed I'd soon have men enough for four battalions and the battalions would expand.

Tired as they were, the men were content to work and grumble. I saw no shirking. No one deserted.

People came out of the fortress and other camps to watch. The men Narayan sent to gather firewood and timber and stone ignored their undisciplined cousins. Skulls looking down moved the curious to keep their distance. Sindhu babysat Swan, Mather, and Smoke. Blade took his appointment seriously. The men in his battalion accepted him. He was one of the heroes of the desperate hours before the coming of the Company.

It was almost too sweet.

But nothing crept up. I watched the watchers.

The camp was three-quarters complete, including a ditch and embankment and the rudiments of a palisade faced with locust thorns and wild rose canes. Jahamaraj Jah rode out of his camp, watched for fifteen minutes. He didn't look pleased by our industry.

I summoned Narayan. "You see Jah?" He was hard to miss. He was as gaudy as a prince. He'd carried all that with him on campaign?

"Yes, Mistress."

"I'll be on the other side of camp for a while. If some of your men—especially Shadar—suffered a lapse of discipline and called him coward and deserter I doubt their punishments would be onerous."

He grinned, started to dart away.

"Hold it."

"Mistress?"

"You seen to have friends everywhere. I wouldn't be averse to knowing what's going on around here if you found contacts. Maybe Ghopal and Hakim and a few others could desert when you weren't looking. Or otherwise get out and poke around."

"Consider it done."

"I do. I trust you that far. I know you'll do what needs to be done."

His grin faded. He caught the warning edge.

From Narayan I went to Swan. "How are you doing?"

"Dying of boredom. Are we prisoners?"

"No. Guests with limited mobility. Now free to go. Or stay. I could use your cachet."

Smoke shook his head vigorously, as though he feared Swan would desert the Radisha. I told him, "You're awfully anxious to hang onto a Black Company spy."

He looked at me and went through some internal change, as though he'd decided to abandon ineffectual tactics. It wasn't a dramatic shift, though. The role he'd been in couldn't have been that far from the real Smoke.

He never said a word.

Swan grinned and winked. "I'm gone. But I got a feeling I'll be back."

The racket started up in Narayan's sector as I watched Swan go. I wondered how Jah was taking it.

Swan was back within the hour. "She wants to see you."

"Why am I not surprised? Ram, get Narayan and Blade. Sindhu, too."

I took Narayan and Blade with me. Sindhu I left in charge, hinting that I'd be pleased if the camp was finished when I got back.

I paused at the gate of the Ghoja fortress, glanced back. It was an hour short of noon. We had been here six hours. Already my camp was the most complete, best protected, most military.

Professionalism and preparedness are relative, I suppose.

Chapter Sixteen

Croaker hobbled to the temple door, looked out. Soulcatcher was nowhere around. He hadn't seen her for days. He wondered if he'd been abandoned. He doubted it. She'd just waited till he was able to care for himself, then had hurried off on some arcane business.

He thought of making a run for it. He knew the surrounding country. There was a village he could reach in a few hours, even at the pace he could make. But that escape would be no escape.

Soulcatcher was away but the crows had stayed to watch. They would stay with him. They would lead her to him. She had the horses. Those beasts could run forever without tiring. She could spot him a week's lead and catch him.

Still . . .

This place was like an island outside the world. It was dark and depressing.

He started walking, going nowhere, moving for the sake of movement. The crows nagged at him. He ig-

nored them, ignored the ache thumping in his chest.
He strolled through the woods, to the countryside
beyond, emerging near the half-dead tree.

He recalled it now. Before Dejagore and Ghoja he
had come south to scout the terrain, had spied Soulcatcher watching, had chased her into these woods.
He'd stood by that tree trying to decide what to do
next—and an arrow had hit it, nearly taking off his
nose. It had carried a message, telling him it wasn't
time for him to catch whomever he was chasing.

Then the Shadowmasters' men had come after him
and he'd been too busy running to give the place any
more thought.

He walked up to the tree. Crows burdened its
branches. He fingered the hole where the arrow had
hit. She'd been watching over him then, hadn't she?
Not interfering but there just in case, maybe laying
on a nudge or two to make sure he was around for
her revenge.

A long, lazy hill lay before. He decided to ignore
the crows. He kept walking.

The pain in his chest became insistent. He wasn't
ready for so much exercise. He couldn't have gone
far even without the crows keeping track.

As he paused to rest he wondered how much Soulcatcher had intruded on his affairs. Could she have
had some hand in the outcome at Dejagore?

Destroying Stormbringer, who had worn the alias
Stormshadow, had been easier than he'd expected.
And getting Shapeshifter had been a breeze, too—
though there'd been a little treachery to that, since
Shifter had been helping Lady. Which reminded him.
That girl. Shifter's apprentice. She'd gotten away.
She could be thinking of evening scores. Did Soul-
catcher know about her? Better mention her next
chance he got.

His heartbeat had fallen off toward normal. The
pain had waned. He resumed walking. He reached
the ridgeline and stood leaning against a gnarly grey
piece of exposed rock, panting while crows circled

and nattered. "Oh, shut up! I'm not going any-where."

Another outcrop nearby vaguely suggested a chair. He shuffled over and sat, surveyed his kingdom.

All Taglios could have been his if he'd won at De-jagore, had that been his ambition.

A flight of three crows arrowed in from the north, coming like racing pigeons, swirled into the flock, cawed some. The whole mob scattered. Odd.

He leaned back, thought about the battle's after-math. Mogaba was alive and holding the city against besieging Shadowmasters, according to Soul-catcher. Maybe a third of the army had managed to get inside the walls. Fine. A stubborn defense would keep them away from Taglios. But he didn't care that much about Taglios. Nice people, but anybody who was anybody was thoroughly treacherous.

He was concerned about the few friends he'd left down south. Had any survived? Had they salvaged the Annals, those precious histories that were the time link cementing the Company? What had be-come of Murgen and the standard and his Widow-maker armor? Legend said the standard had been with the Company since the day it had marched from Khatovar.

What were those damned crows up to? Moments ago there had been a thousand of them. Now he couldn't see a dozen. Those all glided at high alti-tude, drifting back and forth over something up the valley.

Had Khatovar become a hopeless dream? Had the last page of the Annals been written just four hun-dred miles from home?

Sudden memory from the first hours of their jour-ney away from Dejagore. Just an image, of a man floating, writhing upon a lance. Moonshadow? Yes. And Moonshadow had been skewered upon that lance during the fighting. Skewered on the lance that supported the standard.

It wasn't lost! That heirloom more important than

the Annals themselves was down there in the temple somewhere. He hadn't seen it. She must have hidden it.

He glanced at a sky where cumulus marched across a turquoise field. The crows were closer, those few still aloft. He jerked, startled. One was headed his way like a winged missile.

It flapped, fluttered, very nearly suicided, making a landing on a rock pinnacle inches from his left hand. The bird said, "Don't move!" in a perfectly intelligible voice.

He didn't move, though instantly he had a dozen questions. It took no genius to understand that something significant was happening. The birds didn't speak to him otherwise. In fact, they had only once before, bringing the warning that had allowed him to move in time to whip the Shadowmasters at Ghoja ford.

The crow hunkered down and became part of the rock. Croaker eased down a little himself, so he'd present no obviously human form against the skyline, then froze. Moments later he spied movement in the shallow valley before him.

It darted from cover to cover. Then there was more movement, and more. His heart hammered as he remembered the shadows the minions of the Shadowmasters had brought north.

These were no shadows. They were small brown men, but not of the race of the small brown men who had managed the shadows. Those had been cousins of the Taglians. Something familiar about these. But they were so far away.

It didn't occur to them to look up where he was seated. Or if they did they couldn't see him. They moved on down the valley.

Then there were more of them, maybe twenty-five, not sneaking like the others, who must have been scouts. He saw this bunch well enough to recall where he'd seen their kind before. On the great river that ran from the heart of the continent down past

Taglios to the sea. He had fought them a year ago, two thousand miles north of here. They had blockaded the river against all commerce. The Company had opened the way, crushing them in a wild nighttime battle where sorceries flashed and howled.

The Howler!

The main party was in sight. Eight men carried a ninth on a sedan of sorts. The ninth was a small figure so covered with clothing it looked like a pile of rags. As it came abreast of Croaker it let out a prolonged moan.

The Howler. One of the Ten Who Were Taken who had been servants of the Lady in her northern empire, a terrible wizard, thought slain in battle till that night on the river when he'd tried to even old scores against his former empress. Only the intercession of Shifter had driven him off.

Another moan escaped the sorcerer. It was a feeble shadow of the Howler's usual wails. Probably trying to control his cries to avoid attracting attention.

Croaker sat so still his heart almost stopped. There was little in the world he wanted less than to attract attention now. His concentration was so intense he felt no discomfort from rock or chill breeze.

The party passed on, with more small brown men trailing behind, in rearguard. It was an hour before Croaker was confident that he had seen the last of them.

He had counted one hundred twenty-eight swamp warriors, plus the sorcerer. The warriors wouldn't be much use so far out of their element. This terrain was alien to them. But the Howler . . . Terrain and climate and whatnot meant nothing to him.

Where was he headed? Didn't take much to guess. Down to the Shadowlands. Why was more of a mystery, but probably not so great a one.

The Howler had been one of the Taken. Some of the Shadowmasters had been fugitive Taken, too. It seemed likely the survivors had made contact with their former comrade and had negotiated some compact whereby he would replace the Shadowmasters who had fallen.

Lady was alive and at Ghoja, if Soulcatcher hadn't lied. Not forty miles away. He wished he could make that journey. He wished there was some way he could get a message to her. She needed to know about this.

"Crow, I don't know if you know what we just saw, but you'd better get word to your boss. We got trouble." He got up and walked back to the temple, where he amused himself by trying to find the hidden Company standard.

Chapter Seventeen

The everyday business of sorcery is as much stage magic as it is witchcraft. It's misdirection, deceit, what-have-you. I kept an eye on Smoke, expecting him to pass information to the Radisha in some subtle fashion. But if he did he was too crafty for me. Which I doubt.

When you encounter the Radisha you know you're in the presence of a powerful will. It was a shame she was trapped in her culture and had to pretend to be her brother's creature. She might have done interesting things.

"Good afternoon," she said. "We're pleased that you survived."

Was she? Maybe, because there were still Shadowmasters to be conquered. "So am I."

She noted that Blade stood with me instead of his friends. She noted Narayan, of obvious low caste and no cleaner than the day we'd met—though I had no room to criticize. A shadow crossed her brow. "My battalion commanders," I said. "Blade you know.

Narayan, who has been helpful pulling the men together.''

She looked at Narayan intently, maybe because of
his unusual name and the fact that I'd added no
other. I didn't know any other name for him. Narayan was a patronym. We had six more Narayans
among the Shadar troops. Every one of them carried
the personal name Singh, which means Lion.

She caught something with that closer look,
started slightly, glanced at Smoke. The wizard replied with a tiny nod. She looked at Blade. ''You
choose to leave me?''

''I'm going with somebody who can get something
done besides talk.''

That was a long speech for Blade and one that won
him no sympathy. The Radisha glared.

''He's got a point,'' Swan said. ''You and your
brother just keep fiddling.''

''We're more exposed.'' People in positions like
theirs do have to act within constraints or get pulled
down. But try to explain that to men who have never
been anything but momentary captains and didn't
want that power when they had it.

The Radisha rose. ''Come,'' she told us. As we
walked, she told me, ''I *am* pleased that you survived. Though you may find it difficult to continue
doing so.''

That didn't sound like a threat, exactly. ''What?''

''You're in a difficult position because your Captain didn't survive.'' She led us up a spiral stair to
the parapet of the fortress's tallest tower. My companions were as puzzled as I. The Radisha pointed.

Beyond the trees and construction across the river
there was a large, ragtag encampment. The Radisha
said, ''Some fugitives crossed elsewhere and carried
word north. People started arriving the day after
Swan rode south. There are about two thousand already. There'll be thousands more.''

''Who are they?'' Swan asked.

''Families of legionnaires. Families of men the

Shadowmasters enslaved. They've come to find out what happened to their menfolk." She pointed upstream.

Scores of women were stacking wood. I asked, "What are they doing?"

"Building ghats." Narayan sounded nonplussed. "I should have considered that."

"What are ghats?"

"Funeral pyres," Mather said. "The Gunni burn their dead instead of burying them." He looked a little green.

I didn't follow. "There aren't any dead here. Unless somebody makes some." A symbolic gesture? Funerals in absentia?

"The practice is called suttee," Smoke said. I looked at him. He stood straight up and wore a slimy grin. "When a man dies his wife joins him on his ghat. If he dies away from home she joins him in death when she learns of it."

Oh? "Those women are building pyres where they can commit suicide if their husbands have been killed?"

"Yes."

"A damnfool thing to do."

Smoke's smile grew. "It's a custom as old as Taglios. With the force of law."

I didn't like the way he was getting happy. He thought he had a tool to use against me.

"A waste. Who takes care of the children? Never mind. I don't care." The concept was so alien I discounted it. I'm not sure I even believed him.

The Radisha said, "The custom is revered by everyone, even those who aren't Gunni."

"There are crazies everywhere. It's a hideous practice. It should be abolished. But I'm not here to change any social sillinesses. We're at war. We've suffered a setback. A lot of our men are trapped in Dejagore. It's not likely we can save them. More are in flight. We *can* save some of those. And we have to raise new levies so we can cling to what we've gained."

Swan said, "Sweetie, you're missing the point."

"I got the point, Swan. It's irrelevant."

The Radisha said, "You're a woman. You have no friends. Every man of any substance in every priesthood is going to make a point of your relationship with your Captain. A large point of your failure to commit suttee. That will weigh heavily with a large portion of the population."

"It may be the custom. It's an idiot custom and I'll bet it's not universal. I shan't dignify the suggestion—unless I decide that for bringing it up the suggester will be delivered to his suggestion."

Smoke's grin faded.

His eyes narrowed and clouded. His jaw dropped for a second. He was staring at my hand. I realized I'd picked up Narayan's tic, was fingering the bit of yellow cloth peeping from my waist.

Smoke's color turned ghastly.

I said, "Radisha, ask these two about my background." I indicated Swan and Mather. They'd emigrated from my empire while I was at the pinnacle of my power. "Some of the Company have fallen but our contract remains in force. I intend to execute the undertaking."

"Admirable. But you'll find that a lot of people won't want to let you do that."

I shrugged. "What they want doesn't matter. The contract has been made. Better understand that. You people think you know more about us than we do. You must know we don't let anybody back out on a contract."

The Radisha looked at me intently, unafraid, curious about my confident attitude here alone in a sea of enemies.

I said, "I'll present a list of needs tomorrow. Manpower, drayage, animals, weapons, equipment." Half of confidence is the appearance of confidence.

Somebody shouted from the stairwell. The Radisha signalled Mather, who checked it. He came back, said, "Jah's kicking up a fuss. Wants to see you. Guess that means he knows you're here."

I said, "Might as well meet him head on."

"Tell them to bring him, Mather."

Mather passed the word. We waited. The Radisha and I eyed one another like she-leopards. I asked, "Why are you afraid of the Company?"

She didn't bat an eye. "You know quite well."

"I do? I've studied the history of the Company in detail. I don't recall anything that would explain your attitude."

Smoke whispered something. I think he accused me of lying. I was developing an intense dislike for him.

Jahamaraj Jah swept in like a king.

I was curious to see how the Radisha handled the handicap of her sex.

In a moment I was curious to see how Jah handled *his* handicap. He had made his entrance dramatically. He had looked us over. We hadn't responded to the gloriousness of his size, his wealthy apparel, the power he represented. Now he didn't know what to do next.

He was a fool. Croaker hadn't quite erred in ridding the Shadar of his predecessor. That man had been our enemy. But Jah wasn't much of an improvement. He was all appearance without substance.

He was impressive for a Taglian, six feet and two hundred pounds, half a foot taller than average and much more massive. His skin was fairer than most—a desirable trait from the Taglian perspective. Wealthy women often spent their entire lives hiding from the sun. He was handsome even by northern standards. But his mouth was petulant and his eyes gave the impression he was a moment short of breaking into tears because he wasn't getting his own way.

The Radisha gave him ten seconds, snapped, "You have something to say?"

Indecision. He was surrounded by people who had no use for him. Several would have cut his throat happily. Even Smoke found the nerve to look at him like he was a slug.

I said, "Caught by a jury of your enemies. I'd thought you were better at the game."

"What game?" He wasn't good at concealing his feelings. What he thought of me came through.

"Intrigue. That was a poor move, running at Dejagore. Everybody will blame you."

"Hardly. The battle was lost. I made sure a force survived."

"You ran out before it was decided. Your own men say so," the Radisha snapped. "If you give us any grief we'll remind the families of those men who aren't coming home."

Pure hatred. Jah wasn't used to being thwarted. "I'm not accustomed to being threatened. I don't tolerate it from anyone."

I asked, "Do you recall how you came to power? People might be interested in the details."

Among them, everyone there. The others stared, wondering. "You'd be wise to go quietly, abandon the pursuit of arms and power, and content yourself with what you have."

He glared daggers.

"You're vulnerable. You can't erase that. You've made too many poor choices. Keep it up and you'll destroy yourself."

He looked at us, found no sympathy anywhere. His only weapon was bluster. He knew what that was worth. "This round to you." He headed downstairs.

Blade laughed.

He did it knowing Jah couldn't tolerate being mocked. Blade *wanted* trouble.

I sent him a warning look. He stared back impassively. He wasn't intimidated by anyone.

Jah was gone. I said, "I have work to do. We aren't accomplishing anything. We know where we stand. I expect to finish the Company's work. You intend to let that go only as far as it conveniences you, then you plan to backstab me. I don't plan to let you. Blade. You coming or staying?"

"Coming. There's nothing here for me."

Swan and Mather looked croggled, Smoke pained, and the Radisha exasperated.

As soon as we left the fortress, Blade said, "Jah could try something desperate now."

"I'll handle it. He'll vacillate till it's too late. Check on your battalion." Once he was out of hearing, I told Narayan, "He's right. Do we wait for Jah? Or do we move first?"

He didn't respond, just waited for me to answer myself.

"We'll do something when we know he's planning something himself."

I surveyed the camp. The outer enclosure was complete. It would do for the moment. I'd keep making improvements, mainly to keep the men occupied. A wall can never be too high or a ditch too deep.

"I want the Shadar to know I need cavalrymen. Their response will show us what support Jah has. Pass the word amongst all the fugitives that those who join voluntarily will get preferential treatment. We need volunteers from the provinces, too. We need to spread our story before these idiots unleash the hounds of factionalism."

"There are ways to get word out," Narayan admitted. "But we'll have to send some of my friends across the river."

"Do what you have to. Starting now. We don't mark time. We don't let them catch their balance. Go."

I climbed a platform that had been erected near what would become the camp's north gate, surveyed the countryside. My men were as busy as ants.

Their industry hadn't communicated itself to anyone else. Only the builders across the river, and the Gunni women, were doing much.

Smoke curled up from one of the ghats. When the flames were roaring a woman threw herself in.

I had to believe it now.

I retired to the shelter Ram had built, settled to stretch the limits of my talent. I'd be needing it soon.

Chapter Eighteen

The dreams worsened. They were dreams of death.

We all have nightmares but I'd never recalled so many so clearly after I wakened. Some force, some power, was summoning me. Was trying to enlist or subject me.

Those dreams were the creations of a sick mind. If they were supposed to appeal to me, that power didn't know me.

Landscapes of despair and death under skies of lead, fields where bodies rotted and stunted vegetation melted down like slow, soft candlewax. Slime covered everything, hung in strands like the architecture of drunken spiders.

Mad. Mad. Mad. And not a touch of color anywhere.

Mad. And yet with its taint of perverse appeal. For amongst the dead I'd see faces I wished amongst the dead. I strode that land unharmed, vitally alive, its ruler. The ghouls that ran with me were extensions of my will.

It was a dream straight out of the fantasies of my dead husband. It was a world he could have made home.

Always, in the late hours, there'd be a dawn in that land of nightmare, a splash of color on a poorly defined horizon. Always in front of me, it seemed the dawn of hope.

Simple and direct, the architect of my dreams.

There was one dream, less common, that did without the death and corruption, yet was as chilling in its way. Black and white too, it placed me upon a plain of stone where deadly shadows lurked behind countless obelisks. I didn't understand it at all but it frightened me.

I couldn't control the dreams. But I refused to let them influence my waking hours, refused to let them wear me down.

"I've sent word out, Mistress," Narayan said, responding to my question about recruits. We fenced whenever the subject of his brotherhood arose. He wasn't yet ready to talk.

Blade suggested, "Someone ought to be watching things at Dejagore." I understood, though sometimes his brevity caused problems.

Narayan said, "Ghopal and Hakim can take a party down. Twenty men should have no trouble. It'll be quiet now."

I said, "You had them spying on our neighbors."

"They're done. They've made their contacts. Sindhu can take over. He has a higher reputation."

Another of those little oddities about Narayan and his cronies. They had their own hidden caste system. Based on what, I couldn't tell. Narayan was the man of most respect here. Broad, stolid Sindhu ran a close second.

"Send them. If we have spies everywhere why haven't I gotten any information?"

"There's nothing to report that isn't common knowledge. Except that there's a lot of disaffection among Jah's men. A third might defect if you offered to enlist them. Jah's been doing some talking about you ignoring your duties as a wife because you won't commit suttee or go into isolation, as befits a Shadar woman. He's working on a dozen schemes but none of our friends are in his closest councils."

"Kill him," Blade said. And Sindhu nodded.

"Why?" A political victory would be better, long range.

"You don't let the serpent strike if you know where he lies in wait. You destroy him."

A simplistic solution with a certain appeal. It could have a big impact if we took him out where he seemed least vulnerable. And at the moment I didn't feel patient enough to spin out a long game. "Agreed. But with finesse. Do we have good enough friends over there to let us sneak into camp?"

"Close enough," Narayan admitted. "There'd be a question of timing. So the friends would be on duty."

"Set it up. What about other enemies? Jah is just the most obvious because he's right here. There'll be more in the north."

"It'll be handled," Narayan promised. "When there are men and time. We have too much work and too few hands."

Right. But I felt good about my prospects. No one else was doing as much or pushing as hard. I asked, "Can we get any closer to the Radisha and her pet wizard? Smoke? Are Swan and Mather devoted allies of the Radisha's?"

"Devoted?" Blade said. "No. But they've given their word, more or less. They won't turn unless the Woman turns on them first."

Something to consider. Maybe they could be misdirected, though that would work against me if they found me out.

Offered places in my camp and safety from reprisals, two hundred of Jahamaraj Jah's men defected. Another fifty just deserted and disappeared. Several hundred of the other fugitives enlisted the same day the Shadar came over. I got the impression the Radisha wasn't pleased.

Nearly a hundred Gunni women walked into fire the same day. I heard my name cursed from that side of the river.

I went over and spoke to a few women. We had no basis for communication.

Smoke was at the fortress gate when I recrossed the ford. He smirked as I passed. I wondered how much the Radisha would miss him.

There are times when you wonder about the self hidden from yourself. I certainly did as Narayan, Sindhu, and I stole toward the Shadar cavalry camp.

I was excited. I was eager. I was drawn as a moth to flame. I told myself I was doing this because I had to, not because I wanted it. It wasn't a pleasure. Jah's malice had called this down upon him.

Narayan's friends had confirmed that Jah planned to grab the Radisha and me and make it look like I'd carried her off. How he figured he could get to me I don't know. I guessed his plan included me murdering the Radisha—thus eliminating her brother's spine—then being a good girl who committed suttee. With assistance.

So I was moving first, earlier than I'd wanted.

Narayan exchanged whispered passwords with a friendly sentry who turned blind as we stole past. The camp beyond was a pesthole. Ordinarily Shadar set great store by cleanliness. Morale was abysmal.

We stole like shadows. I was proud of myself. I moved as silently as those two. They were surprised a woman could do it. We approached Jah's own tent.

It was oversized and guarded well. The man knew he wasn't popular. A fire burned on each of the tent's four sides. A guard stood near each fire.

Narayan cursed, said something in cant. Sindhu grunted. Narayan whispered, "No way to get any closer. Those guards will be men he trusts. And they'll know who we are."

I nodded, pulled them back, said, "Let me think."

They whispered while I thought. They didn't expect anything from me.

There was a small spell which could be used to blind the unaware briefly. Perfect, if I could manage it. I recalled it all right. One of those children's things that used to be as easy as blinking. I hadn't tried it in ages. There'd be no way to tell if it was working, unless I messed it up so badly the sentry sensed me and gave the alarm.

Nothing to lose but my life.

I went into that spellcasting as though it was the most dangerous demon-summoning I'd ever done. I did it three times to make sure it had a chance to take, but when I finished I didn't know if I'd succeeded or failed. The guard didn't look changed.

Sindhu and Narayan still had their heads together. I said, "Come on," and returned to the edge of the light. No one was in sight but that guard.

Time to test it or chicken.

I walked straight toward the sentry.

Narayan and Sindhu both cursed and tried to call me back. I summoned them with a gesture. The guard couldn't see me.

He didn't see me!

My heart leaped as it had when I'd summoned the horses. I beckoned Narayan and Sindhu, indicating they should stay out of the guard's direct line of vision. He might remember someone he saw head on. And he *would* be questioned later.

They slunk past like dogs, unable to believe he couldn't see them. They desperately wanted to know what I'd done, how I'd done it, if they could learn to do it, too, but they dared not say a word.

I parted the tent flap an inch, saw no one on the other side. The interior was compartmented by hangings. I slipped into what must have been the audience area. It constituted the majority of the interior. It was well appointed, further evidence that Jah had put his own comfort before the welfare of his men and the safety of his homeland.

I had learned better as a child. You win more loyalty and respect if you share the hardships.

Eyes still big, Narayan gestured, reminding me of the layout as he had it from his spies. I nodded. This late Jah should be asleep. We moved toward his sleeping area. I moved the hanging with a dagger. Narayan and Sindhu got their rumels out.

I know I made no noise. I'm sure they didn't. But as we went in Jah boiled up off his cushions, flung himself between Narayan and Sindhu, bowling them aside. He charged me. There was a lamp burning. He saw us well enough to recognize us.

Ever a fool, Jahamaraj Jah. He never yelled. He just tried to get away.

My hand dipped to the triangle of saffron at my waist, yanked, flipped. My rumel moved as if alive, snaked around his throat. I seized the flying end, yanked the loop tight, rolled my wrists and held on.

Luck, fate, or unconscious skill, none of that would have mattered had I been alone. Jah was a powerful man. He could have carried me outside. He could have shaken me off.

But Narayan and Sindhu grabbed his arms and held them extended, twisted them, forced him down. Sindhu's bull strength counted most. Narayan concentrated on keeping Jah's arms extended.

I got my knees into Jah's back and concentrated on keeping him from breathing.

It takes a while for a man to strangle. The skilled strangler is supposed to move so quickly and decisively that the victim's neck breaks and death comes instantly. I did not yet have the wrist roll perfected. So I had to hang on while Jah went the hard way. My arms and shoulders ached before he shuddered his last.

Narayan lifted me away. I was shaking with the intensity of it, the almost orgasmic elation that coursed through me. I'd never done anything like that, with my own two hands, without steel or sorcery. He grinned. He knew what I was feeling. He and Sindhu seemed unnaturally calm. Sindhu was listening, trying to judge if we'd made too much noise. It had seemed a ferocious uproar to me, there in the middle of it, but evidently we'd made less racket than I'd thought. Nobody came. Nobody asked questions.

Sindhu muttered something in cant. Narayan thought a moment, glanced at me, grinned again. He nodded.

Sindhu pawed through Jah's clutter, looking for the ground. He cleared a small area, looked around some more.

While I watched him, trying to figure out what he was doing, Narayan produced an odd tool he'd carried under the dark robe he'd donned for the adventure. The tool had a head that was half hammer, half pick, that weighed at least two pounds. Maybe more if it was the silver and gold it appeared to be. Its handle was ebony inlaid with ivory and a few rubies that caught the lamplight and gleamed like fresh blood. He began pounding the earth with the pick side, but quietly, unrhythmically.

That wasn't a tool that would be used that way ordinarily. I know a cult object when I see one, even if it's unfamiliar.

Narayan broke up the earth. Sindhu used a tin pan to scoop it onto a carpet he'd turned face down, careful not to scatter any. I had no idea what they intended. They were too intent on what they were doing to explain. A litany of sorts, in cant, passed between them. I heard something about auspices and the promise of the crows, more about the Daughter of Night and those people—or whatever they were.

All I could do was keep watch.

Time passed. I had a tense few minutes when the guard changed outside. But those men had little to say to one another. The new men didn't check inside the tent.

I heard a meaty whack and muted crunch, turned to see what they were doing now.

They'd gotten a hole dug. It was barely three feet deep and not that far across. I couldn't guess what they meant to do with it.

They showed me.

Narayan used the hammer face of his tool to break Jah's bones. Just as Ram had been doing with a rock that morning in that draw. He whispered, "It's been a long time but I still have the touch."

It's amazing how small a bundle a big man makes once you pulverize his joints and fold him up.

They cut open Jah's belly and deposited him in the hole. Narayan's final stroke buried the pick in the corpse's skull. He cleaned the tool, then they filled the hole around the remains, tamping the earth as they went. Half an hour later you couldn't tell where they'd dug.

They put the carpets back, bundled up the excess dirt, looked at me for the first time since they'd begun.

They were surprised to find me impassive. They wanted me to be outraged or disgusted. Or something. Anything that betrayed a feminine weakness.

"I've seen men mutilated before."

Narayan nodded. Maybe he was pleased. Hard to tell. "We still have to get out."

The firelight outside betrayed the positions of the guards. They were where they were supposed to be. If my spell worked a second time we'd only need a little luck to get out unseen.

Narayan and Sindhu scattered dirt as we walked toward our camp. "Good rumel work, Mistress," Narayan said. And something more, in cant, to Sindhu, who agreed reluctantly.

I asked, "Why did you bury him? No one will know

what happened to him. I wanted him to become an object lesson."

"Leaving him lie would have told everyone who was responsible. Innuendo is more frightening than fact. Better you're guilty in rumor."

Maybe. "Why did you break him up and cut him open?"

"A smaller grave is harder to find. We cut him open so he wouldn't bloat. If you don't they sometimes bloat so much they come up out of the ground. Or they explode and loose off enough gas so the grave can be found by the smell. Especially by jackals, who dig them up and scatter them all over."

Practical. Logical. Obvious, once he explained it. I'd never had occasion to conceal a body before. I'd surrounded myself with very practical—and clearly very experienced—murderers.

"We have to talk soon, Narayan."

He grinned that grin. He'd tell me some truth when he did.

We slipped back into camp and parted company.

I slept well. There were dreams but they weren't filled with gloom and doom. In one a beautiful black woman came and held me and caressed me and called me her daughter and told me I'd done well. I wakened feeling refreshed and as vigorous as if I'd had a full night's sleep. It was a beautiful morning. The world seemed painted in especially vivid colors.

My exercises with my talent went very well.

Chapter Nineteen

The disappearance, without trace, of the high priest Jahamaraj Jah, so trivial an opponent that I recall him only as a faded caricature of a man, stunned the thousands cluttering the region around the Ghoja ford. A whisper went around saying he had schemed against the Radisha and myself and that had sealed his fate. I wasn't responsible for the rumor. Narayan denied having said anything to anybody. Two days after we buried Jah everybody was convinced I'd eliminated him. Nobody knew how.

They were scared.

The possibility had a big impact on Blade. I got the feeling he thought I'd gone through some rite of passage and he could now devote himself to my cause. I was pleased but had to wonder about a man so devoutly antagonistic toward priests.

I had Narayan spread word that I still needed recruits, especially skilled horsemen. Another two hundred Shadar enlisted. Likewise nearly five hundred survivors of the Dejagore battle, though many just wanted regular meals or the comfort of a known place in the hierarchy. Taglian caste systems encourage dependence upon hierarchy. The chaos at the ford provided none of the benefits of social rigidity, only the handicaps.

I told Narayan to think about expanding the camp. Soon we'd be overcrowded. I told Blade to look for likely leaders. We'd never have enough of those.

The Taglians continued to amaze me. They remained pacifistic in their thinking, yet admired what they thought was the direct and casual way I disposed of enemies. The bigger the violence, the more they would applaud. As long as they were not threatened personally.

The Radisha sent for me the third morning after Jah's death. It was a brief interview, of no consequence except that I left convinced that Smoke was more than a fakir. He'd penetrated the veil of time well enough to assure himself that I'd had a hand in Jah's disappearance. He was more frazzled than ever. For the first time the Radisha was rattled.

She saw her control slipping.

That night she and Smoke and a few followers slipped over the Main and headed north. She left Swan and Mather to pretend she was secluded in the fortress. That deceit was useless. Narayan told me what was happening before the Radisha hit the water.

The day was noteworthy, too, because we enlisted our first nonveterans. There were just three of them. Two were friends of Narayan's friends. But their arrival was a sign that word was spreading and there were Taglians willing to join the cause.

Drills and training continued, as intense as I could make them, always designed to strip each man of all loyalties but those to his comrades and commander.

Former slaves had become the most plentiful volunteers—and best students. They had nothing else. The Shadowmasters had destroyed their world. I thought it might be a good idea to send trusted men

to roam the lands below the Main in search of more
men without strong ties to Taglios.

Narayan and Sindhu told me the Radisha was doing her sneak. I listened, then said, "Sit. The time
has come."

They understood. They didn't look as distressed as
I'd expected. They had talked it over and had agreed
to open up. "Who are you? What are you doing?"

Narayan took a deep breath. He did not look me
in the eye. "Mistress, we are Deceivers. Followers of
the goddess Kina, who has many names and many
guises but whose only truth is death." He went into
a long-winded explanation about the goddess and
how she related to the gods of Taglios and its neighbors. It was an improbable mishmash like that surrounding the genesis and attributes of most dark
gods. Narayan plainly had not thought much about
the doctrine. His explanation didn't tell me much
except that he and Sindhu were devoted to their goddess.

It took some pressure but they admitted they wor-
shipped Kina, in part, by committing murder.

Sindhu volunteered, "Narayan, jamadar of the
Changlor band, is famous among us, Mistress." Evidently he broke the silence because it wasn't good
form for a man to brag about his own accomplish-
ments. "He has given the gift of paradise to more
than a hundred souls."

"One hundred fifty-three," Narayan said. That, apparently, was not considered braggery.

"Paradise? You want to explain that?"

"Those whose lives are taken for the goddess are
freed from the Wheel of Life and ascend to paradise
immediately."

The Wheel of Life was a Gunni concept. You kept
going around and around, rebirth after rebirth, till
the good you did sufficiently outweighed the evil.
Then you were allowed escape. But not to paradise.
Paradise was not a Gunni concept. The Gunni who

escaped the Wheel became one with the generative force that had created the Lords of Light, the gods, who were its champions in the endless struggle with Shadow, which would be defeated only when the generative force had absorbed so many good souls it filled the universe. Shadow, of course, fought back by leading men to evil.

Paradise is a Vehdna notion, something originally imagined by adolescent males and dirty old men. It is stocked with all the comforts a male from a hard world could lust after. In particular it is infested with eager virgins of both sexes so the elevated will have something with which to while away eternity.

The Vehdna paradise gives no gate passes to women. The Vehdna say women have no souls. The gods created them to bear children, serve the lusts of men, and work themselves into early graves.

The Vehdna doctrine is the most perniciously anti-female of Taglios' cults but the most flexible as well. They have their female saints and heroines, and the Vehdna amongst my soldiers adapted to my command more easily than did the Shadar or Gunni. They just cast me in the role of their warrior saints Esmalla (three of the same name, from the same lineage, scattered over a century about eight hundred years back) and concentrated on doing their jobs.

The religions in my end of the world had not made more sense. I did not criticize Taglian beliefs. But I did ask questions. Understanding is an important tool.

Narayan insisted his beliefs were not derivative. He claimed Kina worship antedated all other religions. What I saw were echoes of its primal influence. "Mistress, it is said the Books record the histories of the Children of Kina back to the most ancient times, when men first received the gift of letters. It is said some are in tongues no man has spoken in ten thousand years."

"What books are these? Where are they?"

"The Books of the Dead, they're sometimes called.

They are lost now, I think. There was a very bad time for the Children of Kina a long time ago. A great warlord, Rhadreynak, forged a vast empire. He insulted Kina. She visited vengeance upon his house, but by chance he was spared. He launched a crusade without mercy. The keepers of the Books fled into a hidden place. All who knew where they had gone were devoured by Rhadreynak's wrath before the sainted Mahtnahan dan Jakel broke his neck with the silver rumel."

Sindhu said something in cant, softly, the way men of other paths would say "Praise God" or "Blessed be His Name."

"What's that?" I asked.

"Mahtnahan was the only silver rumel man ever to have lived. The only Deceiver ever to have sent more than a thousand souls to paradise."

Sindhu said, still softly, "Every man, when he plies his rumel for the first time and knows the ecstasy of Kina for the first time, aspires to the heights attained by Mahtnahan."

Narayan brightened, grinned his grin. "And to his luck. Mahtnahan not only freed us of our greatest persecutor, he survived the killing. He lived another forty years."

I led them on through legends and oral histories, interested in the way Croaker would have been interested, intrigued by the dark history. Over and over, Narayan insisted there were true written records somewhere and that it was the great dream of every jamadar in every generation to recover them. "This is a feeble world today, Mistress. The greatest powers afoot are these Shadowmasters and they don't really know what they're doing. The Books . . . Ah, the secrets said to lie within their pages. The lost arts."

We talked about those Books again. I did not swallow their story whole. I'd heard similar legends about books filled with earth-shaking secrets before.

But Narayan did startle me with a description of the place where they had been hidden.

It could have been the caverns I visited in my dreams. As they might have been recalled after a thousand years of oral history.

The history of Kina's cult might deserve some study someday. After I secured myself in today's world.

I had not spent all my time just waiting for Narayan to decide the time was ripe to let me in on a few secrets. Over the weeks I had done my listening among the men, had dropped a question here and there, to hundreds of individuals, and had put together a fair picture of the Kina cult as it was seen from outside.

Every living Taglian had heard Kina's name and believed she existed. Every Taglian had heard of the Stranglers. They thought of them more as bandits and gangsters than as religious fanatics. And not one in a hundred believed the Stranglers existed today. They were something from the past, eradicated during the last century.

I mentioned that to Narayan. He smiled.

"That is our greatest tool, Mistress. No one believes we exist. You have seen how Sindhu and I make little effort to hide from the men. We go among them and say we are the feared and famous Stranglers and they had better not displease us. And they don't believe us. But they fear us even so, because they know stories and think we might try imitating the Deceivers of old."

"There are some who believe." I suspected those included Smoke, the Radisha, and some others in high places.

"Always. Just enough."

He *was* a sinister little man. And probably really a vegetable peddler honored in his community as a good Gunni, good father, good grandfather. But during the dry season, when large portions of the Taglian population were on the move for reasons of trade, he would be, too. With his band, pretending to be travellers like other travellers, murdering those others when the opportunity arose. He was good at that, obviously. That was why Sindhu thought so highly of him.

Now I understood their caste system. It was based on number of successful murders.

Narayan was, likely, secretly, a wealthy man. The followers of Kina always robbed their victims.

They were more egalitarian than other cults. Narayan, of low caste and cursed with a Shadar name, had become jamadar of his band. Because he was a brilliant tactician and favored of Kina—meaning he was lucky, I assumed—according to Sindhu. He was famous among the Stranglers. A living legend.

"He doesn't need arm-holders," Sindhu said. "Only the best black cloths kill so quickly and efficiently that they don't need arm-holders."

A living legend, and my lieutenant. Interesting. "Arm-holders?" He used the word as a title more than as a job description.

"A band consists of many specialists, Mistress. The newest members begin as grave-diggers and bone-breakers. Many never advance beyond that level, for they develop no skill with the rumel. The yellow rumel men are the lowest ranked Stranglers. Apprentices. They seldom have a chance to kill, being mostly assigned as arm-holders for red rumel men and as scouts and victim-finders. Red rumel men do most of the strangling. Few win the black rumel. Those almost always become jamadars or priests. The priests do the divining and take omens, intercede with Kina, and keep the chronicles and accounts of the company. When it becomes necessary they act as judges."

"I was never a priest," Narayan said. "A priest has to be educated."

Never a priest but once a slave. He'd managed to keep his rumel throughout his captivity. I wondered if he had fought back, dealing silent death.

"Sometimes. When the moment was propitious," he admitted. "But Kina teaches us not to slay indiscriminately, nor in anger, but only for her glory. We do not slay for political reasons—except for the safety of the brotherhood."

Interesting. "How many followers do you suppose Kina claims?"

"There is no way to tell, Mistress." Narayan seemed almost relieved by this line of questioning. "We are outlawed. We come under sentence of death the moment we take our oath to Kina. A jamadar will know how many there are in his band and will have contacts with a few other jamadars but he'll have no idea how many bands there are or how strong they might be. There are ways we have to recognize one another, ways we communicate, but seldom do we dare gather in large numbers. The risks are too great."

Sindhu said, "The Festival of Lights is our great gathering, when each band sends men to the rites at the Grove of Doom."

Narayan silenced him with a gesture. "A great holy day but little different than the Shadar festival of the same name. Many of the band captains come but bring few of their followers. The priests attend, of course. Decisions are made and cases judged but I would guess that not one in twenty believers attends. I would guess that there are between one and two thousand of us today, more than half living in Taglian territory."

Not many at all, then. And only a minority of those truly skilled murderers. But what a force to unleash in the darkness if I could make it my instrument.

"And now the true question, Narayan. The heart of the thing. Where do I fit? Why have you chosen me? And for what?"

Chapter Twenty

Crowing and clatter wakened Croaker. He rose and went to the temple entrance. Ghostly dawn light permeated the misty wood.

Soulcatcher had returned. The black stallions were lathered. They had run long and hard. The sorceress was besieged by squawking crows. She cursed them and beat them back, beckoned him. He went out, asked, "Where have you been? Things have been happening."

"So I gather. I went for your armor." She indicated the horse she hadn't ridden.

"You went all the way to Dejagore? For that? Why?"

"We'll need it. Tell me what happened."

"How were they? My men."

"Holding out. Better than I expected. They may hang on for quite a while. Shadowspinner isn't at his best." The voice she chose rasped with irritation. When she continued, though, it had become that of a cajoling child. "Tell me. It'll take forever to get it out of them. They all try to tell me at once."

"The Howler came past yesterday."

She raised that wooden box to eye level, though she didn't make him look at the face inside. "The Howler? Tell me."

He did.

"The game grows more interesting. How did Longshadow lure him out of his swamp?"

"I don't know."

"I was speaking rhetorically, Croaker. Go inside. I'm tired. I was in a bad mood already."

He went. He didn't want to test her temper. Outside, she chattered with a flock of crows so dense she disappeared among them. Somehow she brought confusion out of chaos. Minutes later the temple vibrated to the beat of countless wings. A black cloud flew away south.

Soulcatcher came inside. Croaker kept his distance, kept his mouth shut. Not much intimidated him but he wasn't one to stick his hand in a cobra's mouth.

Morning came. Croaker wakened. Soulcatcher appeared to be sleeping soundly. He resisted temptation. It was less than a flutter of a thought, anyway. He wouldn't catch her off guard that easily. Chances were she wasn't asleep at all. Resting, yes. Maybe testing him. He couldn't recall ever having seen her sleep.

He made himself breakfast.

Soulcatcher wakened while he cooked. He didn't notice. A dramatic pink flash startled him. He whirled. Pinkish smoke swirled beyond the sorceress. A child-sized creature pranced out, flipped the woman a salute, sauntered over to him. "How they hanging, chief? Long time, no see."

"Want an honest answer or one that will please you, Frogface?"

"Hey! You ain't surprised to see me."

"No. I figured you were a plant. One-Eye doesn't have what it takes to manage a demon."

"Hey! Hey! Let's watch our tongue, eh, Cap? I ain't no demon. I'm an imp."

"Sorry about the ethnic slur. You did fool me, some. I thought you belonged to Shapeshifter."

"That lump? What could he offer?"

Croaker shrugged. "You been in Dejagore?" He contained an old anger. The imp, supposedly helping the Black Company, had been absent in the final debacle there. "What's the news?"

The imp stood only two feet tall though he had the proportions of an adult. He glanced at Soulcatcher, received some intangible permission. "That Mogaba is one bad actor, chief. He's giving the Shadowmasters' boys all the trouble they ever wanted. Making them look like fools. Eating them up a nibble at a time. 'Course, it can't last. He keeps getting into it with your old buddies One-Eye, Goblin, and Murgen. They don't like the way he operates. He don't like them all the time telling him about it. You get a split there, or Shadowspinner breaks loose, you got a whole new game."

Croaker settled with his meal. "Shadowspinner breaks loose?"

"Yeah. He got hurt in the fight, you know. His old buddy from down south, Longshadow, got a whammy in on him while he was down. Keeps him from using his talents. Them Shadowmasters was a lovely bunch, all the time trying to slide around behind each other even when they was up to their asses in alligators. Longshadow, he's got a notion he can play Shadowspinner just loose enough to let him wipe Dejagore, then squish the clown and make himself king of the world."

In a voice little more than a whisper the sorceress said, "He has the Howler to consider, now. And me."

The imp's grin faded. "You ain't as secret as you think, boss. They know you're down here. They all did, from the beginning."

"Damn!" She paced. "I thought I'd been more careful."

"Hey! Not to worry. None of them got the faintest where you are now. And maybe when we get done with them they'll wish they was nicer to you in the old days. Eh? Eh?" He laughed, childlike.

Croaker had encountered Frogface first in Gea-Xle, far to the north. One-Eye, one of the Company wizards, had bought him there. Everyone but One-Eye had doubted the imp's provenance and loyalty, though Frogface *had* made himself useful.

Croaker asked Soulcatcher, "You have something planned?"

"Yes. Stand up." He did. She rested one gloved hand against his chest. "Uhm. You've healed enough. And I'm running out of time."

Nervous excitement flooded him. He knew what she wanted and did not want to do it. "I thought that was why he was here. Do you trust him enough to have him watch me?"

"Hey, chief," the imp said, "you hurt my feelings. Sure she does. I done hitched my star."

"One word from me and he spends eternity in torment." Her voice was a merry little girl's. She could be chilling in her choices.

"That too," the imp said, all of a sudden surly. "It's a hard life, Cap. Nobody don't never trust me. Don't never give me no slack. One teensy slip-up and it's roast forever. Or worse. You mortals got it made, man."

Croaker snorted. "What do you think one slip-up will get me?"

"It only hurts for a little while for you."

Soulcatcher said, "Enough banter. Croaker, calm yourself. Get yourself ready for surgery. The imp and I will ready everything else."

Nude and headless, the sorceress floated four feet off the floor, shoulders elevated. Her unboxed head sat on a stone table nearby, eyes alert. Croaker scanned the body. It was perfect though pale and waxy. He'd seen only one to compare. Her sister's.

He glanced at the imp, perched on the head of a stone monster that protruded from the wall. The imp winked. "Show us what you got, Cap." Croaker was not reassured.

He glanced at his hands. They were steady, a legacy of surgeries performed on a dozen battlefields under terrifying conditions.

He stepped to the table. The sorceress had gathered the best surgical instruments the world had to offer. "This will take a while, imp. If I tell you to do something, you do it now. Understood?"

"Sure, chief. Might help if I knew what you were going to do."

"I'll start by removing the scar tissue. That'll be delicate. You'll have to help control bleeding." He didn't know if there would be bleeding or not. He'd never carved on somebody who should have been dead fifteen years ago. He could not believe this operation was possible. But Catcher being alive was impossible.

How much control would she have? How much would she participate? His would be the least part here, physical preparation for the mating of head and neck. The rest, tying nerve to nerve and blood vessel to blood vessel, would be up to her.

It wouldn't work. It couldn't.

He went to work. Soon he was concentrating enough to forget the price of failure.

Chapter Twenty-One

Longshadow watched the upper limb of the sun slide below the horizon. He barked an order. A wrinkly little brown man whispered, "Yes, my lord." He scurried out of the crystal room. Longshadow remained motionless, watched the day fade.

"Welcome the enemy hours." It was summertime. Longshadow preferred summers. The nights were shorter.

He was less troubled, less fearful, now. Those nights after the Stormgard debacle had included a crisis of confidence now past. He was not cocky but was sure of himself now. Everything he touched was turning to gold, unfolding to perfection. The Howler was on his way from the swamps, undetected. The siege of Stormgard continued to enervate Shadowspinner's armies. Spinner remained impotent. *She* seemed to have faded, content to avenge herself on Dorotea Senjak. Senjak was playing her own game unaware that she was playing his. Soon, now, she would stumble. He had just one move to make. And it was time.

Each seventy feet along Overlook's wall stood a tower topped by crystal. Inside each cylinder was a large curved mirror. Fires came to life within those towers. The flames burned brightly. The mirrors hurled light onto the old road descending from the plain of glittering stone. No shadow could move there unseen.

His confidence was back. He could leave the night watch to others. He had other business to conduct. There were reports to receive, orders to send, communiques to issue. He turned his back on the outside world, approached a crystal sphere on a pedestal at the heart of the chamber.

The sphere was four feet in diameter. Channels wormholed through it to a hollow at the heart. Shimmers of light rippled over its surface. Snakes of light wriggled through the channels inside. Longshadow rested withered hands on the sphere. Surface light absorbed them. His hands sank into the globe slowly, as though melting through ice. He grasped serpents of light, manipulated them.

A port opened where the sphere rested on the pedestal, unsealing one channel. Darkness oozed in. It came reluctantly, compelled, fighting every inch. It hated the light as the Shadowmaster hated darkness. It filled the heart of the sphere.

Longshadow spoke to it. The light on the sphere rippled, crept up his arms. The sphere vibrated. A sound weaker than a whisper came off it. Longshadow listened. Then he sent the shadow away and summoned another.

To the fourth such shadow he said, "Take this message to Taglios: 'Create the agent.'"

As the shadow oozed away, fleeing the light, the Shadowmaster suddenly felt that he was no longer alone. Frightened, he tried to turn to look at the road from the plain.

Nothing moved there. The shadowtraps were holding. What, then?

Something inky, glossy, flashed through the nearest beam. "Huh?" No shadow, that. A crow! A lot of crows. What were crows doing here?

It was night. Crows didn't fly at night.

It came, then.

There had been crows around Overlook for weeks, seldom behaving as crows should. "Hers!" He cursed, stamped angrily, childishly. She'd been watching all along. She knew everything!

Fear fled before rage. He'd never had much self-control. He tried to yank his arms free, forgetting there should be no quick movement in the sphere. The crows seemed to laugh at him.

Hell. They swarmed over the surrounding walls, cawing mockingly.

He ripped a hand out of the sphere. Bloody sparks crackled between his fingers. There would be an end to those cackling devils! She wouldn't spy on him again!

He hurled a bolt. A dozen crows exploded. Blood and feathers splattered the tower. The survivors cawed uproariously.

Sense penetrated rage. Something was wrong. They *wanted* him to attack them.

Diversion?

The sphere!

A gap remained where he'd freed his hand. The hole penetrated to the core. A darkness was slithering through already.

He screamed.

He clamped down on his fear, removed his other hand slowly. He closed the deadly gap carefully, but not before the shadow escaped.

It darted through the doorway, out of the chamber, down into the bowels of Overlook, fleeing the light.

There was a shadow loose in the fortress!

Somewhere, a scream. The shadow was hunting.

Longshadow forced an icy calm. It was one lone shadow, small, controllable.

Outside, the crows made merry.

He stifled rage. They would not provoke him again. "Your hour will come," he promised. "Fly to the bitch. Report your failure. I live. I still live!"

Chapter Twenty-Two

When the watchful eye lapses those who are watched invariably sense the instant of freedom.

A prodigious wail escaped the little thing called the Howler. It gobbled at the men carrying it. They raced forward, carried it into the camp of the Shadowmaster Shadowspinner while the watcher in the south was diverted.

The Howler remained just long enough to make contact, speak briefly, exchange views, reach an understanding by which he stood to evade the inevitable treachery of Longshadow, sure to surface the instant the threat from Taglios evaporated.

He was long gone when Longshadow's seekers found him again. The only evidence of his visit was an improvement in Shadowspinner's condition. Spinner kept that well hidden.

Chapter Twenty-Three

The breeze had shifted. It came from the northeast now, carrying smoke from across the river. I asked Narayan, "Could we confiscate their wood?" There had been suicides all morning.

"Unwise, Mistress. Interfering might start a rebellion. Your grip isn't that tight."

And likely would never be, unpleasant as I found that truth. "Just wishful thinking. Tinkering with customs isn't my mission."

Nor his. I had not pressed Narayan about that. I could guess, though. It was implicit in his beliefs. He wanted to bring on the Year of the Skulls. He wanted Kina free. He wanted to become immortal, a Deceiver saint.

"It's all far away, Mistress. What do we do today?"

"We're approaching that point where assembling an army begins snowballing."

"Snowballing?"

I'd used Forsberger for "snowballing," not thinking. I did not know the Taglian for snow. It did not snow here. Narayan had never seen snow. "It starts growing of its own momentum. In another week, ten days, I'd guess, we'll begin getting more recruits than we can handle."

"Even with the Radisha against us?" He was convinced the woman was an enemy.

"That could work for us if we appeal to resentment of the powers that be."

Narayan understood. Such resentments brought recruits to the Deceivers. "There's less of that than you hope. This isn't your land. My people are very fatalistic."

They were. But they had their handles. There would not be two thousand men under my standard now otherwise. "They'll respond to the right spark. True?"

"We all will, Mistress."

"Absolutely. I've provided that spark for you and your friends, haven't I? But how about a spark to fire the masses? One that will make them forget their fear of the Black Company and their objections to a woman commander?" I understood why the Company was feared now. For his sake maybe it was best Croaker had gone before he figured it out. It would have broken his heart.

Narayan had no suggestions.

I said, "We need an electrifying rumor to hand your brotherhood, to whisper everywhere."

"Word should have reached all the jamadars now, Mistress."

"Wonderful, Narayan. So every band captain has heard that your Strangler messiah is come. Assume they all believe because the news came from you, famous and honored master Strangler." My tone was getting sarcastic. "How many men will that bring to a standard that needs thousands? I'd rather have your friends stay where they are, as our hands and knives in hiding. Are there other legends I can exploit? Are there other fears?"

"The Shadowmasters are scary enough, at least in the country, where they remember last year."

True. We were getting volunteers from across the river already, men who'd had no chance to enlist before we marched on Dejagore. The men we had taken down had come from the city or were slaves we had liberated after overrunning Ghoja. The country folk, intimate with the terror of the Shadowmasters, should prove a rich source of manpower. And would be hardier than city folk. But I might have to gather my harvest quickly.

Around here power emanated from the palace and the temples of Trogo Taglios. A few frightened men there could issue bulls and dictates forbidding the faithful from joining me.

"Do you have friends in the city?"

"Not many. None that I know personally. Sindhu may know some."

"Ram came from the city."

"Yes. And a few others. What're you thinking?"

"It might be wise to get established there now, before the Radisha, and especially that whimpering runt Smoke, can swing opinion against us." I said we and us always but meant I and me. Narayan was not fooled much.

"We can't leave Ghoja. Thousands more men will come here. We have to collect them."

I smiled. "Suppose we split what we have? You take half, stay here, do the gathering, and I take half to the city?"

He reacted the way I expected. Almost panicky. He didn't want me out of his sight.

"Or I could leave Blade. Blade is a man of respect, with a strong reputation down here."

"Excellent idea, Mistress."

I wondered who was manipulating whom. "Do you suppose Sindhu is a man of enough respect to leave with him?"

"More than enough, Mistress."

"Good. Blade will have to know something about him. Something about your brotherhood."

"Mistress?"

"If you're going to use a tool you should know its capabilities. Only a priest demands we take things on faith."

"Priests and functionaries," Narayan corrected. "You're right. Blade will take nothing on faith."

He was the last man alive who would. That might come between us someday.

"Are any of your brotherhood cynical enough to be hiding inside other priesthoods?"

"Mistress?" He sounded hurt.

"I have few sources of information. If we had friends within the priesthoods . . ."

"I don't know about Taglios, Mistress. It seems unlikely."

I did miss the old days, when I'd had the unbridled use of my powers, when I could summon a hundred demons to spy for me, when I could recall the memories of a mouse that had been in the wall of a room where my enemies had congregated.

I'd told Narayan that I'd built an empire from beginnings as humble as ours. That was true, but I'd had more weapons. This time I often felt disarmed.

The weapons were coming back, but far too slowly.

"Send Blade to me."

I took Blade for a walk up the river, east of the fortress. He was content to wait on me. He spoke only once, cryptically, as we approached a bankside tree where a fishing pole leaned. "Looks like Swan never got back."

I had him explain. It didn't mean much. I looked at the fortress. Swan and Mather were in there, nominal commanders of all Taglian forces below the river. I wondered how seriously they took that. They hadn't been out much. I wondered if Blade was in touch. He'd hardly had time. He'd been working hours longer than mine, teaching himself as he taught his men. I wondered why he made the effort. I sensed a deep reservoir of irrational hatred inside him.

I suspected he was a man who wanted to change the world.

Such men are easy to manipulate, easier than the Swans, who mostly just want to be left alone.

"I'm thinking of promoting you," I told him.

He responded sardonically. "To what? Unless you're promoting yourself, too."

"Of course. You become legate of the Ghoja legion. I become general of the army."

"You're going north."

He didn't waste words and didn't need many to extract a lot of information. "I should be in Taglios now. To guard my interests."

"It's a bad spot. In the crocodile's jaws."

"I don't follow."

"You need to be here to gather soldiers, to gain power. You need to be there to control the priests who can keep recruits away."

"Yes."

"You need trustworthy lieutenants. But you're alone."

"Am I?"

"Maybe not. Maybe I misinterpret the interest of Narayan and Sindhu."

"Probably not. Their goals aren't mine. What do you know about them?"

"Nothing. They aren't what they pretend."

I thought about that, decided he meant they weren't what they pretended to be to the world. "Have you heard of the Deceivers, Blade? Sometimes called the Stranglers?"

"Death cult. Legendary, probably. The Radisha mentioned them and their goddess. The wizard is terrified of them. The soldiers say they are extinct. That isn't true, is it?"

"No. A few still exist. For their own reasons they're backing me. I won't bore you with their dogma. It's repulsive and I'm not sure it was related to me truthfully."

He grunted. I wondered what went on inside his head. He hid himself well.

I'd met others like him. I will be stunned the day I meet someone entirely new.

"Go north without fear. I'll manage Ghoja."

I believed him.

I turned back. We walked toward camp. I tried to ignore the stench from across the river. "What do you want, Blade? Why are you doing this?"

He shrugged, an uncharacteristic action. "There are many evils in the world. I guess I've chosen one for my personal crusade."

"Why such a hatred for priests?"

He didn't shrug. He didn't give me a straight answer, either. "If each man picks an evil and attacks it relentlessly, how long can evil persist?"

That was an easy one. Forever. More evil gets done in the name of righteousness than any other way. Few villains think they are villains. But I left him his illusion. If he had one. I doubted he did. No more than a sword's blade does.

At first I'd thought him moved as Swan so obviously was when he looked at me. But he hadn't so much as hinted that he considered me anything but a fellow soldier.

He confused me.

He asked, "Will you talk to Willow and Cordy? Or shall I?"

"What do you think?"

"Depends. What you want to discuss? How? You wiggle some, you can lead Swan anywhere."

"Not interested."

"I'll talk to them, then. You go ahead. Do what you have to do."

Sunrise next morning I was on the road north with two incompetent and incomplete battalions, Narayan and Ram, and all the trophies I had claimed from the Shadowmasters' horsemen.

Chapter Twenty-Four

The Radisha waited impatiently while Smoke bustled around making sure his spells were proof against eavesdroppers. The Prahbrindrah Drah lounged in a chair, looking indolent and unconcerned. But he spoke first when the wizard signalled satisfaction with his precautions. "More bad news, Sis?"

"Bad? I don't know. Not pleasant. Dejagore was a disaster. Though experts tell me it hurt the Shadowmasters so badly they can't bother us this year. The woman you lust after did survive, though."

The Prahbrindrah grinned. "Is that the good news or the bad?"

"Subject to interpretation. For once, though, I think Smoke might be right."

"Ah?"

"She insists the defeat neither destroyed the Black Company nor terminated our contract. She gave me a requisition for more men, equipment, and materials."

"She's serious?"

"Deadly. She reminded me of the Company's history and what becomes of those who renege on contracts."

The Prahbrindrah chuckled. "Bold wench. All by herself?"

Smoke squeaked something.

The Radisha said, "She's already recruited a force two thousand strong. She's training them. She's dangerous, dear. You'd better take her seriously."

Smoke squeaked again, apparently unable to articulate what he wanted to say.

"Yes. She killed Jahamaraj Jah. Jah tried giving her some trouble. Poof! She made him disappear."

The prince took a deep breath, blew it out between puffed cheeks. "Can't fault her taste. But that's no way to make friends with priests."

Smoke gobbled again.

The Radisha said, "She doesn't intend to try. She got Blade to defect. He's her number two man, now. You know his attitude. Dammit, Smoke! One thing at a time."

"Swan and Mather?"

"They stuck. I think. But Swan is taken with her, too. I really don't know what you see in her."

The Prahbrindrah chuckled. "She's exotic. And gorgeous. Where are they now?"

"I left them in charge. Supposedly. It's meaningless. She considers herself the Captain and free to do whatever she pleases. With those two there I'll have eyes on the scene. They can keep us informed. All right, Smoke. All right."

"What's he lathered about?"

"He thinks she's made an alliance with the Stranglers."

"The Stranglers?"

"Kina worshippers. Like Smoke's been whining all along."

"Oh."

"First time she visited me she brought two of them with her. Or men who appeared to be Stranglers."

Smoke managed a clear statement. "She carried a strangling cloth herself. I believe she slew Jah personally. I believe she disposed of his corpse in a Deceivers' rite."

"Let me think." The prince steepled his fingers before his lips. Finally, he asked, "Were they men she'd recruited? Or did she make an alliance with the whole cult?"

Smoke gobbled. The Radisha contradicted him. "I don't know. Who knows how that cult works?"

"It's not monolithic."

Smoke said, "She carried a rumel herself. She posed as Kina during the fight with the Shadowmasters' cavalry."

The Radisha had to explain that.

The prince observed, "So we assume the worst? No matter how unlikely?"

"Even if she has access to only a few Stranglers, dear, she's acquired an unholy power. They have no fear of death. If they're told to kill, they'll kill. Disregarding any cost to themselves. And we have no way of knowing who might be one of them."

"The Year of the Skulls," Smoke piped. "It's coming."

"Let's don't get carried away. You talked to her, Sis. What does she want?"

"To continue the war. To fulfill the Black Company's commission, then see us meet our end of the agreement."

"Then we're in no immediate danger. Why not let her have her head?"

"Kill her now," Smoke said. "Before she grows any stronger. Destroy her! Or she will destroy Taglios."

"He seems to be overreacting. Don't you think, Sis?"

"I'm not so sure anymore."

"But . . ."

"You didn't talk to her, her with all the confidence of a tidal wave. She's turned damned scary."

"And the Shadowmasters? Who'll handle them?"

"We have a year."

"You think *we* could build an army?"

"I don't know. I think we made a lethal mistake dealing with the Black Company the way we did. Quiet, Smoke. We wove webs of deception. That will come back on us because we're in too deep to retreat. Swan, Blade, and Mather were convinced we were treacherous in our promises. I'm sure Blade shared his opinions with the woman."

"We'll step carefully, then." The Prahbrindrah reflected. "But right now I don't see the threat. If she wants to get the Shadowmasters, I say let her go after them."

Smoke had a fit. He ranted. He cursed. He issued dire prophecies. Every sentence included the words, "The Year of the Skulls."

His histrionics were so craven they drove the Radisha toward her brother's position.

Brother and sister left him to his humors. As they moved toward their part of the palace, the Prahbrindrah asked, "What's gotten into him? He's lost his nerve completely."

"He never had much."

"No. But he's gone from a mouse to a jellyfish. First it was fear of getting found out by the Shadowmasters. Now it's the Stranglers."

"They scare *me*."

The prince snorted. "We have more power than you suspect, Sis. We have the power to manipulate three priesthoods."

The Radisha sneered. She knew what that was worth. So did Jahamaraj Jah, now.

Chapter Twenty-Five

Eight men sat around the fire in the room without a roof. That room was on the top floor of a four-storey tenement in Taglios' worst slum. The landlord would have suffered apoplexy had he seen what they had done.

They had been there only a few days. They were wrinkled little brown men unlike any Taglian native. But Taglios lay beside a great river. Strangers came and went. Unusual people seldom drew a second glance.

They had opened the room to the elements and now some regretted it.

A summer shower had come down the river. It was not a heavy rain but the clouds had stalled over the city. They shed a steady drizzle. Taglios' people were pleased. Rain cleared the air and carried away the trash in the streets. Tomorrow, though, the air would be muggy and everyone would complain.

Seven of the eight brown men did nothing but stare into the flames. The eighth occasionally added a bit of fuel or a pinch of something that sent sparks flying and filled the air with aromatic smoke. They were patient. They did this for two hours each night.

Suddenly, shadows rippled in over the tops of the walls, danced behind and among the men. They did not move, did nothing to admit they sensed the new presence. The one added another pinch of aromatic, then rested his hands in his lap. Shadows gathered around him. Shadows whispered. He replied, "I understand." The language he spoke was not Taglian. It was spoken nowhere within six hundred miles of Taglios.

The shadows went away.

The men did not move till the fire died. The rain became a blessing then. It quenched the flames quickly.

The one who had fed the fire spoke briefly. The others nodded. They had their orders. Discussion was unnecessary. In minutes they were out in the Taglian streets.

Smoke muttered curses as he stepped into the rain. "Story of my life. Nothing goes right anymore." He scuttled along, head down. "What am I doing out here?" He ought to be inside trying to make the Radisha see sense so she could make her brother see sense. They were going to ruin everything. All they had worked toward was going to fly away if they didn't do something about that woman.

They were going to destroy Taglios by default. Why couldn't they see that?

Sometimes a walk helped clear the mind. He needed to be out, away, alone, free. Some new avenue would present itself. There was a way to get through, he was sure. There had to be.

A bat zipped past so close he felt the air stirred by its wings. A bat? On a night like this?

He recalled a time, before the legions marched, when bats had been everywhere. And someone had made a considerable effort to eliminate them. Someone like maybe those wizards who had travelled with the Black Company.

He halted, suddenly nervous. Bats in weather when bats should not fly? Not a good omen.

He had not come far. One minute and he'd be safely in the palace.

Another bat whipped past. He turned to run.

Three men blocked his path.

He whirled.

More men. Everywhere, men. He was surrounded. For half a minute they seemed a horde. But there were only six. In very bad Taglian one said, "A man want see you. You come."

He looked around wildly. There was no escape.

The paradox of being Smoke, Smoke thought. Terrified when the danger was insubstantial, calm now with it concrete, he moved through streets dark and wet, surrounded by men no bigger than he. His mind worked perfectly. He could break away whenever he willed. One small spell and he could be gone, safe.

But something was afoot. It might be crucial to know what. That spell could be loosed later as well as now.

He pretended to be as rattled and craven as ever.

They took him to the worst part of the city, to a tenement that looked like it could collapse any second. He was more frightened of it than of them. They led him up four creaky flights. One man tapped a code on a door.

The door opened. They went inside. Smoke eyed the man waiting. He looked just like the six who had brought him. Nor did the man who had opened the door seem any different. All hatched in the same nest. But the man who waited spoke passable Taglian.

He asked, "You are the one called Smoke? The fire marshall? I cannot recall the full title."

The wizard supposed they knew who and what he was, else he would not be here. "I am. You have me at a disadvantage."

"I have no name. I can be called One Who Leads
Eight Who Serve." Ghost of a smile. "Unwieldy, yes?
It is of no importance. I am the only one here who
can speak your language. You won't confuse me with
anyone else."

"Why did you interrupt my stroll?" Keep it cool,
casual, he thought.

"Because we have a common interest in dealing
with a peril so great it could devour the world. The
Year of the Skulls."

Now Smoke knew who they were.

He controlled himself but his mind went wild. His
efforts to maintain his anonymity had gone for
naught. The Shadowmasters knew him.

Maybe Swan was right. Maybe he was just a coward . . . He was. He had known that always. But he
was no puling craven. He could manage his fear if
he had to.

Still . . . It rankled that Swan could be right about
anything. Willow Swan was an animal that walked
on its hind legs and made noises like a man.

"The Year of the Skulls?" he asked. "What do you
mean?"

The man smiled thinly. "It will save time if we
don't pretend. You know Kina is stirring. And when
she stirs, ripples go out and waken other things best
left undisturbed. The first whisper of Kina passes
over the world. Soon the woman who is her avatar
will become aware of what she is."

"Do you think me simple?" Smoke demanded. "Do
you believe I can be weaned from my loyalty so easily? Do you believe an appeal to my fears will sub-
vert me?"

"No. Subversion is not the point. He who sent me
is to you as you are to a mouse. *He* is afraid. He has
cast the bones of time. He has seen what may be.
That woman can bring on the true Year of the Skulls.
What she was once she can become again, filled with
the breath of Kina. Before that terror all else pales.
The contention of armies becomes the squabbling of

children. But he who sent me has no power to reach out where the danger abides. She has surrounded herself with Kina's Children. She grows stronger by the hour. And he who sent me must remain where he is, holding back the tide of darkness that laps at Shadowcatch. He can do nothing but register his appeal for help and offer his friendship, which you may test as you will and call upon as you see fit."

A scheme. A tortuous scheme, surely. But he dared not reject it out of hand. There was sorcery in this place. He hadn't time to take its measure. If he turned them down flatly he might not get out alive.

"Which Shadowmaster do you call lord?" He thought he knew. The man had mentioned Shadowcatch.

The brown man smiled. "You call him Longshadow. He has other names."

Longshadow, master of Shadowcatch. The Shadowmaster whose demesne was farthest from Taglios, who was the least known of the four, rumored to be insane. He hadn't been much involved in the attacks upon Taglios.

The foreigner said, "He who sent me has not been involved in this war. He opposed it from the beginning. He has refused to participate. There are more pressing dangers, more deadly concerns, which preoccupy him."

"Men much like you have attacked Taglians several times."

"Stipulated. On the river. In the southern Taglian territories. Can you guess the common denominator, wizard?"

"The woman."

"The woman. Kina's fulcrum. He who sent me cast the bones of time. And as she becomes a greater danger he becomes more pressed elsewhere, less able to fight. He needs allies. He is desperate with fear. He will give more than he takes. The weed of doom has taken root in Taglios and he can do so little. It must be expunged by Taglians."

"There's a war on. Taglians didn't initiate it."

"Neither did he. But that war can be ended. He has that power. Of the three who wanted war, two are dead. Stormshadow and Moonshadow are gone. Shadowspinner lingers. He controls their combined armies but he is injured. He can be compelled to accept peace. He can be expunged, if that is the price of peace. Peace *can* be restored. Taglios *can* be as it was before the madness began. But he who sent me will *not* invest resources in making these things come true if there is nothing to be gained by letting some of his attention be diverted."

"From what?"

"Glittering stone. Khatovar. You are no unlettered peasant. You have read the ancients. You know the Shadar Khadi is but a pale shade of Kina, though Khadi's priests deny it. You know Khatovar, in the old tongue, means Khadi's Throne and is supposed to be the place where Khadi fell to earth. He who sent me believes the legend of Khatovar is an echo of an older, truer tale of Kina."

Smoke controlled his emotions and fears. He forced a smile. "You've given me a great deal to digest. A veritable feast."

"Only a first course. Truly, he who sent me is desperate. He needs a friend, an ally, who has influence here, who has some chance to cut the weed before it flowers. He will do what he has to do to demonstrate his good faith. He has told me to tell you he will even bring you to him so you can judge his honesty for yourself if that is your wish. If you are able to feel safe doing so. He'll agree to whatever safeguards you feel you need if you wish to speak to him directly."

"A lot to digest," Smoke said again, just wanting to get out of there before somebody turned vicious.

"I expect so. Enough to overturn your world. And more to come. And you have been gone a long time now. We wouldn't want your absence to become an object of concern. Go. Think. Make decisions."

"How should I get in touch?"

The brown man smiled. "We will find you. We will move from this place after you leave, lest you suffer some shortsighted inspiration to make yourself a hero. A bat will find you when it is time. Place yourself where you cannot be watched and these others will meet you."

"All right. You're right. I'd better get back." He eased toward the door, still not sure where he stood. But no one interfered with his departure.

He had a lot to mull over. And the interview had been productive if for no other reason than that it proved the Shadowmasters had put new agents into the city after the Black Company's wizards rooted out those that had been there before.

The little brown man who spoke bad Taglian asked his leader, "Will he take the bait?"

The leader shrugged. "The appeal was broad enough to touch him somewhere. His fears. His ego. His ambitions. He's been handed the chance to destroy what he fears and hates. He's been offered the chance to make himself big as a peacemaker. He's been offered the opportunity to fatten his own power with potent friends. If he has any need to become a traitor we've touched it."

The man smiled. His companions did, too. Then all eight began packing. The leader was sure the wizard's conscience would move him to report this initial approach.

He hoped the wizard would not take long seducing himself. The Shadowmaster was concerned about wasting time. He was not pleasant when he was worried.

Chapter Twenty-Six

The Radisha had only a day's start on us. Though a thousand men should find it harder to stop and start than a smaller party, we gained ground. Narayan had supplied us with the most efficient and motivated men. We were only two hours behind when the Radisha reached the city.

I marched in boldly, trophies displayed, and went straight to the barracks the Company had used when we were training the legions. The barracks were occupied by men we had left behind, men who had been injured in the battle at the Ghoja ford, and men who had volunteered after our departure. Most were commuting from their homes for daytime self-training but the barracks were still crowded. Enrollment exceeded four thousand.

"Get them under control," I told Narayan as soon as I grasped the situation. "Make them ours. Isolate them as much as possible. Work on them." Bold words, but how practical?

"Word of our arrival is spreading," he said. "The whole city will know soon."

"No avoiding it. I've been thinking. Between them the men ought to have some notion what happened to almost everybody who didn't come home. A lot of Taglians will want to know what happened to their men. We could make a few friends telling them."

"We'd be swamped." He was forgetting to offer an honorific more and more often. *He* thought he was a partner in my enterprise.

"Maybe. But let it out that we welcome inquiries. And push news that a lot of Taglians are trapped in Dejagore and I could get them out if I could get a little help."

Narayan looked at me oddly. "No chance, Mistress. Those men are dead. Even if they're still breathing."

"We know it. But the world doesn't. Anybody asks, to get them out we just put together enough men and arms quick enough. That will fix anybody who wants to interfere with me. Someone opens his mouth, he says he doesn't care about those men. Blade says the people here all think their priests are thieves. They might get real upset if the priests start playing with their sons' and brothers' and husbands' lives. We take advantage of religious friction. If a Gunni priest gets on me, we just appeal to the Shadar and Vehdna laity. And never stop mentioning that I'm the only professional soldier around."

Narayan grinned that repulsive grin. "You've given this a lot of thought."

"Wasn't much else to do on the way here. Get moving. We have to take control before anybody wonders if we really ought to. Before troublemakers think up ways to give us grief. Get feelers out to members of your brotherhood. We need information."

Narayan had some organizational skills though he was no charismatic leader. He could rise in a small group by demonstrated ability but he'd never get a large gang to follow him just because he cut a bold figure.

Thinking that made me think of Croaker. Croaker hadn't been charismatic. He'd been a workaday sort of commander. He'd identified the task to be accomplished, had considered his options, had put the best-suited men to work. He usually guessed right and got the job done. Except for that last time, at Dejagore, when his weakness became obvious.

He didn't think fast on his feet. He didn't intuit well.

Past tense, woman. He's gone.

I didn't want to think about him. It still hurt too much.

There was plenty of work to occupy me.

I began looking at the manpower resources that had fallen into my lap.

Not promising. Plenty of spear carriers, determined young men, but hardly anyone who stood out as an immediate leader. Damn, I missed the military engine I'd had back home.

I started wondering what I was doing here, why I had come. Pointless, woman. I could not go back. That empire had moved on. It had no place for me now.

I missed more than my armies. I had no intelligence machine. No way to ferret out secrets.

Ram remained my shadow, as much as he could. Determined to protect me, Ram was. Probably under the most dire orders of jamadar Narayan. "Ram, do you know the country around Taglios?"

"No, Mistress. I never went out till I enlisted."

"I need men who do know. Find them, please."

"Mistress?"

"This place is indefensible. Most of the men are drilling out of their homes." Why was I explaining? "We need to get away from distractions and vulnerabilities." Ideally on a hill near the south road, water, and a large wood.

"I'll ask around, Mistress." He was reluctant to

leave me but no longer had to be ordered away. He
was learning. Give him another year.

Narayan materialized before Ram returned. "It's
going all right. A lot of excitement. The men who
were there—there must be at least six hundred of
them now—are telling inflated stories about how we
beat those cavalrymen. There's talk about relieving
Dejagore before the rainy season. I didn't have to
start it."

During the rainy season the Main became impassable. For five or six months it was Taglios' wall
against the Shadowmasters. And theirs against Taglios.

What would happen if I got caught south of the
river when the rains came? That would give me time
to get the army whipped into shape.

On the other hand, it would not leave me anywhere to run.

"Narayan, get me . . ."

"Mistress?"

"I forget you haven't been with me forever. I was
going to send you after something we compiled before we went south."

One of our great enterprises had been a census of
men, materials, animals, skills, and other resources
an army needs. The results should be around somewhere still.

There was a way around the high water dilemma
if the right men and materials were available.

"Mistress?" Narayan asked again.

"Sorry. Just wondering what I'm doing here. I have
these moments."

He took me literally. He started in on revenge and
rebuilding the Company.

"I know, Narayan. It's just fatigue."

"Rest, then. You'll have to be at your best later."

"Oh?"

"Those who want to know about their men are
gathering already. Surely the news of our arrival has
reached all the false priests and even the palace. Men

will come to see how they can take advantage of you."

"You're right."

Ram returned with a half dozen men and some maps. None were men who had come north with me. They were nervous. They showed me three sites they thought might suit my purpose. I dismissed one immediately. It had a hamlet there already. Neither of the others had much to recommend it either way. Which meant I had to go look for myself.

Something to kill time.

I was getting as sarky as Croaker in my old age.

I thanked everybody and sent them away. A few minutes' rest would be useful. Like Narayan said, the siege would begin soon. We might have problems with men who could not wait to see their loved ones.

I dragged my things into the quarters I had occupied last time, one small room I refused to share. I plopped on the cot. It had not changed while I was gone. Still a rock within a mask of linen.

I'd just relax for a few minutes.

Hours fled. I dreamed. I was confused when Narayan wakened me. He came while I was visiting the caverns of the ancients. The voice calling me was louder, clearer, more insistent, more pressed.

I got hold of myself. "What is it?"

"The crowds of relatives. I was having them visit the gate one by one, but they've started pushing and shoving. There must be four thousand people out there and more arriving all the time."

"It's dark. Why did you let me sleep?"

"You needed it. It's raining, too. That may be a blessing."

"It'll keep some people home." But this would cost time however we handled it. "There's a public square where we paraded before we went south. I don't recall the name. Find out. Tell those people to assemble there. Tell the men to prepare for a short march in the weather. Tell Ram to ready my armor but forget the helmet."

There were five thousand people in the square. I managed to intimidate them into keeping quiet. I faced them on my stallion, looking at a sea of lamps and lanterns and torches while the soldiers formed up behind me.

I said, "You have a right to know what happened to your loved ones. But the soldiers and I have a great work before us yet. If you'll cooperate we'll handle this quickly. If you don't remain orderly we'll never get it done." My Taglian had improved dramatically. No one had trouble understanding me.

"When I point you out name the man you want to know about in a clear, loud voice. If one of the soldiers knew him he'll speak up. Go to that soldier. Talk quickly and quietly. If the news is bad, contain yourself. There are others who want news, too. They have to be able to hear."

I doubted it would go smoothly for long but it was just a gesture meant to get me mentioned kindly outside the corridors of power.

It worked well for longer than I expected, but Taglians are pliable people, used to doing what they're told. When disorder did develop I just announced that we would leave if it did not stop.

Some of my men were the objects of queries. I had Narayan moving through the formation. Those he knew were industrious, cooperative, hard-working, and loyal he could grant a short leave. He was supposed to remind the less diligent why they would remain on duty. Carrot and stick.

It held up. Even the greenest behaved. It took all night but we satisfied half the crowd. I reminded everyone frequently that Mogaba's legion and who knew how many more men were trapped in Dejagore, thanks to the desertion of Jahamaraj Jah. I made it sound like everyone not accounted for was among the besieged.

Most were probably dead.

Whips and carrots and emotional manipulations.
I'd been at it so long I could do it in my sleep.

A messenger came. There were priests at the barracks to see me. "Took them long enough," I muttered. Were they late because they were off balance
or because they waited till they were ready for a
confrontation? No matter. They would wait till we
finished.

The rain stopped. It was never much more than a
drizzling nuisance.

Once we cleared the square I dismounted and
walked with Narayan. We were seventy fewer now.
He had let that many go. I asked, "Did you notice
the bats?"

"A few, Mistress." He was puzzled.

"Are they special among the omens of Kina?"

"I don't think so. But I was never a priest."

"They're significant to me."

"Eh?"

"They tell me, plain as a shout, that the Shadowmasters have spies here. General order to the men.
Kill all bats. If they can, find out where they're roost-
ing. Watch out for foreigners. Pass the word to the
populace, too. There are spies among us again and I
want to lay hands on a few."

We'd probably end up swamped with useless reports about harmless people, but . . . A few wouldn't
be harmless. And those needed their teeth pulled.

Chapter Twenty-Seven

The men waiting included delegations from all three religious hierarchies. They were not pleased that I had kept them waiting. I did not apologize. I was not in a good humor and did not mind a confrontation.

They'd had to wait in the mess hall because there was nowhere else to put them. Even there they had to crowd up because they had to get out of the way of men who had nowhere else to spread their blankets.

Before I went in I told Narayan, "First score to my credit. They came to me."

"Probably because none of them want you making a private deal with the others."

"Probably." I put on my best scowl, laid on a light glamor, clanked into the mess hall. "Good morning. I'm honored but I'm also pressed for time. If you have something to discuss please get to the point. I'm an hour behind schedule and didn't budget time for socializing."

They didn't know how to take me. A woman talking hard was something new.

Somebody shot an obnoxious question from the back.

"All right. A position statement. That should save time. My religious attitude is indifference. I'll stay indifferent as long as religion ignores me. My position on social issues is the same. I'm a soldier, one of the Black Company, which contracted with the Prahbrindrah Drah to rid Taglios of the Shadowmasters. My Captain fell. I replaced him. I will fulfill the contract. If that statement doesn't answer your questions then you probably have questions you have no right to ask.

"My predecessor was a patient man. He worried about offending people. I don't share those qualities. I'm direct and unpleasant when aroused. Questions?"

They had them. Of course. They yammered. I picked a man I recognized, one who was offensive and was not loved by his peers. He was a bald Gunni in scarlet. "Tal. You're being unpleasant. Stop it. You have no legitimate business here. None of you have, really. I said I have no interest in religion. You have little cause to be interested in things military. Let's leave each other to our own competences."

Beautiful Tal played his part as though rehearsed. His response was more than offensive, it was a direct challenge predicated upon my sex, speaking to my failure to commit suttee.

I tossed him a Golden Hammer, not to the heart but to the right shoulder. It spun him around and knocked him down. He screamed for more than a minute before he passed out.

It got real quiet. Everyone, including poor fuddled Narayan, stared at me wide-eyed.

"You see? I'm not my predecessor. He would have remained polite. He would have clung to persuasion and diplomacy long past the point where a demonstration is a more effective way to communicate. Go tend to priestly matters. I'll tend to making war and to wartime discipline.''

That should not be hard for them to figure out. The Company's contract made the Captain virtual military dictator for a year. Croaker had not used the power. I did not expect to. But it was there if needed.

"Go. I have work to do."

They went. Quietly. Thoughtfully.

"Well," Narayan said after they left. "Well."

"Now they know I'm no fainter. Now they know I'm mission-oriented and don't care who I stomp if they get in the way."

"They're bad men to make enemies."

"They make the choice. Yes! I know. But they're confused. It'll take them a while to decide what to do. Then they'll all get in each other's ways. I've bought time. I need intelligence sources, Narayan. Find Ram. Tell him I want those men he brought to me earlier. It's time to look at those sites." Before he could argue, I added, "And tell him if he plans to keep on being my shadow he'd better learn to ride. I expect to be moving around a lot, now."

"Yes, Mistress." He hurried off, paused just before he left, looked back, frowned. He was wondering who was using who and who had the upper hand. Good. Let him. While he was wondering I'd get my foundations set solidly.

The men in the mess hall all stared at me with varying degrees of awe. Few met my gaze. "Rest while you can, soldiers. The sands are running through the glass."

I went to my quarters to wait for Ram.

Chapter Twenty-Eight

Croaker stared into the drizzly night, fingers nervously twisting strands of grass. One of the horses made a sound out there. He thought about walking over there, mounting up bareback, riding away. He would stand a fifty-fifty chance of staying ahead.

Except that things had changed. Now Catcher did not have to catch up physically.

He held up the figure he had made, a man shape two inches tall. The grass gave off a garlic odor. He shrugged, flipped it out into the rain, took more strands of grass from a pocket. He had made hundreds now. Grass figures had become a sort of measure of time.

A steady banging came from behind him. He turned away from the night, walked slowly toward the woman. She had produced a set of armorer's tools from somewhere. This was the second day running she had spent building something. Obviously black armor, but why?

She glanced at the horse figure he was twisting. "I may get you some paper and ink."

"Would you?" There was a lot he wanted to set down. He had grown used to keeping a journal.

"I may. That's no pastime for a grown man."

He shrugged, put the horse aside. "Take a break. Time to check you over."

She no longer wore robes. She was outfitted as she had been when first he had met her, in tight black leather that somehow left her sex ambiguous. Her Soulcatcher costume, she called it. She hadn't bothered with the helmet yet.

She set her tools aside, looked at him with mischief in her eyes. "You sound depressed." The voice she chose was merry.

"I am depressed. Stand up." She did. He peeled away the leather around her neck. "It's healing quickly. I'll remove the sutures tomorrow, maybe."

"Will there be much scarring?"

"I don't know. Depends on how well your healing spells work. I didn't know you were vain."

"I'm human. I'm a woman. I want to look nice." Same voice but less merry.

"You do look nice." He did not think before he spoke. Just making a statement of fact. She looked nice in the sense that she was a beautiful woman. Like her sister. He had become very conscious of that since she had changed her style of dress. That left him nagged by low-grade guilt.

She laughed. "I'm reading your mind, Croaker."

She was not, literally. She would not be pleased with him if she was. But she had been around a long time and had studied people. She could read books from a few physical clues.

He grunted. He was getting used to it. There was no point trying hard to hide from it. "What are you making?"

"Armor. We'll be healed enough to go soon. We'll have great fun."

"I'll bet." He felt a twinge in his chest. He *was* almost healed. There had been none of the complications he had expected. He had begun taking forced exercise.

"We're the gadflies here, love. The chaos factor. My beloved sister and the Taglians know nothing about us. Those clubfooted Shadowmasters know I'm here but they don't know about you. They don't know what you've accomplished. They think I'm a nuisance floating around in the dark. I doubt they've entertained the notion that I could be restored."

She rested a hand on his cheek. "I'm more basic than you think."

"Oh?"

Change of voice, businesslike, masculine, at odds with the invitation. "I have eyes everywhere. I know every word spoken by anyone who interests me. A while back I arranged for Longshadow to be diverted while Howler visited Spinner and cut Longshadow's webs of control."

"Damn! He'll hit Dejagore with everything."

"He'll lie low and pretend he's unchanged. The siege costs him nothing. He'll be more interested in improving his position in relation to Longshadow. He knows Longshadow will destroy him when he's no longer useful. We'll have fun. We'll poke around and make them chase their tails. When the dust settles, maybe there'll be no Longshadow, no Shadowspinner, no Howler, just you and me and an empire of our own. Or maybe the spirit will move me some other direction. I don't know. I'm just having fun with it."

He shook his head slightly. Hard to believe, but it sounded true. Her schemes could kill thousands, could distress millions, and to her it was play.

"I'll never understand you."

She giggled the giggle of a girl with nothing between the ears. She was neither young nor emptyheaded. "I don't understand myself. But I gave up trying a long time ago. It's distracting."

Games. From the first she had been involved in tortuous maneuvers and manipulations, to no obvious end. Her great pleasure was to watch a scheme flower and devour its victim. Her only plot to fail had been the one meant to displace her sister. And she had not failed completely then because she had survived, somehow.

She said, "Soon Kina's followers will start arriving. We'll have to be somewhere else. So let's go down to Dejagore and cause some confusion. We ought to get there about the time Spinner figures he's ready to make an independent move. Be interesting to see how it goes."

Croaker did not understand but did not ask. He was used to her talking in riddles. She let him know what she wanted him to know when she was ready to tell him. No point pressing her. He could do little but bide his time and hope.

"It's late," she said. "We've done enough for today. Let's turn in."

He grunted, not eager. The place gave him the creeps when he thought about it, which meant every night as he fell asleep. Which meant at least one potent nightmare. He would be glad to get out.

Maybe out there he could vanish—if he could think of a way to hide from the crows.

Fifteen minutes after the lamp went out Soulcatcher asked, "Are you awake?"

"Yeah."

"It's cold in here."

"Uhm." It always was. Most nights he fell asleep shivering.

"Why don't you come over here?"

The shivering worsened. "I don't think so."

She laughed. "Some other time."

He fell asleep worrying about how she always got her way instead of about the temple. His dreams were more troubling than nightmares.

Once he wakened momentarily. The lamp was alive again. Soulcatcher was murmuring with a clatch of crows. The subject seemed to be events in Taglios. She appeared pleased. He drifted off without understanding what it was about.

Chapter Twenty-Nine

Neither potential campsite was perfect. One had been fortified before, in ancient times. For centuries people had carried the stone off for use elsewhere. I chose that site.

"Nobody remembers the name," I told Ram as we rode toward town. "Makes you think."

"Huh? About what?"

"The fleeting nature of things. Taglios' entire history could have been influenced by what happened there and now nobody remembers the name."

He looked at me oddly, straining for understanding. He wanted to understand but he didn't have the capacity. The past was last week, the future tomorrow. There was no reality in anything that happened before he was born.

He was not stupid. He seemed big and dull and slow but possessed an average intellect. He just had not learned to employ it.

"Never mind. It doesn't matter. I'm just being

moody." He understood moody. He expected it. His wife and mother had been "moody."

He did not have time now to think, anyway. He was too busy staying on his horse.

We returned to the barracks. There was another crowd looking for their loved ones. Narayan was handling them efficiently. They eyed me curiously. Not at all the way they had looked at Croaker. Him they had hailed Liberator everywhere. Me, I was a freak without the sense to know she was not a man.

I would grow on them. Just a matter of creating a legend.

Narayan caught up with me. "There was a messenger from the palace. The prince wants you to dine with him tonight. Someplace called the grove."

"Oh?" That was where I had met him first. Croaker had taken me. The grove was an outdoor place frequented by the rich and influential. "Request or order?"

"Invitation. Will you do me the honor of, like that."

"Did you accept?"

"No. How could I guess what you'd want to do?"

"Good. Send a message. I accept. What time?"

"He wasn't specific."

It would slow me down but I might accomplish something that would save fussing and feuding later. At least I'd learn how much grief I could expect from the state. "I'm going to sketch out the camp I want built. We'll send one company plus five hundred recruits to start. Pick whoever you think we should get out of the city. That mess outside. How's it going?"

"Well enough, Mistress."

"Any volunteers showing?"

"A few."

"And intelligence? Have you gotten anything started?"

"Lot of people want to tell us things. Mostly about foreigners. Nothing really interesting."

"Keep at it. Let me do those sketches. After that I'll make a list to give the Prahbrindrah. After that I'll make myself presentable." Around here somewhere would be my imperial getup, that I'd worn last time, and my coach, that we had brought down from the north and had left here when we had marched on Ghoja.

"Ram, before we went south I had several men help me make special armor. I need to find them again."

I went to work sketching and estimating.

The coach was not as impressive with a four-horse team but people did gawk. I had enough skill to make hooves strike fire and to set a glamor running the coach's exterior. The fire-breathing skull of the Company blazed on both doors. The steel-rimmed wheels and pounding hooves rumbled thunderously.

I was satisfied.

I reached the grove an hour before sunset, entered, looked around. Just like last time, the cream of Taglian society had come out to rubberneck. Ram and a red rumel man named Abda, of Vehdna background, were my bodyguards. I did not know Abda. He was with me because Narayan said he was good.

They had spruced up. Ram cleaned up nicely when you held a knife to his kidneys. Bathed, hair and beard trimmed, in new clothes, he cut a handsome figure. But Abda did not improve much. He was a shifty-eyed little villain who looked like a villain no matter what.

I wished I had brought a Gunni bodyguard, too, to make a symbolic statement. You can't think of everything when you're rushed.

The Prahbrindrah rose as I strode up to him. He smiled. "You found me. I was concerned. I wasn't specific about where we'd meet."

"It seemed logical I'd find you where we met before."

He eyed Ram and Abda. He had come alone. A measure of his confidence in his people's reverence? Misplaced confidence, maybe.

"Make yourself comfortable," he invited. "I've tried to order things I think you'll like." He glanced at Ram and Abda again, perplexed. He did not know what to do about them.

I said, "Last time I was here somebody tried to kill Croaker. Forget them. I trust their discretion." I had no idea whether I could trust Abda or not. Didn't seem smart to make a point of it, though.

Servitors started with refreshments and appetizers. From the state of the grove you could not tell Taglios was a nation threatened with extinction.

"You look radiant this evening."

"I don't feel it. I feel worn out."

"You should relax more. Take life easier."

"Have the Shadowmasters decided to take a holiday?"

He sampled something that looked like shrimp. Where had shrimp come from, here? Well, the sea was not that far away.

Which sparked a germ of an idea. I set it aside for later examination.

The prince swallowed, dabbed his lips with a napkin. "You seem determined to make my life difficult."

"Oh?"

"You roar ahead like the whirlwind, giving no one time to think. You rush headlong. Everyone else has to concentrate on keeping their balance."

I smiled. "If I give anyone time to do anything but run along behind me I'll be up to my ears in grief. None of you seem to understand the magnitude of your enemy. You all have your priorities inverted. Everybody wants to dance around and get the angle on everybody else. Meantime, the Shadowmasters are planning to exterminate all of you."

He nibbled and pretended to think. "You're right. But people are human. Nobody here has ever had to think in terms of external enemies. Or really deadly enemies."

"The Shadowmasters count on that, too."

"No doubt."

A new course arrived, more substantial. Some kind of bird. I was surprised. The prince's background was Gunni. The Gunni were determined vegetarians.

Watching my surroundings I spied two things I did not like. There were dozens of crows among the trees. And that priest Tal I had embarrassed earlier, with several of his cronies, was watching us.

The Prahbrindrah said, "I'm under a lot of pressure because of you. Some from close quarters. It puts me in a delicate position."

Where was his sister? Were she and Smoke riding him? Probably. I shrugged and ate.

The prince said, "It would help if I knew your plans."

I told him.

"Suppose some important people don't approve or don't feel you're the right champion?"

"It wouldn't matter. There's a contract in force. It will be fulfilled. And I don't distinguish between enemies foreign or domestic."

He understood.

Nothing got said during the next course. Then he blurted, "Did you kill Jahamaraj Jah?"

"Yes."

"My gods! Why?"

"His existence offended me."

He gulped some air.

"He deserted at Dejagore. That cost us the battle. That was reason enough. But he also planned to kill your sister and blame me. He had a wife. If Shadar women are foolish enough to kill themselves over men, you can tell her to fire her ghat. Any priest's wife who has a husband like Jah had better start collecting firewood. She'll need it."

He winced. "You'll start a civil war."

"Not if everybody behaves and minds his own business."

"You don't understand. Priests consider everything their business."

"How many men are we talking about? A few thousand? You ever watch a gardener prune? He snips a twig here, a branch there, and the plant grows stronger. I'll prune if I have to."

"But . . . There's only you. You can't take on . . ."

"I can. I will. I'm going to fulfill the contract. And so are you."

"What?"

"I've heard that you and your sister didn't negotiate in good faith. Not smart, my friend. Nobody cheats the Company."

He did not respond.

"I'm not really good at games. I'm not subtle. My solutions are forthright and final."

"Forthright and final begets forthright and final. You kill a Jah, the other Jahs will get the idea their only option is to kill you."

"Only if they ignore the option of minding their own business. And where's my risk? I have nothing to lose. That's the fate planned for me once I'm used up, anyway. Why cooperate in my own destruction?"

"You can't just keep killing people who don't agree with you."

"I won't. Only people who disagree and try to force their ideas on me. Here in Taglios, now, there's no legitimate cause for conflict."

The prince seemed surprised. "I don't follow."

"Taglios must be preserved from the Shadowmasters. The Company contracted to do that. Where's the problem? We do what we agreed, you pay up as agreed, we go away. That ought to make everyone happy."

The prince looked at me like he wondered how I could be so naive. "I'm starting to think we have no basis for communication. This dinner may have been a mistake."

"No. It's been productive. It'll keep on being productive if you *listen* to me. I'm not beating around the bush. I'm telling you how it is and how it's going

to be. Without me the Shadowmasters will eat you
alive. You think they'll be impressed by which cult
got a leg up on what with a boondoggle wall construction grant? I know how those people think. If
they reach Taglios they'll slaughter everybody who
could possibly make trouble ever. You should understand that. You saw what they did elsewhere."

"It's impossible to argue with you."

"Because you know I'm right. I have a list of things
I need right away. I have to build an encampment
and prepare a training ground immediately."

This could lead to a quick confrontation. The resources would have to come from that absurd wall
project. The city was too big to surround effectively.
The project could not be justified. It was a tool for
transferring the wealth of the state to a few individuals.

I said, "The men and resources devoted to the wall
can be more profitably employed."

He understood. I was asking for trouble. He
grunted.

I said, "Why don't we just enjoy our meal?"

We tried but it never turned into a festive evening.

A few courses along, with the conversation darting
between his younger years and mine, I took the offensive again. "One more thing I want. The books
Smoke hid."

His eyes got big.

"I want to know why you're afraid of the past."

He smiled weakly. "I think you know. Smoke is
sure you do. He believes it was the point of your
coming."

"Give me a clue."

"The Year of the Skulls."

I was not entirely surprised. I feigned bewilder-
ment. "Year of the Skulls? What's that?"

He glanced at Ram and Abda. Doubt appeared. I
recalled toying with my rumel while talking to his
sister. He would not doubt long.

"If you don't know you should find out. But I'm

not the best authority. Talk it over with your friends."

"I have no friends if I don't have the Prahbrindrah Drah."

"A pity."

"Do you have?"

That baffled him again. He forced a smile. "Perhaps I don't. Perhaps I ought to try to make some." The smile changed.

"We all need a few. Sometimes our enemies won't let us find them. I should be getting back. My number two is inexperienced and handicapped by his place in your caste system."

A hint of disappointment? He had wanted more than a discussion of princes and warlords.

"Thank you for the dinner, Prahbrindrah. I'll treat you in kind, soon. Ram. Abda." They stepped close. Ram offered a hand up. They had stayed behind me, unseen. I was pleased that they were alert. Ram would have been if only because of where we were. A man of his station had no hope of visiting the grove ordinarily. "Have a pleasant evening, Prince. I expect to hand you the heads of Taglios' enemies within the year."

He wore a sort of sad, yearning look as he watched us go. I knew what he was feeling. I had felt it often while I was empress in the north. But I had hidden it better.

Chapter Thirty

Ram waited till he was confident we were out of earshot. "Something is going to happen, Mistress."

"Trouble?"

"We were watched by sneaking Gunni priests all the time. They acted like they were up to no good."

"Ah." I did not question his estimate. He did not have too rich an imagination. I snapped fingers at a nearby servitor. "Fetch Master Gupta."

Master Gupta ran the grove, a benign dictator. He was attentive to his guests—especially those who were close to the Prahbrindrah Drah. He appeared almost instantly.

Bowing like a coolie, he asked, "What could the great lady want of this lowly worm?"

"How about a sword?" Dressed as a woman and empress I had not come heavily armed. I had one short dagger.

His eyes got huge. "A sword? What would I do with a sword, Mistress?"

"I haven't the faintest. But I want to borrow one if you can provide it."

Eyes even bigger, he bowed several times. "I'll see what can be found." He scooted off, throwing uncertain looks over his shoulder.

"Ram, help me shed some of this showpiece."

He was scandalized. He refused.

"Ram, you're pushing for the opportunity to spend your army time digging latrine trenches."

He took my word for it, accepted the disapproval of several dozen watchers as he helped me shed my most cumbersome garments. He was embarrassed.

Abda, not asked to participate, pretended blindness.

Gupta materialized. He had a sword. It was someone's show toy. "I borrowed this from a gentleman who was gracious enough to permit me to carry it to you." He was blind, too. I expect he had seen everything over the years. The grove was a place where lovers managed clever assignations.

"I shall harbor kind thoughts toward you forever, Gupta. Am I correct in assuming the staff sent for my coach when they saw me getting ready to leave?"

"The men responsible will be seeking employment elsewhere if it isn't there when you arrive, Lady."

"Thank you. I'll send this toy back shortly."

Ram again waited till he thought no one could hear, grunted a question. I replied, "If there's to be trouble it'll come just inside the gate. If we reach the coach we'll be safe."

"You have a plan, Mistress?"

"Spring the trap. If there is one. We wipe them out or take them prisoner and carry them off, never to be seen again. How many might there be?"

Ram shrugged. He did not waste time looking at me now. He had eyes for trouble only.

Abda said, "Eight. And the one you embarrassed. But he'll avoid getting too close. He might have to explain if someone saw him."

"Oh?"

"I was involved in two similar schemes when I was an acolyte."

I had no idea what he meant. It did not seem like the best time to fill myself in on his past. We were approaching a brushy area that crowded the path to the exit.

I say brushy but I'm no devotee of formal gardening. The area consisted of heavy vegetation four to eight feet high. Every single leaf was tended and considered daily. Its function was to mask the grove from the world so Taglios' lords would not be defiled by common eyes.

I started a spell as soon as we left Gupta. I was ready when we reached the shrubbery. It was another child's plaything but my most ambitious effort yet. I spoke the initiator and threw the resulting fireball into the growth to my left.

By the time the ball went ten feet it was hot enough to melt steel. It broke into fragments that broke into smaller fragments.

Someone screamed.

Someone else screamed. A man plunged out of the growth pounding his side.

I got another ball ready, threw it the other way.

"Wait," I said. "Let them come out. We'll push them down the path to the gate." There were three men on that path now, wild-eyed. Then three more came out like spooked cattle. The brush was burning. "That's long enough. Let's move."

We hustled forward. The baffled would-be assassins retreated. They piled up against the closed gate. The gatemen stared at the flames, stunned, unsure what to do.

"Ram. Bang them over the head. Put them in the coach." A guard recognized me, did his job by rote as Ram waded into the six.

"Mistress."

Abda was behind me. I turned. A man afire was charging us with an upraised tulwar, a weapon I had not seen here before. It looked like an antique.

Abda ducked, darted, had his rumel around the man's neck in a blink. I did not get to use my borrowed blade. The assassin's impetus broke his neck.

That was it. Ram tossed bodies into the coach. I told the least rattled gate guard, "Thank master Gupta for the loan." I gave him the sword. "And extend my apologies for the damages. The priest Chandra Chan Tal should be happy to make them good. Ready, Ram?"

"Yes, Mistress."

"Abda, get that carrion loaded." I walked to the coach, climbed up beside my driver, looked around, spotted Tal. He and two other priests in red were standing streetside eighty feet away, bug-eyed. I saluted them.

"Loaded, Mistress," Abda called up.

I got some amusement from him and Ram. They did not want me up there, exposed, but did not want me inside with the dead and captive, either. "Shall I run along behind like a good Taglian woman, Ram?"

Embarrassed, he shook his head.

"Climb aboard."

We rolled right past Tal and his cronies. I called down, "Get what pleasure you can from the hours you have left."

Tal blanched. The other two were made of sterner or stupider stuff.

Chapter Thirty-One

It was a gorgeous day. A few clouds above to break up the sky, a gentle breeze, the air unseasonably cool. If you stayed in the shade you could remain sweat-free. It was midafternoon. Work on the camp had begun at dawn. Four thousand men made progress obvious.

First we would provide shelter, mess halls, stables, storage. I had planned ambitiously, for a garrison of ten thousand. Even Narayan was worried that I wanted to grab too much too soon.

I had spent the morning administering oaths to the soldiers in small groups, by cult, having them pledge everything in the sacred defense of Taglios. Wormed into the oath was a line about unquestioning obedience to commanders.

Narayan's cleverer cronies weeded out the priests and religious fanatics beforehand. The dross we isolated in what was supposed to be a special unit. There were about three hundred such men. They were on the field below the hill, being given "accelerated" training. As soon as I found a good one I would send them off on a bold and dramatic mission somewhere far away. I sat in the shade of an old tree observing and directing. Ram hovered.

I spied Narayan approaching. I had left him in the city. I rose, asked, "Well?"

"It's done. The last one was found an hour before I left."

"Good." Tal had been easy but his companions had been hard to trace. Narayan's friends had disposed of them. "That's good. Has it caused excitement?"

"Hard to tell yet, though a Gunni emissary did show up just before I left."

"Oh?"

"He wanted to arrange the release of the men from the grove."

"And?"

"I told him they'd been released. He'll figure it out."

"Excellent. Any word on the Shadowmasters' spies?"

"No. But people have seen the wrinkled little brown men you mentioned. So they must be here."

"They're here. I'd give a couple of teeth to know what they're up to. Anything else?"

"Not yet. Except a rumor that the Prahbrindrah Drah called in the big men in the wall project and told them they have to build you a fortress instead. I've located a friend who works in the palace occasionally, when their normal resources are taxed. Our prince doesn't maintain a household in keeping with his station. He won't get much if the prince doesn't entertain, and probably not much then."

"Look into the possibility of arranging for your friend to become employed full time. Have there been many more volunteers?"

"Only a few. It's still too early. People want to see how you manage with the powers that be."

"Understandable. Nobody wants to sign on with a loser."

Be interesting to know what they said about me at that meeting. A pity I did not command the resources I once had.

I was not going to get them back loafing. "I'll ride back with you. I have things to do." I had recalled one thing my husband had done to secure his rule. A version here just might make everyone forget politics for a while.

I would need a suitable theater. I had to start looking. As we rode, I asked Narayan, "Do we have many archers?" I knew we did not but what I lacked he had a knack for finding.

"No, Mistress. Archery wasn't a skill much encouraged. A hobby for Marhans, that's all." He meant the top-dog caste.

"We had a few, though. Find them. Have them teach the most reliable men."

"You have something in mind?"

"A new twist on an old story. Maybe. I may never need them but if I do I want to know they're there."

"As always, we shall endeavor to provide." He grinned that grin I wished I could scrub off his face forever.

"To create a body of archers you'll need bows and arrows and all the ancillary paraphernalia." That would keep his mind occupied. I did not feel like talking. I did not feel ready to wrestle lions today. Had not for several days, in fact. I supposed it was lack of sleep, bad dreams, and the fact that I had been driving myself to the limit.

The dreams persisted. They were bad but I just shoved them aside in my mind, took the unpleasantness, and got on with getting on. There was just so much I could do in the time available. I would deal with the dreams when I finished with more immediate concerns.

For a while I thought about my one-time husband, the Dominator, and his empire-building techniques, then about my own plight. Lack of leaders continued to plague me. Every day men were handed tasks beyond their training, based on my or Narayan's gut feelings. Some worked out, some folded under the pressure. That was heavier now that we meant to digest a horde with no idea what was happening.

As we neared the city, approaching scaffolding where wall construction had started, Narayan observed, "Mistress, it's less than a month till the Festival of Lights."

He lost me for a moment. Then I recalled the festival as the big holy day of his cult. And remembered him hinting around that I should be there if I wanted the support of the Stranglers. I had to go convince the other jamadars that I was the Daughter of Night and could bring on the Year of the Skulls.

I had to learn more about the cult. To find out what Narayan might be hiding.

There was no time to do everything that had to be done.

We had gotten our first message from the men watching Dejagore last night. Mogaba was holding out. Stubborn Mogaba. I did not look forward to seeing him again. Sparks would fly. He would claim the Captaincy, too. I knew that as sure as I knew the sun rose and set.

One step at a time. One step at a time.

Chapter Thirty-Two

The meeting with the priests had not gone well. The Radisha was in a blistering rage. Her brother looked grim. Smoke squeaked, "Something has to be done about that woman."

They were in a shielded room but something had installed itself amongst clutter on a high shelf. Those below did not notice the one yellow crow eye watching.

"I'm not so sure," the Prahbrindrah Drah replied. "We talked extensively. I think she was truthful. My gut feeling is that we should give her her head."

"Gods!" Smoke swore. "No!"

The Radisha remained neutral. For the moment. "We were inches from getting thrown out tonight. We couldn't drive a wedge between them. The fact that we might be able to point her in their direction was all that saved us. We can't get rid of her, Smoke."

The Prahbrindrah Drah said, "We've got the tiger by the tail. Can't let go. I feel like I'm in a big bowl and all around the rim are people who want to roll boulders down on me."

"She will devour us," Smoke said. He kept his tone reasonable. Panicky talk had worked against him before. The Prahbrindrah Drah and Radisha had to be convinced intellectually. "She traffics with Stranglers."

"Of whom there are maybe only a few hundred in the whole world," the Radisha observed. "How many men are there in the Shadowlands? How many shadows? There're more backstabbing priests here in the city than there are Stranglers anywhere."

"Read those old chronicles again," Smoke suggested. "How numerous were the Black Company when they came here before? Yet before they were driven out our ancestors very nearly witnessed the Year of the Skulls. You can't traffic with this darkness. It wakens the devil in everyone. You can't invite the tiger into your house to keep the wolf away. There are no greys. There is no tightrope to walk. No one can hope to play this off against other darknesses. This is the deep and ultimate evil beyond all evils. Consider what the woman did last night."

The Prahbrindrah Drah said, "I was put out by the damage done. Master Gupta and his predecessors worked on that for a century."

"Not the damned plants!" Smoke almost lost control. "A man is dead, killed by sorcery. Seven more were carried off to who knows what fate? Tal and his cronies were slain in their very temples. Strangled!"

"They asked for it," the Radisha said. "They did something stupid. They paid for it. You notice the other Gunni priests weren't put out."

"Ghapor's bunch? They probably encouraged Tal and didn't mind when he came out on the short end."

"Probably."

"Don't you see what she's done? A year ago no priest would have considered murder. Now it's accepted. Nobody is distressed.

"Tal is gone. You say he was stupid and asked for it and you're right. But he was one of the most important men in Taglios. So was Jahamaraj Jah. He asked for it, too. When she picks off the next one, well, maybe everybody will say the same thing again. He asked for it. And the next one and the next and then it's you and the Prahbrindrah Drah and after that the deluge. Never mind professionalism as a soldier. She might be the best that ever was. Maybe she can ruin the Shadowmasters in her sleep. But even if they never cross the Main again, if they never come north of Dejagore, if they never win another skirmish, if she's in charge, Taglios will lose as certainly as if we hadn't resisted at all."

The Prahbrindrah Drah started to speak. The Radisha jumped in first. "He has a point. Taglios won't ever be the same."

"Oh?"

"If we give the woman a free hand she'll make Taglios over into the image of the Shadowlands because that's what it will take to win. Smoke, I see that. Even if you're obsessive about the Stranglers and the Year of the Skulls. I've watched the woman. I doubt if anyone but that man Croaker ever had any influence on her. Brother, he's right. She'll turn us into what we fear in order to save us."

"Then we're damned if we do and damned if we don't. We let her go on, we're done. We don't, the Shadowmasters eat us."

Smoke said, "There's another way. . . ." But he could not tell them. He had not told them everything when he had reported the approach by Longshadow's agents. Too late now. If he brought up overlooked details they would no longer trust him. They might even think his opposition to the woman had been ordered by Taglios' enemies.

That wrinkled little man had foreseen this. Damn him.

"Well?" the Radisha demanded.

"I had a thought. It was impractical. Emotion guiding the mind. Forget it. Kina is stirring. The Daughter of Night walks among us. We must silence her."

The Prahbrindrah Drah said, "We can talk about this all night. None of us will change our minds. We'd better concentrate on staying a step ahead of the priests till we do agree."

Smoke shook his head. That would not do. The woman would keep everyone confused and divided; then it would be too late. That was the way of darkness. Deceit. Endless deceit.

No point talking anymore. There was only one choice left.

They would hate him if they caught him. They would brand him traitor. But there was no other answer.

He had to pray for courage and a clear head. The Shadowmasters were masters of deceit themselves. They would use him if they could. But if he played the game carefully he could serve Taglios better than any dozen armies.

He started trying to cut the conversation short.

As brother and sister were leaving, the prince said, "Smoke, I meant to ask. Why would she put a bounty on bats all of a sudden?"

"A what?"

"The Shadar Singh mentioned it. He heard it on his way here. She put out word that any children who wanted could pick up a few coppers by bringing her dead bats. Every poor family in town will start hunting them. And the treasury will have to pay for them. Why?"

"I have no idea," Smoke lied. His heart was in his throat. She *knew*. That business about reporting strangers . . . It wasn't a propaganda ploy. She knew. "A few exotic spells use bat parts powdered. Fur, claws, livers. But they're the kind that make your neighbor's cattle sterile or his hens stop laying. Nothing of use to her."

But live bats were useful to the Shadowmasters.

He barely waited till the prince and his sister turned a corner down the hall. Then he headed for the world outside, before there were no bats left to find him.

Chapter Thirty-Three

Croaker sat on a rock in the wood, leaning against a tree, twisting an animal figure. He finished it and tossed it at a stump. Crows watched. He paid them no heed. He was thinking about Soulcatcher.

She was not great company: She had spent ages turned inward. She could be amiable and animated for brief periods but did not know how to keep it up. Neither did he. Sometimes it seemed they were moving in parallel rather than together. But she would not let him go just because they weren't soulmates. She had uses for him.

She had been bustling around the temple all day. He did not know why. He felt no urge to find out. He was depressed. He came to this spot when his mood was at low ebb.

The imp Frogface materialized. "Why the long face, Cap?"

"Why not?"

"You got me there."

"What's happening in Dejagore?"

"Got me there, too. I've been busy."

"Doing what?"

"Can't say." The imp aped his morose stance. "Last time I was there your boys was doing fine. Maybe fussing and feuding a little more than before. Old One-Eye and his sidekick don't get along with that Mogaba, not even a little. They been talking about doing a fade and letting him go to hell his own way."

"He'd get wiped out if they did."

"He don't appreciate them enough, that's sure."

"She says we're going down there."

"Well. Then you can look for yourself."

"I don't think that's what she's got in mind. She call you in?"

"Came to report. Interesting things happening. You could ask. She might tell you."

"What's she doing?"

"Fixing the place up so it don't look like somebody's been living there. That Festival thing is coming up. Them weirdos will be getting here real soon."

Croaker doubted he would get a straight answer but he asked anyway. "How's Lady?"

"Fine. Keeps on, she'll be running the whole show in six months. Got every poobah in Taglios so confused she's doing any damned thing she pleases."

"She's in Taglios?" He hadn't known that. Catcher hadn't told him. He hadn't asked.

"Has been for weeks. Left that Blade character in charge at Ghoja and went up to the city and started taking over."

"She would. She isn't the kind to wait for things to happen."

"Tell me about it. Whoa! I hear the boss calling. Better get on over there. Pack up your things."

"What things?" He did not have much but the clothes he wore. And those were rags.

"Whatever you have to take with you. She's leaving in an hour."

He did not argue. That was as futile as arguing

with a stone. His wants and interests did not count. He had less freedom than a slave.

"Take it easy, Cap," the imp said. And vanished.

They rode till Croaker collapsed. They rested, then rode again. Soulcatcher ignored such niceties as restricting travel to daylight hours. She permitted a third halt only after they entered the hills northwest of Dejagore. She spoke seldom except to her crows, and to Frogface briefly after they arrived, while Croaker was sleeping.

She wakened him as the sun rose. "We reenter the world today, my love. Sorry I haven't been as attentive as I should." He could tell nothing from her choice of voices. This one he thought was her own, much like her sister's, always neutral. "I've had a lot on my mind. I should bring you up to date."

"That would be nice."

"Your flair for sarcasm hasn't disappeared."

"It keeps me going."

"Maybe. This is how things stand. Last week Spinner attacked Dejagore in force. He was thrown back. He would have succeeded if he'd used all his skills. But he couldn't without Longshadow finding out he's not as feeble as he pretends. He'll try again tonight. He could succeed. Your One-Eye and Goblin have broken with their commander.

"My beloved sister has obtained a strong position in and around Taglios. She has five or six thousand men, none of them worth a damn.

"She left the man Blade at Ghoja when she headed north. He has the same problems and none of her expertise but some of the men he has have legionary experience. He's decided to let them learn the hard way. He's begun occupying surrounding territories, especially southward along the road to Dejagore."

"Makes it easier to feed his men, probably."

"Yes. He has a force exceeding three thousand men now. His scouts have skirmished with Shadowspinner's patrols.

"And the big news, of course, is that the wizard Smoke has been seduced by Longshadow."

"Say what? That little bastard. I never did trust him."

"Longshadow appealed to his idealism. And to his fear of my sister and the Black Company. Offered him assurances he couldn't help but believe, made him think he could become a hero by saving Taglios from its supposed saviors while he made peace with the Shadowlands."

"That man is a fool. I thought you had to be smart to be a wizard."

"Smart doesn't mean sensible, Croaker. And he isn't a complete fool. He didn't trust Longshadow. He used every device he could to make Longshadow keep his word. His real mistake was going to visit Longshadow at Shadowcatch."

"What?"

"The Howler and Longshadow combined their talents to create a flying carpet like those we had back when, before they were destroyed. It's a puny one but good enough for Howler to fly the wizard to Shadowcatch and to drop spies into Taglios. Smoke is down there now. Frogface is watching him. Longshadow is trying to do a poor man's Taking of Smoke. He'll go back to Taglios as Longshadow's creature."

Croaker did not like the sums he came up with. Three major wizards against Taglios now, and Taglios' only magical defender was a creature of the enemy. Lady might be doing well but could not be doing as well as she must to manage both the Shadowmasters and her enemies behind her.

Doom would be stalking Taglios long before anyone expected it.

Khatovar was farther away than ever.

He could not manage that mission on his own. Taking the Annals back ... He did not have them. They were trapped inside Dejagore. He could not get to them.

Was Murgen keeping them up? He'd better be.

"You haven't said anything about our part in all this."

"But I have. Often. We're just going to have fun with it. We're going to kick the props out from under people. Tonight we'll have this whole end of the world wondering what's going on and who's doing what to who."

He began to understand soon after she told him to start getting ready.

"Ready how?"

"Get your armor on. It's time to scare the shit out of Spinner's men and save Dejagore."

He just stood there, puzzled. She asked, "Would you rather let them be wiped out?"

"No." The Annals were in the city. They had to be preserved. He unpacked the armor they had lugged all the way from the temple. "I can't get this on by myself."

"I know. You'll have to help me with mine, too."

With hers? He had assumed she would use her old Soulcatcher guise. He began to see her subtlety.

The armor she had made at the temple was a copy of Lady's Lifetaker rig. Their appearance would leave all the principals completely confused. His Widowmaker was supposed to be dead. Lady's Lifetaker was supposed to be in Taglios. Neither was supposed to amount to anything in sorcerous terms. The besieged would be stunned. Spinner's men would be dismayed. Longshadow might suspect the truth but would not be sure. Smoke and the Taglian prince and his sister would be baffled. Even Lady would be confused.

He was sure she believed him dead.

"Damn you," he said as he settled her helmet over her head. "Damn you to hell." He could not refuse to cooperate. Dejagore would fall and its defenders would be massacred if he and she did not intercede.

"Relax, my love. Relax. Put emotion aside. Have fun with it. Look. The lance." She pointed.

It was the lance that had carried the Company standard for centuries. He had searched in vain for it at the temple. He had not seen it coming down. Now it stood beyond the fire they had lighted for illumination. It glowed gently. A banner hung from it but he could not make it out.

"How did you . . . ?" To hell with her. Sorcery. He would play her game only as far as he had to. He would give her no pleasure.

"Get it, Croaker. Mount up. It's time." She'd even conjured the armor that went with the stallions, baroque and beginning to show highlights of witchfire.

He did as he was told. And was startled. Her armor had a subtly different look from that which Lady had created for her Lifetaker character. This was more intimidating. It radiated menace. It had the feel of an archetypal doom.

Two huge black crows settled on his shoulders. Their eyes burned red. More crows circled Catcher. Frogface materialized on the neck of her horse, chattered briefly, vanished. "Come. We should arrive just in time to save the day." The voice she used was that of a happy kid contemplating a prank.

Chapter Thirty-Four

Mather stuck his head into the room. "He's on his way, Willow."

Swan grunted, opened shutters for more light. He looked out at Blade's camp and its satellites. The gods themselves were on Blade's team. Recruits had been arriving in droves. None of them wanted to enlist in the Radisha's guard. He'd had high hopes when he had invented that. But the Radisha's name carried less weight here than Blade's. And, damn him, he was as stubborn about sticking with Lady as Cordy was about the Radisha.

"Cordy, Cordy, why the hell don't we just go home?" he muttered to himself.

Blade came in, escorted by Mather. That human stump Sindu was right behind them. He was like Blade's shadow, anymore. Swan did not like the man. He was creepy.

Blade said, "Cordy says you have something."

"Yeah. We finally got one up on you." He had begun fielding patrols of his own after Blade started expanding southward. "Our boys grabbed some prisoners."

"I know."

Of course he did. There was no hiding from each other here. They did not try. They remained friends, however much they disagreed. Blade did most of his planning in that room, on the map table there. Anything Swan wanted to know he could see right there.

"There was a big dust-up at Dejagore the other night. Shadowspinner hit the burg with everything he had. He grabbed our friends by the short hairs. Then what should pop up but two giant fire-breathing riders in black armor flinging thunderbolts around and kicking ass wholesale. When the smoke cleared away it was the Shadowlanders that got whupped. One of the prisoners saw it with his own eyes. He said Shadowspinner had to yank everything out of his trick bag to hold those two off. Here's the way they say it went down."

Swan kept a close eye on Blade while he chattered. There was some emotion showing through that bland facade.

He finished his tale. "What you think, old buddy? Those two miracle visitors sound like anybody we know?"

"Lady and Croaker. In their costume armor."

"Bingo! But?"

"He's dead and she's in Taglios."

"Two in a row. Give the man a prize. I think. So what the hell really went down? Sindhu. What you grinning about, man?"

"Kina."

The others looked hard at the broad man. Mather said, "Descriptions again, Willow."

Swan repeated.

Mather said, "Kina. The way she's described by people who know her."

"Not her," Sindhu said. "Kina sleeps. The Daughter is bound in flesh." Sindhu's association with the Deceivers was an open secret. But he was not much help. Usually it was like this. He would say one thing, then contradict himself.

Swan said, "I'm not going to try to figure that out, buddy. Somebody fits the description went in and tore them new buttholes down there. Kina or not-Kina, I don't care. Somebody wanted people to think Kina. Right?"

Sindhu nodded.

"So who was that with her? That fit anywhere?"

Sindhu shook his head. "This confuses me."

Mather hoisted himself to a seat in the window. Swan shuddered. Cordy had a forty-foot drop behind him. He said, "Be quiet. Let me think."

Swan echoed, "Quiet. Let him." Cordy was a genius when he took the trouble.

They waited. Swan paced. Blade studied the map. He let no time waste. Sindhu remained impassive and still, yet seemed shaken.

Mather said, "There's another force in the field."

"Say what?" Swan chirped.

"Only way it adds up, Willow. The Shadowmasters are out to get each other but they wouldn't go that far. Helps us too much. Our side doesn't have anybody who could pull off the sorcery angle. So somebody else did it."

"What the hell for?"

"To confuse things?"

"They did that. Why?"

"I couldn't guess."

"Then who?"

"I don't know. Just like everyone else won't know, and will be chasing their tails trying to figure it out."

Was Blade listening? Didn't seem like it. He asked, "How bad were the Shadowlanders hurt?"

"Huh?"

"Shadowspinner's armies. How bad off are they?"

"Bad enough they can't take a crack at Dejagore again till they get replacements. But not so bad our guys have a crack at breaking out."

"Just enough interference to keep the balance, then."

"Our guys got cut up bad, way the prisoners talked. As many as half of them killed. Meaning the Shadowmasters' men really got mauled."

"But they could still send out patrols for you to catch?"

"Shadowspinner is scared we'll move on him. He doesn't want any more surprises."

Blade paced. He returned to the map, tapped out the garrisons and posts he had established as much as a hundred fifty miles south. He paced. He asked Mather, "Is it true? Or is it something they want us to believe? Bait for a trap?"

Swan said, "The prisoners believed it."

Blade said, "Sindhu, why haven't we heard from Hakim? Why did this news reach us this way?"

"I don't know."

"Find out. Go talk to your friends right now. If this is true we should have known before their patrol got here with the prisoners."

Sindhu departed, disturbed.

Swan said, "Now you got rid of him, what's on your mind?"

"Is the story true? That's what's on my mind. Sindhu has people babysitting Dejagore. They should've had a messenger moving the minute the dust-up started. Another should've brought a complete report when it was over. One might not have gotten through but two wouldn't have failed. We made that road safe. We enlisted most of the bandits and feistier peasants."

"You think the prisoners are plants?"

Blade paced. "I don't know. If they are, why on you? Mather?"

Cordy thought. "If they're a plant we shouldn't have been the captors. Unless their purpose is to cause confusion. Or they don't know the difference. It could be they're telling the truth but we're not supposed to believe it because you haven't heard from your scouts. It could be a device to buy time."

"Illusion," Swan said. "You remember what Croaker used to say? That his favorite weapon was illusion?"

"That's not quite what he said, Willow," Mather corrected. "But close enough. Somebody wants us to see something that isn't there. Or to ignore something that is."

Blade said, "I'm moving."

Swan squawked. "What do you mean, moving?"

"I'm heading down there."

"Hey! Man! What are you, crazy? You're getting a little carried away, chasing that tail."

Blade walked out.

Willow spun on Mather. "What do we do, Cordy?"

Mather shook his head. "I don't know about friend Blade anymore. He's looking to get killed. Maybe we shouldn't have taken him away from those crocs."

"Yeah. Maybe. But what do we do now?"

"Send a message north. Then go with him."

"But . . ."

"We're in charge. We can do whatever we want." Mather hustled out.

"They're both crazy," Swan muttered. He looked at the map a minute, went to the window, watched the excitement in Blade's camp, eyed the ford and the swarming engineers setting wooden pylons for Lady's temporary bridge. "Everybody's gone crazy." He laid a finger between his lips and wiggled it furiously while saying, "Why the hell should I be any different?"

Chapter Thirty-Five

"That's it," I said. "I've had it." I'd just gotten word that a Vehdna priest, Iman ul Habn Adr, had ordered Vehdna construction workers to abandon my camp and report for work on that absurd city wall. It was the second defection of the day. The Gunni contingent had walked an hour after starting time. "The Shadar won't show tomorrow. They've finally decided to test me, Narayan. Assemble the archers. Ram, send those messages I had the scribes prepare."

Narayan's eyes got big. He could not get himself moving. He did not believe I would do it. "Mistress?"

"Move."

They went.

I prowled, trying to walk off my anger. I had no reason to be mad. This was no surprise. The cults had given me no grief since I had taken care of Tal. That meant they were working things out between them before they tested me again.

I took advantage of the respite, recruiting two hundred men a day. I got the camp established in temporary form. The stonework of the fortress, meant to replace it, was well started. I'd gotten some of the men through the first stages of their training. I had cajoled or extorted weapons and animals and money and materials from the Prahbrindrah Drah. In that area I had more than I needed.

I had stretched my talent considerably. I was still no threat even to Smoke but my progress excited me.

The big negatives were the dreams and an incessant mild nausea I could not shake. It might be the water at the campsite though it persisted when I returned to the city. Probably it was mostly reaction to lack of sleep.

I refused to yield to the dreams. I refused to pay attention. I made them something to be suffered through, like boils. Someday I would have the chance to do something about them. Then balances would be redressed.

I watched my messengers trot toward town. Too late to back down now.

Succeed or fail, I would get their attention.

Ram helped me don my armor. A hundred men watched. The barracks remained as overcrowded as ever, though I had moved five thousand men to the campsite. "More volunteers than I know what to do with, Ram."

He grunted. "Lift your arm, Mistress."

I raised both. And spied Narayan pushing through the press. He looked like he had seen a ghost. "What is it?"

"The Prahbrindrah Drah is here. By himself. He wants to see you." He tried to whisper but men heard. Word spread.

"Quiet! All of you. Here? Where?"

"I told Abda to bring him around the long way."

"That was thoughtful, Narayan. Keep working, Ram."

Narayan fled before Abda brought the prince. I started in on the appropriate public courtesies. He said, "Forget that. Can you clear this out some? I'd like a little privacy."

"Fire drill. Something. You men, outside. Abda, see to it."

The crowd started moving reluctantly. The prince eyed Ram. I said, "Ram stays. I can't get dressed without him."

"Surprised to see me?"

"Yes."

"Good. It's time somebody surprised you."

I just looked at him.

He demanded, "What's all this bull about you quitting?"

"Quitting what?"

"Resigning. Going away. Leaving us to the Shadowmasters."

That had been the implication but not the substance of the messages I'd had delivered. "I don't know what you mean. I'm going to make a speech to some priests. Just to straighten them out. Where did you get the idea I was deserting?"

"That's the talk. They're all excited. They think they've beaten you. That they just stood up to you, stopped letting you walk over them, and you're going to say good-bye."

Exactly what I wanted them to think. What *they* wanted to think. "Then they're going to be disappointed."

He smiled. "I've had nothing but trouble from them all my life. I've got to see this."

"I wouldn't recommend it."

"Why not?"

I could not tell him. "Trust me. If you're there you'll regret it."

"I doubt it. They couldn't give me much more trouble than they have already. I want to see them when you disappoint them."

"You do, you'll never forget. Don't go."

"I insist."

"I warned you." Him being there would not do him

any good but it would be good for me. I told myself
I'd done my best. My conscience was clear.

Ram finished dressing me. I told him, "I need Narayan. Abda! Would you look after the prince? If
you'll excuse me?"

I got Narayan into a corner where we could whisper. I told him what had happened. He grinned that
damned grin of his till I was ready to rip it off his
face. But he jumped to another subject. "The Festival is almost upon us, Mistress. We have to make
travel plans soon."

"I know. The jamadars want to look me over. But
I have too much on my mind now. Let's get through
tonight first."

"Of course, Mistress. Of course. I didn't mean to
press."

"The hell you didn't. Is everything set?"

"Yes, Mistress. Since early this afternoon."

"Will they do it? When it comes to the moment of
decision, will they?"

"You never know what a man will do till he's faced
with a decision, Mistress. But the men are all former
slaves. Very few of them Taglian."

"Excellent. Go. We'll be leaving in a few minutes."

The square was called Aiku Rukhadi, Khadi Junc-
tion. It had been a crossroads long ago, before the
city swamped the countryside. It was Shadar then
but Vehdna now. It was not a big square, being a
hundred twenty feet in its greatest dimension. It had
a public fountain in its center, water for the neighborhood. It was crowded with priests.

The cult leaders had come and had brought all the
friends they wanted to witness the humiliation of the
female upstart. They had dressed for the occasion.
The Shadar wore white, simple shirts and pantaloons.
The Vehdna wore kaftans and glamorous turbans. The
most numerous contingent, the Gunni crowd, was sub-
divided by sect. Some wore scarlet robes, some saffron, some indigo, some aquamarine. Jahamaraj Jah's

successors wore black. I guessed the crowd at between
eight hundred and a thousand. The square was packed.

"Every priest who's anybody is here," the prince told
me. We entered the square behind a half dozen incompetent drummers. They were my only bodyguards.
Even Ram was absent. The drummers cleared a space
against a wall.

I told the prince, "That's the way I wanted it." I
hoped I looked sufficiently impressive in costume. Atop
my great black stallion I loomed over the Prahbrindrah, whose chestnut was no dwarf. The priests noticed him and started whispering. Eight hundred men
whispering make as much noise as a swarm of locusts.

I positioned us with the wall behind and the drummers in front.

Would it work?

It had, wonderfully, for my husband, so long ago.

"Soul lords of Taglios." Silence fell. I had that
spell right. My voice carried well. "Thank you for
coming. Taglios faces a severe test. The Shadowmasters are a threat that cannot be exaggerated. The
tales out of the Shadowlands are ghosts of the truth.
This city and nation has one hope: turn a single face
toward the enemy. In faction lies defeat." They listened. I was pleased.

"In faction, defeat. Some of you feel I'm not the champion for Taglios' cause. More of you have been seduced
by lust for power. By factionalism. Rather than let that
worsen and distract Taglios from its grand mission I've
decided to eliminate the cause of factionalism. Taglios
will present one face after tonight."

I donned my helmet while they were waiting for me
to announce my abdication. I set the witchfires free.

They began to suspect then. Someone shouted,
"Kina!"

I drew my sword.

The arrows began to fall.

While I was talking Narayan's picked men had
placed barricades in the narrow streets entering the

square. When I drew my sword, soldiers inside the surrounding houses let fly. Priests screamed. They tried to flee. They found the barricades too high. They tried to turn on me. My talent was enough to hold them off, beyond my terrified drummers. The arrows continued to fall.

They surged this way and that. They fell. They begged for mercy.

The arrowfall continued till I lowered my sword.

I dismounted. The Prahbrindrah Drah looked down, face bloodless. He tried to say something, could not speak. "I warned you."

Narayan and his friends joined me. I asked, "Did you send for the wagons?" It would take dozens to haul the bodies to an unhallowed mass grave.

He nodded, no more able to speak than the prince. I told him, "This is nothing, Narayan. I've done lots worse. I'll do worse again. Check them out. See if anybody important is missing." I walked across the killing ground to tell the bowmen they could release the people who lived in the houses.

The Prahbrindrah never moved. He just sat there and stared, painfully aware that his presence made it seem he approved.

Ram found me there. "Mistress," he gasped. He had run all the way from the barracks.

"What are you doing here?"

"There is a messenger from Ghoja. From Blade. He rode night and day. Come immediately." He was not affected by the mass of bodies. He might have been watching the neighborhood women at the well instead of Narayan's cronies finishing the wounded.

I went. I spoke with the messenger. For a minute I was furious with Blade. Then I saw the silver lining.

Blade's actions gave me an excuse to move the troops out before they got wind of what had happened here tonight.

Chapter Thirty-Six

The Prahbrindrah Drah sat there an hour, staring at his bedchamber wall. He would not respond to his sister's questions. She was shaken. What had happened?

He looked at her at last.

"Did she go through with it? Did you hope she wouldn't? I told you not to go."

"She didn't resign. No. She didn't." He laughed squeakily. "Not by a long shot." His tone was spooky.

"What happened?"

"She resolved our problems with the priests. Not permanently, but it'll be a long time before . . ." His voice trailed off. "I'm as guilty as she is . . ."

"What happened, dammit! Tell me!"

"She killed them. Every last one of them. She lured them there by making them think they were going to humiliate her. She had archers cut them down. A thousand priests. And I was there. I watched her walk among them afterward, cutting the throats of the wounded."

For a moment the Radisha thought it was some grisly joke. *That* was impossible.

He said, "She made her point. Did she ever make her point. Smoke was right."

The Radisha began pacing, lending only half an ear to his self-flagellation. It was grotesque. It was an atrocity surpassing comprehension. Things like that did not happen in Taglios. They couldn't.

But what an opportunity! The religious hierarchies would be in disarray for years. Atrocity or not, this was a chance to achieve all they had worked for. It could mean the return of the primacy of the state.

He heard a sound. She whirled, startled, gawked.

The woman was there, having penetrated the palace who knew how. She still wore her bizarre armor, covered with blood. "He's told you."

"Yes."

"The Shadowmasters attacked Dejagore. They were repelled with heavy losses. Blade is moving south to relieve the city before they gather reinforcements. I'm going to join him. I have no one to leave here to continue my work. You two will have to handle it. Send the construction crews back to the fortress. Continue enrolling volunteers. There's a slim chance we may get past the worst in the coming few weeks, leaving no one but Longshadow to deal with. But it's more likely we'll face a prolonged struggle that will require every man and resource available."

The Radisha could not speak. The woman had the blood of a thousand priests on her hands. How could you argue with someone like that?

"I've handed you an opportunity you always wanted. Grab it."

The Radisha willed herself to speak. Still nothing came out. Never had she been so terrified.

The woman said, "I have no ambitions here. You have no need to fear me—so long as you don't interfere with me. I *will* destroy the Shadowmasters. I *will* fulfill the Company's undertaking. And I *will* collect its reward."

The Radisha nodded as though a hand had grabbed her hair and forced her to move her head.

The woman said, "I'll come back after I've seen what's happening at Dejagore." She moved to the Prahbrindrah, rested a hand on his shoulder. "Don't take it on yourself. They wrote their own destinies. You're a prince. A prince must be stern. Be stern now. Don't let chaos claim Taglios. I'll leave you a small garrison. Their reputation should be enough to enforce your will."

She strode out.

The Radisha and her brother stared at one another. "What have we done?" he asked.

"Too late to cry about it. Let's do what we can with it."

"Where's Smoke?"

"I don't know. I haven't seen him for days."

"Was he right? Is she really the Daughter of Night?"

"I don't know. I just don't know. But we're on the tiger's back now. We can't let go."

Chapter Thirty-Seven

I moved out before dawn. I took every man I could round up—except those who had helped despatch the priests. Those I left as a garrison, with orders to remain in the city a week, then to move to the remote Vehdna-Bota ford across the Main. I did not want them talking to the other men, who did not yet know about the massacre.

There were six thousand men in the force. They were scarcely more than an armed rabble. They were enthusiastic, though. They wanted to relieve Deja-gore.

I tried to teach them on the march.

Narayan did not like the move. He brooded. He came to me late the third day of the march. We were twenty miles from Ghoja. "Mistress?"

"You've finally decided to talk about it?"

He pretended not to be surprised. He tried to accept everything about me. On the surface. Did he regret his snap decision that I was his Strangler messiah? I am sure he wanted more control. He did not want his Daughter of Night to be independent of his own ambitions and wishful thinking.

"Yes, Mistress. Tomorrow is Etsataya, first day of the Festival. We're only a few miles from the Holy Grove. It is *important* that you present yourself to the jamadars."

I guided him out of the human stream. "I haven't been trying to duck it. I've been preoccupied. You said the first day. I thought this was a one-day holy festival."

"It's three days, Mistress. The middle day is the actual high holy day."

"I can't afford a three-day delay, Narayan."

"I know, Mistress." Funny how the honorifics showed up so much more often when he wanted something. "But we do have men capable of keeping the mob moving. All they have to do is follow the road. With your horses we can overtake them quickly."

I masked my feelings. This was something I had to do but not something I wanted to do. Narayan's cult had not been much use yet.

But Narayan himself was a valuable aide. I had to keep him happy. "All right. Get this mob pointed in the right direction and going on its own momentum. I'll want Ram and my gear."

"Yes, Mistress."

We left the column half an hour later.

It was dark when we reached the Stranglers' holy grove. I did not see much of it but I felt it. Seldom had I encountered a place with a darker aura. Some of Narayan's brotherhood were there already. We joined them. They watched me sidelong, afraid to look at me directly.

There was nothing to do. I went to sleep early.

The dreams were worse than ever before, unrelenting, continuous. I did not escape till the sun rose, probed through the mist and dark trees. Ten thousand crows bickered and squawked overhead. Na-

rayan and his cronies thought that a hugely
favorable omen. The crow was Kina's favorite bird,
her messenger and spy.

Was there a connection with the crows that had
followed the Company so long? According to Croaker
they had picked us up before we had crossed the Sea
of Torments. The Sea lies seven thousand miles north
of the grove.

As soon as I wakened I was sick. I vomited as I
tried to sit up. Men bustled around, solicitous, unable to do anything helpful. Narayan looked scared
to death. He had a lot invested in me. He would be
a nothing if he lost me now. "Mistress! Mistress!
What's the matter?"

"I'm puking my guts up!" I snarled. "Get me something."

There was nothing anyone could do.

The worst passed. After that it was just nausea
that worsened drastically if I moved suddenly. I
passed on breakfast. After an hour I was able to get
up and around without too much discomfort—if I
took it slowly.

Being sick was new to me. I had not been, ever
before. I did not like it.

There were a hundred men in the grove already,
maybe more. They all came for a glimpse at their
ragged messiah. I don't think they were impressed.
I would not have been, in their shoes. Nobody could
measure up to an anticipation of millennia. Ragged
as I was I had to be a double dose of disappointment.

Narayan did a fair job of arguing his case. They
did not cut my throat.

They were a mixed bag, all religions, all castes,
and as many of them foreigners as Taglians, all sinister in that grove. It reeked of darkness and old
blood.

Nobody seemed festive. They seemed to be waiting
for something to happen. I isolated Narayan and
asked.

"Nothing much happens before nightfall," he said.

"Most of the men will arrive today. Those who are here already will make preparation. There will be a ceremony tonight, to open the festival and let Kina know that tomorrow is her day. The ceremonies tomorrow are meant to invoke her. Candidates will be presented to her, to accept or reject. After the ceremonies the feast will begin. All during Festival the priests will judge petitions presented. There aren't many this year. An old dispute between the Ineld and Twana bands is up for judgment, though. That will attract a lot of attention."

I frowned.

"Bands sometimes come into conflict. The Ineld band is of Vehdna stock, the Twana of Shadar. Each accuses the other of heresy and poaching. It's an old dispute that grew much worse after the Shadowmasters invaded. In parts of their territories the bands are the only law, which makes for bigger stakes."

It was a long story, not pretty, too human, serving to illustrate that the Deceivers were more than a lot of deadly fanatics. In some areas they ruled the underworld. The bands in question hailed from populous Hatchpur State, where the Deceivers were relatively strong. Their true feud was a contest of criminal gangs over territories.

"Anyway," Narayan said, "Iluk of the Ineld band stunned everyone by insisting the conflict be handed to the justice of Kina."

The way he said it was ominous. Kina's must be a very final justice. "That's unusual?"

"Everyone thinks it's a bluff. Iluk expects Kowran, jamadar of the Twana band, to refuse. That would leave the judgment to the priests, who would take his refusal into account."

"And if he doesn't back down?"

"There's no appeal from the judgment of Kina."

"I thought so."

"Are you feeling better?"

"Some. I'm still nauseous but I've got it under control."

"Can you eat? You should."

"A little rice, maybe. Nothing heavily spiced." They liked their spices in Taglios. Cooking odors could be overwhelming in the city.

He handed me over to Ram. Ram hovered. I kept my composure. Well I did. While I nibbled, letting each bite settle, Narayan brought a parade of priests and jamadars for formal introduction. I memorized names and faces carefully. I noted that few of the jamadars boasted the black rumel. I met only four men who did. I mentioned that to Ram.

"Very few are honored, Mistress. And jamadar Narayan is foremost among those. He's a living legend. No other man would have dared bring you here."

Was he warning me? Maybe I had best watch myself. There could be politics here, too. Some band captains might resist me simply because I was associated with Narayan.

Narayan. The living legend.

How had our paths come to cross? I'm no believer in fate or gods, in the accepted senses, but there are powers that move the world. That I know well. Once I was one.

The sender of my dreams arranged it, no doubt. She, or it, had been interested in me long before I became aware of that interest.

Could it have been she who had struck Croaker down? To rid me of an inconvenient emotional entanglement?

Maybe. Maybe when the Shadowmasters fell I might turn to another target.

The anger rose in me. I controlled it and rode it, let Ram finish feeding me, went exploring the grove. I went to its heart and examined the temple for the first time.

It barely passed muster. It was so buried in creepers it was barely recognizable. Nobody challenged my presence outside. I did not press my luck by climbing the steps. Instead, I rambled around.

I found a man willing to get Narayan for me. I did not want to enter the holy place uninvited. He came out looking irritated. "Take a walk with me. I have a few questions. First, will anyone get upset if I go inside?"

He thought. "I don't think so."

"Anybody saying I can't be what you claim? Do you have the kind of enemies who will oppose you on everything?"

"No. But there *are* doubts."

"I'm sure. I don't look the part."

He shrugged.

I'd led him to the area where I wanted him. I suggested, "You'd need a fair hand at woodcraft to survive your summer travels, wouldn't you?"

"Yes."

"Look around."

He did. He came back perplexed. "Someone kept horses here."

"Anyone else come on horseback?"

"A few. High-caste Deceivers from afar. Yesterday and today."

"That's not fresh. Is there a regular guard?"

"No one comes here but us. No one dares."

"Somebody did. And it looks like they stayed awhile. That's a lot of manure for a casual visit."

"I have to tell the others. This will mean purification rites if the temple was profaned." As we ascended the steps to the temple, he said, "You noticing will be a point in your favor. No one else did."

"You don't see what you don't expect to see."

The temple was poorly lighted inside. Just as well. It was ugly in there. The architects had dreamed some of my dreams, then had re-created them in stone. Narayan collected several jamadars, told them what I had found. They fussed and cussed and grumbled, spread out to see if the infidels had defiled their temple.

I wandered.

They found where the invaders had done their cooking. The place had been cleaned but smoke stains are hard to erase. The stains suggested that someone had camped there for a long time.

Narayan sidled up, gave me his grin. "Now would be a good time to impress them, Mistress."

"Like how?"

"By using your talent to find out something about whoever was here."

"Sure. Just like that. I've maybe got enough skill to find their latrine and garbage pit."

He eyed me, wondering how I could know they had had one, then reasoned it out. There was no garbage or human waste around. "That could tell us a lot."

One of the jamadars told us that now they were looking they had found plenty of evidence of an extended occupation. "One man and one woman. The woman slept near the fire. The man stayed near the altar. They don't appear to have bothered that. Mistress? Would you look?"

"An honor." I did not immediately understand how they knew a woman had slept near the fire. Then one produced a few strands of long black hair. "Can you tell anything from this, Mistress?"

"Yes. She didn't have naturally curly hair. If it was a she." Some Gunni men let their hair grow long. Shadar and Vehdna tended toward curls. Vehdna men wore their hair short. But everyone at this end of the earth had black hair, or very dark brown when it was clean.

Swan was a real curiosity with his golden locks.

My sarcasm did not escape my companions. I said, "Don't expect me to see the past or future. Yet. Kina comes to me only in dreams."

That even startled Narayan.

"Let's see the other place."

They showed me where the man had slept. Again, they had determined sex by length of hair. They had found one strand three inches long, fine, a medium brown. "Hang onto those hairs, Narayan. They could be useful someday."

Deceivers scurried around seeking more signs. Narayan suggested, "Let's find that pit."

We went out. We wandered. I located the place. Some lowlife candidates to the cult got to open it. I wandered while I waited.

"Mistress. I just found this." A jamadar offered me a small animal figure someone had made by bending and braiding and twisting strands of grass, the kind of time-killing thing people do when they have nothing to do. But the man looked disturbed.

"It's just something somebody did for the hell of it. It has no power. But if there are more around I'd like to see them. They might tell us something about whoever made them."

Less than a minute passed before another turned up. "It was hanging from a twig, Mistress. I guess it's supposed to be a monkey."

I had a brainstorm. "Don't move anything. I want to see them right where they are."

Over the next few hours we found scores of those things, some made of grass, some twisted from strips of bark. Someone had had a lot of time and nothing to do. I knew a man once who did that with paper and never realized he was doing it.

Most of those things were stick figures, monkeys hanging from twigs, four-legged beasts that could have been anything. But a few of the four-leggers carried riders. The riders always carried twig swords or spears.

I must have made a noise. Narayan said, "Mistress?"

I whispered, "There's something important about those things. But I'll be damned if I understand what."

Someone found a whole mob of figures where someone had sat on a rock leaning against a tree making them and maybe daydreaming. It was a little clearing about ten feet across. A stump stood in the middle.

I knew I was onto something the instant I arrived. But what? Whatever, it stayed way down below consciousness. I told Narayan, "If there's anything to be learned, it's here." I whispered again. "Get everybody back to what they're supposed to be doing." I perched on the rock. I pulled some grass and started twisting a figure. The men went away. I let my mind drift into the twilight state. Wonder of wonders, dreams did not intrude.

Minutes passed. More and more crows dropped into the trees. My interest must have been too obvious.

Were they watching to see if I found out something? Like maybe something about those who had been staying here? Ah! The birds had more to do with them than with the Deceivers. They were not omens—in the sense the Stranglers hoped. They were messengers and spies.

Crows. Everywhere and always, crows, seldom behaving the way crows should. Tools. Their sudden interest suggested they feared I would learn something I ought not. Which meant there *was* something.

My mind leaped from stone to stone across a brook of ignorance. If I did discover something I had best not be obvious.

Realization.

The clearing felt familiar because it recalled a place I had lived. If that stump represented the Tower, whence I had ruled my empire, then the scatter of stones might represent the badlands I had created so the Tower could be approached along just one narrow, deadly path.

Patterns emerged. They were almost imperceptible, as though put there by someone who knew he was watched. Someone surrounded by crows? If I let my imagination loose, that scatter of rocks, debris, and twisted figures did make a fair representation of the Tower's surroundings. In fact, a couple of sticks and a scatter and a boot scuff and a little soil pushed into a mound described a situation that had existed only once in the history of the Tower.

I had trouble pretending calm and indolence.

If the rocks and twigs and such were significant,

so must be the creatures of grass and bark. I stood up for a better view.

One thing jumped right out.

A leaf lay at the foot of the stump. A tiny figure sat upon it. A lot of care had gone into creating that figure. More than enough to make the message clear.

The Howler, my then master of the flying carpet, was supposed to have been killed by a fall from the heights of the Tower. I had known that was not true for some time now. The message had to be that the Howler was somehow involved in current events.

Whoever set this up knew me and expected me to visit the grove. That should mean that someone knew what I was doing. That someone must have access to what the crows reported but was not their master. Else there was no reason for such an elaborate and iffy means of passing a message.

There was more.

Many great sorcerers had been involved in the battle where the Howler was supposed to have died. Most of them were supposed to have been killed. Since then I have discovered that several had fled after faking their deaths. I checked the figures again. Some were identifiable as representing some of those sorcerers. Three had been crushed underfoot. Those known to have been destroyed?

I gave it all the time it needed and still nearly missed the critical message. It was almost dark when I spied the clever little figure carrying what appeared to be a head under its arm. It took a while after that to understand the significance of the figure.

I had told Narayan that we do not see what we do not expect to see.

A lot of things fell into place once I realized that the impossible was not impossible at all. My sister was alive. I saw a whole new picture of what was going on. And I was frightened.

And, frightened, I missed the most important message of all.

Chapter Thirty-Eight

Narayan was not in a pleasant mood. "The whole temple has to be purified. Everything has been defiled. At least they committed no willful sacrilege, no desecration. The idol and relics remain undisturbed."

I had no idea what he was talking about. All the men had long faces. I looked at Narayan over our cookfire. He took my look for a question.

"Any unbeliever who found the holy relics or the idol would have plundered them."

"Maybe they were afraid of the curse."

His eyes got big. He glanced around, made a gesture urging silence. He whispered, "How did you know that?"

"These things always have curses. Part of their rustic charm." Pardon my sarcasm. I did not feel good. I did not want to spend any more time hanging around the grove. It was not a pleasant place. A lot of people had died there, none of them of old age. The earth was rich with their blood and bones and screams. It had a smell, psychic and physical, probably pleasing to Kina.

"How much longer, Narayan? I'm trying to cooperate. But I'm not going to hang around here the rest of my life."

"Oh. Mistress. There will be no Festival now. The purification will take weeks. The priests are distraught. The ceremonies have been moved to Nadam. It's only a minor holiday usually, when the bands break up for the off season, and the priests remind them to invoke the Daughter of Night in their prayers. The priests always say the reason she hasn't come yet is we haven't prayed hard enough."

Was he going to dole it out in driblets forever? I guess no one of any religion would have spent much time explaining holidays and saints and such, though. "Why are we still here, then? Why aren't we headed south?"

"We came for more than the Festival."

We had indeed. But how was I supposed to convince these men I was their messiah? Narayan kept the specifications to himself. How could the actress act without being told her role?

There was the trouble. Narayan *believed* I was the Daughter of Night. He wanted me to be. Which meant that he would not coach me if I asked. He expected me to know instinctively.

And I did not have a clue.

The jamadars seemed disappointed and Narayan nervous. I was not living up to expectations and hopes, even if I *had* discovered that their temple had been profaned.

In a whisper, I asked, "Am I expected to do holy deeds in a place no longer holy?"

"I don't know, Mistress. We have no guideposts. It's all in the hands of Kina. She will send an omen."

Omens. Wonderful. I had had no chance to bone up on omens the cult considered significant. Crows were important, of course. Those men thought it wonderful that Taglian territory was infested by carrion birds. They thought that presaged the Year of the Skulls. But what else was significant?

"Are comets important to you?" I asked. "In the north, last year, and once earlier, there were great comets. Did you see them down here?"

"No. Comets are bad omens."

"They were for me."

"They have been called Sword of Sheda, or Tongue of Sheda, Sheda-linca, that shed the light of Sheda upon the world."

Sheda was an archaic form of the name of the chief Gunni god, one of whose titles was Lord of Lords of Light. I suspected the Deceiver cult's beliefs had taken a left turn off the trunk of Gunni beliefs a few thousand years ago.

He said, "The priests say Kina is weakest when a comet is in the sky, for then light rules heaven day and night."

"But the moon . . ."

"The moon is the light of darkness. The moon belongs to Shadow, put up so Shadow's creatures may hunt."

He rambled off into incomprehensibility. Local religion had its light and dark, right and left, good and evil. But Kina, despite her trappings of darkness, was supposed to be outside and beyond that eternal struggle, enemy of both Light and Shadow, ally of each in some circumstances. Just to confuse me, maybe, nobody seemed to know how things really lay in the eyes of their gods. Vehdna, Shadar, and Gunni all respected one another's gods. Within the majority Gunni cult the various deities, whether identified with Light or Shadow, got equal deference. They all had their temples and cults and priests. Some, like Jahamaraj Jah's Shadar Khadi cult, were tainted by the doctrines of Kina.

As Narayan clarified by making the waters murkier he got shifty-eyed, then would not look at me at all. He fixed his gaze on the cookfire, talked, grew morose. He was good at hiding it. No one else no-

ticed. But I had had more practice reading people. I
noted tension in some of the jamadars, too.

Something was about to happen. A test? With this
crowd that was not likely to be gentle.

My fingers drifted to the yellow triangle at my belt.
I had not practiced much lately. There had been lit-
tle time. I realized what I had done, wondered why.
That was hardly the weapon to get me out of trouble.

There *was* danger. I felt it now. The jamadars were
nervous and excited. I let my psychic sense sharpen
despite the aura of the grove. It was like taking a
deep breath in a hot room where a corpse had been
rotting for a week. I persevered. If I could take the
dreams without bending I could take this.

I asked Narayan a question that sent him off on
another ramble. I concentrated on form and pattern
in my psychic surroundings.

I spotted it.

I was ready when it happened.

He was a black rumel man, a jamadar with a reputation nearly rivalling Narayan's, Moma Sharra-el,
Vehdna. When we'd been introduced I'd had the feeling he was a man who killed for himself, not for his
goddess. His rumel moved like black lightning.

I grabbed the weighted end on the fly. I took it
away before he recovered his balance, snapped it
around his neck. It seemed I'd played this game always, or as though another hand guided my own. I
did cheat a little, using a silent spell to strike at his
heart. I wasted no mercy. I sensed that that would
be an error as deadly as not reacting at all.

I would have had no chance had I not sensed the
wrongness gathering around me.

No one cried out. No one said a word. They were
shaken, even Narayan. Nobody looked at me. For no
reason apparent at the moment, I said, "Mother is
not pleased."

That got me a few startled looks. I folded Moma's
rumel as Narayan had taught me, discarded my yel-

low cloth and took the black. No one argued with my self-promotion.

How to reach these men without hearts? They were impressed now, but not indelibly, not permanently. "Ram."

Ram came out of the darkness. He did not speak for fear of betraying his feelings. I think he might have stepped in if Moma's attack had succeeded, though that would have been the end of him. I gave him instructions.

He got a rope and looped one end around the dead man's left ankle, tossed the rope over a branch, hauled the corpse up so it hung head down over the fire. "Excellent, Ram. Excellent. Everyone gather round."

They came reluctantly as the summons spread. Once they were all there I cut Moma's jugular.

The blood did not come fast but it came. A small spell made each drop flash when it reached the fire. I seized Narayan's right arm, forced him to put his hand out and let a few drops fall on his palm. Then I turned him loose. "All of you," I said.

Kina's followers do not like spilled blood. There is a complex and irrational explanation having to do with the legend of the devoured demons. Narayan told me later. It has a bearing only because it made the evening more memorable for those men once they had the blood of their fellow on their hands.

They did not look at me while they endured my little ceremony. I used the opportunity to hazard a spell that, to my surprise, came off without a hitch. It turned the stains on their hands as indelible as tattoos. Unless I took it back they would go through life with one hand marked scarlet.

The jamadars and priests were mine, like it or not. They were branded. The world would not forgive them that brand if its meaning became known. Men with red palms would not be able to deny that they had been present at the debut of the Daughter of Night.

Nowhere did I see any doubts, now, that I was what Narayan claimed.

The dreams were powerful that night but not grim. I floated in the warmth of the approval of that other who wanted to make me her creature.

Ram wakened me before there was light enough to see. He and Narayan and I rode out before the sun rose. Narayan did not speak all day. He remained in shock.

His dreams were coming true. He did not know if that was what he wanted anymore. He was scared.

So was I.

Chapter Thirty-Nine

Longshadow had fallen into a permanent rage. The wizard Smoke, a trivial little nothing, was stubborn. He was determined not to be enslaved. He might die first.

A howl echoed through Overlook. The Shadowmaster glanced up, imagined mockery in the cry. That bastard Howler. He had pulled a fast one somehow. No one else could have freed Shadowspinner. Treachery. Always treachery. He would pay. How he would pay. His agony would go on for years.

Later. There was damage to be undone. There was that damnable little wizard to be broken.

What *had* happened at Stormgard?

The obvious assumption was that the Lifetaker character had been *her*. Dorotea Senjak had been in Taglios. Of that there was no doubt. But *she* did not have the powers to battle Shadowspinner to a draw while ensuring the defeat of his armies.

Who had that been with her, bearing the Lance? The real power?

A flicker of fear. He dropped his work, climbed to his crystal chamber, looked out on the plain of glittering stone. Forces were moving. Not even he could grasp them all. Maybe that had not been *her.* Maybe she was gone. The tamed shadows had seen no sign of her for some time. Maybe she had gone north again after taking her revenge. She'd always wanted to rule her sister's empire.

Was there an unknown player in the game? Were Lifetaker and Widowmaker more than phantoms conjured by Senjak? The shadows thought some power was guiding her. Suppose Lifetaker and Widowmaker were real beings? Suppose they had put the notion into her head to create imitations so everyone would believe them unreal, actors, till it was too late?

Grim presentiments. Grim questions. And no answers.

Sunlight danced among the pillars on the plain. The Howler wailed. The wizard's groans echoed through the fortress.

It was closing in.

He had to capture Senjak. She was the keystone. Her head held the keys to power. She knew the Names. She knew the Truths. She contained secrets that could be hammered into weapons capable of stemming even that dark tide waiting to break out of the plain.

But first, the wizard. Before all else, Smoke. Smoke would give him Taglios and maybe Senjak.

He returned to the room where the little man battled his terror and pain. "There will be an end to this foolish resistance. Now. I have lost patience. Now I will find what you fear and feed you to it."

Chapter Forty

Blade's army moved in twenty-mile stages. He scouted heavily, used his cavalry exhaustively. Sindhu's men, who had hurried ahead to discover what had become of the Deceivers watching Dejagore, reported finding no sign of those men.

Blade took the news to Mather. "What do you think?"

Mather shook his head. "Probably killed or captured."

Swan and Mather had their own scouts out, farther south. Swan said, "Word we have is the Shadowlanders really did get whipped bad. Our guys got past their pickets and checked their camp. There's only two-thirds as many of them as there should be. Half of those are dinged up. That character Mogaba keeps hitting them with sorties, too. They never get to relax."

"Are they watching us? Do they know we're coming?"

Mather said, "You have to assume they do. Shadowspinner is a sorcerer. They don't call him a Shadowmaster for nothing. And there's the bats. Croaker thought they controlled the bats. There have been plenty of those around lately."

"Then we should be very careful. How many effectives can they field if they decide to meet us?"

"Listen to this guy, Cordy," Swan said. "He's starting to sound like a pro. Effectives. My, oh my. She's going to turn him into a real ass-kicking warlord."

Blade chuckled.

"Too many of them if you ask me," Swan continued. "If they sneak them away without Mogaba noticing they probably could put eight or ten thousand veterans in our way."

"With the Shadowmaster?"

Mather said, "I doubt he would leave. That would be an invitation to disaster."

"Then the thing to do is advance cautiously, scout thoroughly, try to know as much about them as they know about us. Right?"

Mather chuckled. "That's what the book would say. We have one factor in our favor. Their scouts don't move during daylight. And the days are long now."

Blade grunted thoughtfully.

Blade halted thirty miles north of Dejagore. Scouts brought word that Shadowspinner had moved troops into the hills ahead, at night, when the city's defenders could not see them go. The men who had stayed behind were making a show of preparing another assault.

"Where are they?" Blade asked. The scouts could not tell him. Somewhere along the road as it snaked through the hills. Waiting. Only four thousand, apparently, but that was enough against this mob.

"You going to mess with them?" Swan asked. "Or just hang around and keep some of them off Mogaba?"

"That would make sense," Mather suggested. "Keep some tied up while Mogaba does the fighting. If we could get a message to him . . ."

"I've tried," Blade said. "There's no way. They have the city sealed up. Sitting down there in the middle of that bowl like that . . ."

"Well?" Swan asked. "What do we do?"

Blade assembled his cavalry officers. He sent them to find the enemy. When they encountered no immediate resistance he moved his army ten miles southward and camped. Next morning, as soon as the bats went away, he formed line of battle but did nothing else. His scouts worked the hills carefully. He repeated that the next day and the day following. Late that afternoon a rider came in from the north. His news put a smile on Blade's face. He did not tell Swan or Mather immediately.

The fourth morning his battle line advanced. He entered the hills slowly, made sure his formations stayed integrated. There was no hurry. The cavalry stayed out front.

Contact came shortly before noon. Blade did not push. He let his men skirmish but avoided a general engagement. His cavalry harassed the enemy with missiles. The Shadowlanders were not inclined to attack them.

The sun dropped westward. Blade let the skirmishes grow.

The enemy commander gave the order to attack.

Blade's own officers had orders to stage a fighting withdrawal as soon as the enemy came out to play. They were to stop retreating only if the enemy stopped coming. If he did that they were to start harassing him again.

That game went on till the Shadowlanders lost all patience.

Chapter Forty-One

I halted the column, gathered Narayan and Ram and those men who passed for officers. "This is the place. On the back of the swale. We put me and the standard on the road, spread the men out to either side."

Narayan and the others looked puzzled. Nobody knew what was going on. It seemed wise to keep it that way till it was too late for anybody to worry.

I set it up, practically having to show each squad leader where I wanted him. Narayan finally figured it out. "It won't work," he decided. He had been on a negative kick since the grove. He did not believe anything was going to go right ever again.

"Why not? I doubt they know we're here. I was able to confuse their bats and shadows."

I hoped.

Once I had everybody in place I got into my armor, got Ram fixed up, led him and Narayan to where we could see what lay beyond the crest.

I saw what I expected to see, a lot of dust headed

my way. "They're coming. Narayan, go tell the men that in less than an hour they'll get their chance to drink Shadowlander blood. Tell them as soon as Blade's men slip through the aisles in the formation they're to plug those up."

The dust came closer fast. I watched Narayan off to spring the surprise. I watched the nervousness spread among the men. I was especially interested in the small troops of horsemen on the wings. If they followed Jah's old example I was in for another disaster.

Blade's men were almost upon me. I took my position, set witchfires burning on my armor. Ram came up beside me, impressive in the Widowmaker armor I'd had made for him. I put fires upon him but could do nothing about giving him the crows that always attached themselves to Croaker's shoulders when he turned into Widowmaker. I doubted the Shadowlanders would notice.

Blade's men poured over the crest. There was a lot of confusion till they realized we were on their side. Willow Swan galloped up, hair flying, laughing like the demented. "Right on time, sweetheart. Right on time."

"Go get your men under control. Cavalry to the wings. Move it!"

He went.

There were Shadowlanders among the men coming now. Chaos held court. They tried to stop but their comrades behind forced them forward. They tried hard to stay away from Ram and me.

Where was Blade? Where was his cavalry?

The Shadowlanders pelted my line in no order, like hail, then turned to flee. Once they had their backs to us the outcome was not in doubt. I signalled for the cavalry to advance. I made no effort to keep my men in formation. I let them chase the enemy.

When I crested the rise I saw Blade and his cavalry. He had had them flee to the flanks, distancing the footbound Shadowlanders, then had brought them back behind our enemies, scattered so they could cut down fugitives. My own cavalry had the Shadowlanders cut off on the flanks.

Only a few got away.

It was over before darkness fell.

Chapter Forty-Two

Swan could not get over it. "Our man Blade's done turned into a real live general. You had it figured all the way, didn't you?"

Blade nodded.

I believed him. He might actually make a commander—unless he'd had a once in a lifetime stroke of genius.

Swan chuckled. "Old Spinner ought to have the word by now. Bet he's foaming at the mouth."

"Very likely," I said. "And he might take steps. I want a strong guard posted. The night still belongs to the Shadowmasters."

"What can he do, hey?" Swan demanded.

"I don't know. I'd rather not find out the hard way."

Blade said, "Calm down, Swan. We didn't win the war."

You would have thought so from the celebrating. I told Blade, "Tell me more about this other Widowmaker and Lifetaker."

"You know as much as I do. Shadowspinner attacked and should have taken the city. But they rode out of the hills. Lifetaker kept him fighting for his life. Widowmaker rode around killing his men. They couldn't touch him. They rode away after our men drove the attackers out of the city. Mogaba tried a sortie. They didn't help. He took heavy casualties."

I checked a crow in a nearby bush, careful not to be obvious. "I see. We can't do anything about it. Let's ignore it and get on with plans for tomorrow."

"Is that wise, Mistress?" Narayan asked. "The night *does* belong to the Shadowmasters." Meaning there were shadows among us, listening, and bats whisking overhead.

"There are tools available." I could take care of the bats—and the crows—but I could not get rid of the shadows. To do anything more than confuse them was beyond my limited powers. "But does it matter? He knows we're here. He knows we'll come there. He just has to sit and wait. Or run away, if that suits him."

I had no hope Shadowspinner would elect that option. He retained the preponderance of force—if not in numbers, certainly in power. The stunt I had pulled was the limit. I would not send these men into a maelstrom of sorcery.

The victory would increase their confidence but could lead to trouble if I overvalued it. That was partly why Croaker lost his last battle. He got lucky several times and began to count on it. Luck has its way of running out.

"You have a point, Narayan. No need to ask for trouble. We'll talk about it tomorrow. Pass the word. We'll make an early start. Rest. We may have to do it again." The men had to be reminded: there were battles yet to come.

The others went, leaving Ram, Blade, and me. I looked at Blade. "Well done, Blade. Very well done."

He nodded. He knew that.

"How are your friends taking it?" Swan and Mather were off with their band of Radisha's Guards.

He shrugged. "Taking the long view."

"Uhm?"

"Taglios will be there after the Black Company goes. They've set down roots there."

"Understandable. Will they be trouble?"

Blade chuckled. "They don't even want to trouble Shadowspinner. If there was any way, they'd be running their tavern and staying out of everybody's way."

"But they take their pledge to the Radisha seriously?"

"As seriously as you take your contract."

"Then it behooves me to make sure there's no tension."

He grunted. "Shadows don't need ideas."

"True. Tomorrow, then."

He rose, went.

"Ram, let's take a ride."

Ram groaned. In about a hundred years, maybe, he would make a horseman.

We were both in armor still, uncomfortable as that was. I touched up the glamors. We rode among the men. Had to keep their minds fixed on me. I paused to thank men who had been pointed out as having done well. When the show was over I returned to my own place in the camp, indistinguishable from any other, and gave myself up to night's dreams.

I was sick again. Ram did his best to keep it from the men. I noticed Narayan whispering with Sindhu about it. I did not care at the moment. Sindhu glided away, presumably to tell Blade. Narayan came over. "Perhaps you ought to consult a physician."

"You have one handy?"

His grin was a shadow of itself. "No. There isn't one here."

Which meant some of the wounded would die needlessly, often as not victims of their own home remedies. Medical discipline had been something Croaker had started pounding into his men when they were learning to keep in step. And he'd been right.

I have dealt with a great many soldiers and armies. Infection and disease are deadlier enemies than foreign arms. Determined health discipline had been one of the strengths of the Company before Croaker's passing.

Pain. Damn me. It still hurt. I had never grieved over anybody before.

It was light enough to drive away bats and shadows. "Narayan. Are they fed?" Damn the sickness. "Let's get them moving."

"Where are we going?"

"Get Blade. I'll explain."

He got Blade. I explained. I rode out with the cavalry, leaving Blade to bring the rest. I headed ten miles, turned into the hills. Crows followed. I was not concerned about crows. They were not reporting to the Shadowmasters.

Ten miles into the hills I halted. I could see part of the plain. "Dismount. Rest. Keep the noise down. Cold food. Ram, come with me." I moved forward. "Quiet. There may be pickets."

We did not encounter any before I could see the whole panorama.

There had been changes. When we had come before the hills had been green with farms and orchards. Now they were spotted brown, especially to the south. The canals were not delivering water as they should.

"Ram, get those two red rumel men, Abda and whatever his name is."

He went. I studied the prospect.

Shadowspinner's camps and siegeworks surrounded the city. Near the north gate the besiegers had raised an earthen ramp to the top of the wall, no mean achievement. Dejagore squatted atop a high mound, behind walls forty feet high. The ramp had been damaged badly. Men were hauling earth up to repair it.

Presumably that had been the point of attack the night whatever had happened had happened.

The besiegers looked ragged. The condition of their camps suggested low morale. Could I take advantage? Had word of yesterday's misadventure reached the line troops? Knowing that, knowing a large force could hammer them against the anvil of the city, they ought to be ripe for a rout.

I could not place Shadowspinner. Maybe he was holed up in the remnants of the permanent camp south of the city. It had its own rampart and ditch. If not, he was careful not to stand out. Maybe Mogaba had a habit of picking on him.

Ram returned with Abda and the other man. I said, "I want to find a way to get down there unseen. Spread out, try to find one. Watch for pickets. If we can get down there we can give them a nasty surprise tonight."

They nodded and slipped away, Ram with his customary worried look. He still did not believe I could take care of myself.

Sometimes *I* wondered.

I gave them a head start, then moved westward. I had a surprise for the Shadowmasters—if my limited talent was up to it.

It took longer than I hoped but it looked workable, "it" being a bat trap that would call and kill like a candle does moths. I'd been thinking about versions since we'd left Taglios. It should work on crows, too, with adjustments.

Which left only the shadows.

We had not encountered it but rumors of old, out of the Shadowlands in the days of conquest, said those shadows could be assassins as well as spies. Captains and kings had died too opportunely, with no other explanation. Maybe the deaths of two Shadowmasters had taken that weapon away. Maybe

a killing took a combined effort. I hoped so but did
not count on it.

I set the trap working and hurried back to where
I had parted with Ram. The others were there waiting. Ram scolded me. I suffered it. I'd grown fond of
him in a sisterly way. It had been a long time since
anyone had been concerned about me. It felt good.

When Ram finished, Abda interjected, "We've
found two routes down. Neither one is ideal. The
better one might be used by the horsemen. We
cleared the pickets. I sent a few men down in case
there's a changing of the guard."

That could be a problem.

Blade materialized, dogged by Narayan and Sindhu. "You made good time," I told him.

He grunted, studied the city. I explained what I
wanted to do. "I don't expect to accomplish much.
The point is to harass Shadowspinner, demoralize
his men, and let ours inside know there's an army
out here."

Blade glanced at the westering sun, grunted again.

Swan and Mather joined us. I said, "Get some men
moving. Abda, explain the routes. Mr. Mather, take
charge of the infantry. Sindhu, you take the horsemen. Swan, Blade, Narayan, Ram, come with me. I
want to talk."

Mather and Sindhu got things moving. We got out
of their way. I asked Swan, "Swan, your men
brought home the news about the row down here.
Run through what you know."

He did. I entered questions, did not get half the
information I wanted. Not that I expected to.

Swan said, "Some third party is playing his own
game."

"Yes." There were crows nearby. I could not mention names. "The attackers definitely masqueraded
as Lifetaker and Widowmaker?"

"Absolutely."

"Then those men down there should panic if they
see them again. Get the armor, Ram."

Narayan prowled restlessly while we talked, putting in nothing, keeping one eye on the city. He said, "They're starting to move around."

"We've been discovered?"

"I don't think so. They don't act like they expect trouble."

I went and looked. After watching awhile I hazarded a guess. "The news is out. They're shook. Their officers are trying to keep them busy."

"You really going to take a whack?" Swan asked.

"A little one. Just big enough to let Mogaba know he has friends on the outside."

The day was getting on. I passed orders for the men to eat cold and keep moving. Ram showed up with our armor and animals. "Two hours of light. We ought to do something while they can see us."

Narayan said, "There's a group of four, five hundred headed out south, Mistress."

I checked. Hard to tell from so far away but they looked more like a labor battalion than armed men on the march. Curious. A similar group was forming north of the city.

Sindhu appeared. "They got the word about yesterday. They're bad rattled."

I lifted an eyebrow.

"I got close enough to hear some talk. They're making a move. Don't know what it is."

Daring, Sindhu. "You didn't hear where we could find Shadowspinner, did you?"

"No."

I sent everybody off with instructions. Ram and I donned our armor. Ram said nothing the whole time. Usually he had some small talk, thoughtless but comforting.

"You're awfully quiet."

"Thinking. All what's happened in just a couple months. Wondering."

"What?"

"If the world really is so black it's time for the Year of the Skulls."

"Oh, Ram." He was not a fast thinker but an inexorable one, now suffering a crisis of faith brought on by events in the grove but sprouting from seeds that had fallen earlier. He cared again. Kina was losing her hold.

And damn me, I let Croaker get past my defenses and turn me soft inside, too. I felt enough now that I could not just use and discard.

Maybe that soft center was there all the time. Maybe I was like an oyster. Croaker always thought so. Before we hardly knew one another he wrote about me in ways that suggested he thought there was something special inside me.

Those people down there took him. They destroyed his dreams and hamstrung mine. I did not give a damn about the Year of the Skulls or Kina. I wanted restitution.

"Ram, stop." I stepped close, placed a hand on his chest, looked him in the eye. "Don't worry. Don't tear your heart out. Believe me when I tell you I'll try to make everything work out."

He did trust me, damn him. A big damn faithful dog look came into his eyes.

Chapter Forty-Three

The Prahbrindrah Drah took Smoke's advice. He re-read the old books about the Black Company's first visit. They told a tale of death and heartbreak but reread as he might he found nothing to indict the Company returned from the north. The more he studied the more he veered from the attitude Smoke wanted him to adopt.

The Radisha joined him. "You're going to wear those things out."

"No. I don't have to read any more. Smoke is wrong."

"But . . ."

"Never mind the woman. I'd bet my life—and I am—that she has no intention of becoming the Daughter of Night. It's subtle. You have to read this stuff over and over before it sinks in, but there're signs missing that would be there no matter how hard they tried to hide them. They were exactly what they pretended."

"Oh?" the Radisha asked. "Didn't they mean to return to Khatovar?"

"Without knowing what it is. Could have been interesting seeing what would have happened if they'd made it."

"We still might find out. If anyone can pull down the Shadowmasters that woman can."

"Maybe." The prince smiled. "Peaceful as it's been, I'm tempted to ride south myself. There's no one left here to bother me."

"Don't let it go to your head."

"What?"

"People being scared of you. It won't last. Better win their respect before their fear wears off."

"Just once I'd like to go off and do something because I want to do it, not because it will strengthen the office."

That sparked an exchange halfway between argument and discussion. Smoke arrived in its midst. He stepped into the room, stopped, stared stupidly.

They stared back. The Radisha demanded, "Where the hell have you been?"

The prince silenced her with a touch. "What's happened, Smoke? You look awful."

Smoke was stunned. His thoughts oozed too slowly. This was the last thing he expected, walking right into those two. He needed time to get hold of himself.

He opened his mouth.

Longshadow flashed behind his eyes. The terror and pain closed in. He could not tell them. He could do nothing but carry out his orders. And pray.

"Where the hell have you been?" the Radisha demanded again. "Do you have any idea what's happened while you've been off fooling around?"

She was angry. Good. That would distract her some. "No."

She told him.

He was dismayed. "She murdered them? *All* of

them?" It was a chance to press his point with passion but he did not have the strength or will. He just wanted to lie down and sleep all night for the first time since . . . since . . .

"All of them that counted for anything. Right now she could do anything she pleased with Taglios. If she was here."

"She isn't?" Longshadow had not kept him posted. "Where is she?"

"By now she may be in Dejagore."

Slowly, slowly, he milked the Radisha of news. A lot had happened. Perhaps Longshadow had told him none of this because he did not know himself. Which might place the situation beyond reclamation.

Who broke up Shadowspinner's attack on Dejagore?

The prince never said a word. He just sat there looking sleepy. An awful sign. The prince was most dangerous when he seemed indifferent.

He was not going to pull it off.

He did not want to. But if he failed . . . The face of the Shadowmaster burned in his brain. Terror unmanned him. He gobbled, "We have to do something. We have to control her before she devours this whole nation. . . ." The Prahbrindrah had opened his eyes. There was no sympathy in them.

"I took your advice, Smoke. I reread those old books six times. They've convinced me."

The wizard nearly collapsed with joy.

"They've convinced me you're full of shit. This Company has nothing to do with that. I'm on her side."

Chapter Forty-Four

I scattered the spell that baffled shadows, though it was not yet dark. It would be dark before we finished.

The horsemen were in place. The Shadowlanders did not appear suspicious. They were up to whatever with those work parties. Both had vanished into the hills, taking a thousand men out of my way.

What temper possessed Shadowspinner? Not a good one, surely. Having four thousand men nipped off an undermanned siege force had to stick in his craw.

Blade had spread enough infantrymen around to cover the cavalry withdrawal. I told Ram, "It's time."

He nodded. He did not have much to say now.

I urged my stallion onto an outcrop from which we would be visible all over the plain. He followed. I hoped he would do nothing clumsy. Falling off your horse takes something away from high drama.

I drew my sword. It blossomed fire.

Trumpets sounded. The horsemen broke cover.

The Shadar element were very nearly veterans now, Blade had them in shape. I was pleased by their performance.

Chaos broke its chains down below.

It seemed the Shadowlanders would never get together. I feared I would have another unexpected victory on my hands. It was full dark before I lowered my sword and the trumpets sounded recall. The Shadowlanders did not pursue my horsemen.

Blade showed up quickly. "What now?"

"The message has been delivered. Maybe we should back off." A gangrenous glow formed inside the walled camp beside the city. "Before that gets here." I cancelled the spells illuminating Ram and myself, dismounted, led the way out of there.

I stumbled into Sindhu, who had come from Narayan with the question Blade had asked. I told him, "I want Narayan and your friends to join me. Evacuate the cavalry. The infantry should come out behind them. We'll take tomorrow off."

I needed the rest. I felt drained all the time. All I wanted to do was lie down and sleep. I had been going on will power for so long I feared I would collapse at a critical moment.

There had been no time to filter all the infantry down the slope. Once it had become apparent that was impossible I had sent the majority back to make camp. I longed to be there now. But the night was not yet done.

The valley glowed as though a cancerous green moon was rising there. The green grew brighter. "Down!" I snapped, and hit the dirt.

A ball of ugly light crashed into the eminence from which I had observed the fighting. Earth and vegetation melted. Smoke filled the air. Fires started but burned out quickly. My companions were awed.

I was pleased. Shadowspinner had missed by two hundred yards. He did not know where I was. His bats were flying to my kill trap and his shadows were confused. Sometimes little tricks can be as useful as ones like Spinner's fireball.

"Let's move out," I said. "He'll need time to ready another shot. Take advantage of it. Ram, let's get out of the way and out of these costumes. They're too damned cumbersome."

We did that. Horsemen moved past, talking softly, wearily, in good spirits. They had made a big mess out there. They were pleased with themselves.

Narayan's friends gathered, one now, one then. By the time the infantry started out, there were eighty of them. "Mainly men of my band," he explained. "They came to Ghoja in answer to my summons. What do you plan now?"

"Down." Shadowspinner was pasting the hills with random sorceries, hurling his darts blind. From beside Narayan, with stones grinding into my belly and breasts, I murmured, "We're going to infiltrate their camp and try for the Shadowmaster."

I could not see his face. Just as well, probably. The idea did not thrill him. "But . . ."

"Never have a better chance. Longshadow knows everything that happens as soon as it happens. His resources haven't been tapped. He sees Shadowspinner in bad trouble, he'll do something." Send the Howler, probably. "We'd better get what we can while we can get it."

He did not want to try. Damn him. If he refused, his Stranglers would, too.

But he had sewn himself into a sack. I was his Daughter of Night. For his own sake he dared not argue. He grunted, whispered, "I don't like it. If it has to be done, please don't you go. The risk is too great."

"I have to. I'm the messiah, remember? It's still that time when I have to win support by demonstration."

I did not *want* to go. I just wanted to lie down and sleep. But my role demanded I play it totally.

He selected twenty-five men whose abilities he

knew. The rest he dismissed. They joined the soldiers headed for camp. Lucky bastards.

"Sindhu. Take four men and scout ahead. As carefully as you can. Don't take anybody out without
checking. Unless you have to." He chose the men to
accompany Sindhu. We followed in a tighter crowd,
with flankers out. Narayan knew his small-unit tactics.

Shadows fluttered around us, still blind to our
presence. But I did not trust their blindness. Had I
been Shadowspinner I would have had them pretend.

Chaos still reigned. Spinner kept pounding the
hills. Maybe his shadows did not know where we
were, only that we had not all departed.

Sindhu drifted back from the point. "Ground's wet
ahead."

That made no sense. It had been dry before sun-
down. It had not rained. "Water?" I asked.

"Yes."

"Strange." But no way to see what it meant before
morning. "Be careful." He went forward again. We
resumed moving. Soon I was in water an inch deep.
The earth beneath was not waterlogged.

The reason for part of the confusion became apparent. The Shadowlanders were trying to stay away
from the hills. When they got too close to the city
archers sniped at them. But the disorder was sorting
itself out.

Sindhu had to eliminate several sentries.

Shadowspinner stopped hammering the hills.
Narayan guessed, "His shadows were watching his
sentries."

Not so. Their confusion was caused by my prox-
imity. It would envelop the sentries. But maybe he
sensed our approach some other way. I sent word to
Sindhu to run for it the instant he thought we were
walking into something.

I was a hundred yards from the old walled camp.
Sindhu was at its shattered gate. He thought the way

was clear. We might actually get our shot at Shadowspinner.

All hell broke loose.

Half a hundred fireballs jumped straight up to push back the night. Their light betrayed a hundred men stealing toward the camp. Taglian men and big black men. Some were in hand-shaking distance of my Stranglers.

I looked into the eyes of their commander, Mogaba the Nar, from thirty feet away. He had had the same idea as I'd had.

Chapter Forty-Five

Longshadow glanced across a table where a bowl of mercury sat, reflecting the frightened, wavering face of his slave Smoke. The Howler floated over there. Between them they had just enough strength to communicate with the little wizard. The Howler was amused.

The slave had nothing good to report. Senjak not only was not available, she had evaded his eye well enough to have moved south perhaps as far as Stormgard. Longshadow flung a hand out above the bowl and broke the pattern. Smoke faded, chaotic colors melting.

Howler chuckled. "You should have seduced him. You're too enamored of brute force. Took more time to do it the hard way. And now he's a bent tool. And they don't trust him."

"Don't tell me how to . . ." This was not one of his powerless minions. This one was almost as strong as he. He would not endure attempts at intimidation. He had to be placated, lulled. Seduced.

"Let's check on our colleague at Stormgard."

They joined talents. Though Longshadow could reach that far without help, help did forge the connection more quickly.

It was apparent Shadowspinner was preoccupied. He responded only sporadically. The magnitude and scope of his troubles became clear only slowly.

"Damn it all!" Four thousand men lost. Chaos among the besiegers. Who knew how many more men lost tonight. Shadowspinner falling back on his last desperate device for keeping the city sealed. . . . "That's Senjak herself this time. Has to be. And she's recovered some of her skills."

"Or she's found someone to provide them."

That was Howler, always finding extra explanations, confusing issues. Damn him. It would be a pleasure killing him. Maybe it would take a century to finish him.

"Whatever. She's there. We can end the threat she poses. Have you completed the new carpet?"

"It's ready."

"I'll give you three capable men from my Guard. Bring her here. We will enjoy her for ages to come." Would Howler accept that? He was not naive.

It was a risk, sending him. He might run off with Senjak. The knowledge she possessed . . .

Forewarned is forearmed. He would send his best three men.

"Fail in this and there will be but one answer left. I shall have to loose one of the big ones off the Plain."

The Howler's concentration broke momentarily. A terrible wail tore through his lips. Then the little bundle of rags chuckled. "Consider her caught. I have a score to settle myself."

Longshadow watched the ragbag drift out, taking its odor with it. Maybe its first torment would consist of soap and water.

He sent for his best three Guards and briefed them, then tried contacting Shadowspinner again.

Spinner did not respond. He was preoccupied. Or dead.

He retreated to his crystal tower. Crows perched on its top peered down. It was time he did something about them. Permanently. After he sent shadows to Dejagore.

Chapter Forty-Six

Mogaba was much more surprised to see me than I was to see him. An immense displeasure marred his features, a grand measure of his surprise. He was always in control of what he showed the world.

The look persisted only a moment. He altered his course to join me. Before he reached me Ram was beside me, between him and me, and Abda had materialized to my left. Narayan was making certain no outsider caused me grief.

Up ahead Sindhu cursed the light and ordered men to move. It was hit fast or die.

"Lady," Mogaba said. "We thought you dead." He was a big man without an ounce of waste on him, muscled like a fictional hero. He was blacker than Blade and a consummate commander, one of the Nar, descendants of the original Black Company. Croaker had enlisted him in Gea-Xle during our southward journey. The Nar constituted a separate warrior class there. With a thousand Nar I could have cleaned the Shadowmasters out as fast as the men could march.

There were only fifteen or twenty left alive, I guessed. All loyal to Mogaba.

"Did you? I'm tougher than you think." His men piled into the camp with mine, trying to reach Shadowspinner before he reacted. I suspected Mogaba's men had triggered the lights. In Spinner's place I would have expected an attack from him before one from me.

"Do you have the Lance?" he asked. The question took me from the blind side. I would have thought he'd want to talk about the siege or which of us had the stronger claim to the Captaincy.

"What lance?"

He smiled. Relieved. "The standard. Murgen lost it."

He was stretching the truth somehow. I turned the conversation to business. We would not have much time. The Shadowlanders were getting ready to interrupt. "How bad off are you? I have no veterans and few trained men. I can only harass them, not break you out."

"We aren't in good shape. Their last assault nearly overcame us. Where did you get your power? Who are you riding with? Murgen saw Croaker die."

"The enemies of the Shadowmasters are my friends." Better to be cryptic than to hand him free information.

"Why don't you put an end to the Shadowmasters?"

I could not answer without lying. I lied. "My friend is no longer with me."

"Who was up there today?"

"Anyone can wear armor."

He smiled tightly, showing a thin strip of sharp teeth. "The Captaincy, then. You don't plan to let me get out of here. Do you?"

We spoke the language of the Jewel Cities, both

disinclined to let our companions in on our conversation.

Men started screaming inside the encampment. I shouted, "Narayan! Come on!" The Shadowlanders west of us would be ready to move any moment. I told Mogaba, "There's no problem with the Captaincy. The progression was established. When the Captain dies the Lieutenant steps into his shoes."

"The tradition is for the Captain to be elected."

We were both right.

Mogaba shouted, "Sindawe! Let's go! It won't work." His archers and artillerymen on the wall were hard at work, laying down fire to cover his withdrawal. "We know where we stand, Lady."

"Do we? I have no enemies but those who choose to make themselves my enemies. I'm interested only in the destruction of the Shadowmasters." My men flew past me. Mogaba's flew past him. A wall of Shadowlanders hurtled toward us.

Mogaba showed me that smile, turned, headed for the city and the safety of ropes hanging down the wall.

Ram gouged me. "Move, Mistress!"

I moved.

A gang of Shadowlanders came after my band, thinking us the easier meat. In the hills some observer had initiative enough to bluff them by sounding trumpets. They slackened the chase. We vanished into the dark ravines.

We assembled. I asked Narayan, "Did we get close?"

"We would have had him if those others hadn't alerted him. Sindhu wasn't ten feet from him."

"Where is he?" Sindhu had not come back. I hated to lose him.

Narayan grinned. "He's healthy. We lost only two Stranglers. Those you don't see got caught in the confusion and fled to the city."

For once I did not mind his grin. "Quick thinking, Narayan. You think he'll find many friends there?"

"A few. Mostly I wanted him to get to your friends. Those who might not be enchanted with that Mogaba."

Mogaba was not much of a problem yet. He was in no position to trouble me. The cure for him was to let him rot. I could just pretend to look for ways to relieve the city while actually only training my men till they suffered the illusion they were soldiers. Meantime, Mogaba could wear the enemy down for me.

The flaw, of course, was that Shadowspinner had allies who might decide to help him.

Dejagore and its surroundings were not worth much anymore but the city did have symbolic value. The Shadowlands were more heavily populated down south. The peoples there would be watching. The fate of Dejagore could decide the fate of the Shadowmasters' empire. If they lost the city and we looked likely to move south again the oppressed might revolt.

All that passed through my mind while I tried to muster strength enough to cross the hills to our camp.

I could not make it. Ram had to help me.

Chapter Forty-Seven

The riders paused to consider the hill beside the road. The woman said, "She's sure gotten them busy." What had been a bald hilltop a few weeks ago now boasted a maze of stonework. Construction looked like a day and night project.

"She gets things done." Croaker wondered how Lady was getting on down south. He wondered why they had come here.

"She does. Damn her." The sorceress touched him gently, like a lover. She did that all the time now. And she looked so much like Lady. He had trouble resisting.

She smiled. She knew what he was thinking. He had his justifications lined up. She had the battle halfway won.

He ground his teeth, stared at the fortress and ignored her. She touched him again. He tried to remark on the layout of the fortress, found nothing would come out. He looked at her again, wide-eyed.

"Just a precaution, my love. You haven't surrendered your heart. But in time you'll come around. Come. Let's visit our friends." She urged her stallion forward.

Circling crows led the way. Catcher wanted to attract attention. She got it. She was a beautiful and exotic woman.

He understood when she spoke to a man as though she knew him. She meant to pass as Lady. No wonder she wanted him mute.

No one paid him any heed. As they passed through the press of sweating men and animals, dust and clatter, the stench of labor and dung, only the insects noticed him.

In this he might disappear. If her attention lapsed. If the crows became distracted. Could they pick him out of such a mob?

She led the way toward the works atop the hill, already nearing completion. She paused again and again to speak to men, usually about matters of no consequence. She was not playing the role right if she meant to usurp Lady. Lady's manner was distant and imperious unless she was striving for a specific result . . . Of course. She wanted word spread that Lady was back.

What was she up to?

His conscience told him he had to do something. But he could think of nothing.

Nobody recognized him. That did his ego no good. Only months ago all Taglios had hailed him Liberator.

Word ran ahead. As they approached the inner fortress a man came out. The Prahbrindrah Drah himself! He was here directing construction? That was not like him. He stayed holed up where the priests could not get to him. The prince said, "I didn't expect you back right away."

"We've won a small victory north of Dejagore. The Shadowmasters lost four thousand men. Blade planned the operation and carried it out. I decided to leave him in charge. I came back to recruit and train new formations. You've done well here. I take it the priests abandoned their obstructionism?"

"You convinced them." The prince looked troubled. "But you don't have any friends now. Don't leave your back unguarded." His gaze kept drifting to Croaker. He seemed puzzled. "Your man Ram seems odd today."

"Touch of dysentery. How is the recruiting going?"

"Slow. Most of the volunteers are helping here. Most men are holding off, waiting to have their minds made up for them."

"Let them know about the victory. Let them know the siege *can* be broken. Shadowspinner has no strength left. He's getting no help from Longshadow. He's on his own with an army so battered only its fear of him holds it together."

Croaker glanced up at a few clouds sliding east from the sea. Nothing remarkable about them but they did cause thoughts to click. The subtle bitch! He knew exactly what she was doing.

Lady was down there sparring with Shadowspinner, beyond the Main, which became impassable during the rainy season. A touch here, a nudge there, and that contest would go on till it was too late for Lady to get back over the river. The season was not that far away, now. Two months at the most. Lady would be trapped over there with the Shadowmasters. Catcher would have five months to take control here, without interference. Probably without anyone discovering who she was. Her crows would watch the routes north. Messengers would be intercepted.

The bitch! The black-hearted bitch!

The prince frowned at him, sensing his turmoil. But he was preoccupied with the woman. "Maybe we can do the garden again sometime."

"That would be lovely. But remember, it's my turn to put on the spread."

The prince smiled weakly. "If they'll let you. After last time."

"I didn't start it."

What was that about? Something involving Lady had happened in the gardens? Soulcatcher did not tell him everything. Only what would leave his heart raw.

He sensed someone watching, spied Smoke lurking in shadows. The wizard's face was a mask of hatred. That faded when he realized he had been spotted. He started shivering, slipped away.

Crows followed, Croaker noted. Of course. Wherever Smoke went he would be watched. Soulcatcher knew all about him.

Catcher asked, "Have my quarters been completed? It's been a long, dusty road. It'll take me two hours to get human."

"They're not finished but they should do. Shall I have someone take your horses and give you a hand with your things?"

"Yes. Of course. Kind of you." She did some trick with her eyes. The prince went shy. "There are some men I want to see." She named names unfamiliar to Croaker. "Send them to my quarters. Ram will entertain them till I'm cleaned up."

"Of course." The prince summoned his hangers-on, sent them to find the men she wanted.

At Catcher's gesture Croaker dismounted and handed his horse over. He followed her as she followed the prince. The crows did a good job scouting, he admitted. Grudgingly. She was pulling it off without a hitch.

In Lady's quarters he discovered why he could be called "Ram," why no one knew him. He encountered a mirror. He did not see himself in it. He saw a big, dirty Shadar with hair enough for a gorilla.

She had laid a glamor on him.

The men Catcher asked for were low caste, skin and bone, nervous little creatures unable to meet her eye. As he introduced himself each added words in cant that Croaker did not recognize. The honorifics were puzzling enough. Daughter of Night? What did that mean? Too much was happening and he had no way of knowing what, nor any control.

Catcher told those men, "I want you to watch the wizard Smoke. At least two of you should be within sight of him all the time. I especially want to know if he goes near the Street of the Dead Lamps. If he enters it, stop him. By whatever means necessary, though I'd rather he didn't make an early entrance into paradise."

The men all plucked at bits of colored cloth peeking from their loincloths. One said, "As you will, so shall it be, Mistress."

"Of course. Get on with it. Find him. Stick tight. He's dangerous to us."

The men hurried out, obviously eager to be away from her. "They're terrified of you," Croaker observed. His voice came back when he was alone with her.

"Naturally. They think I'm the daughter of their goddess. Why don't you get cleaned up? I can smell you from here. I'll have them bring you new clothes."

The bath and clothes were the only good things that happened that day.

Chapter Forty-Eight

I did not get the sleep I needed. The dreams were bad. I wandered the caverns under the earth, awash in the stench of decay. The caverns were no longer cold. The old men were rotting. They were still alive but decaying. When I passed through their line of sight I felt their appeal, their blame. I really tried. But I could get no nearer whatever my destination was supposed to be.

The thing trying to recruit me was getting impatient.

Narayan wakened me. "I'm sorry, Mistress. It's important." He looked like he had seen a ghost.

I sat up. And started vomiting. Narayan sighed. His friends moved to mask me from the men. He looked worried. He feared his investment was going to come up short. I was going to die on him.

I was not worried about that. More the opposite, that I would not die and never escape the misery. What was wrong with me? This was getting old, every morning sick—and not that great the rest of the day.

I didn't have time to be sick. I had work to do. I had worlds to conquer. "Help me up, Ram. Did I mess myself?"

"No, Mistress."

"Thank the goddess for small favors. What is it, Narayan?"

"Better you see for yourself. Come, Mistress. Please?"

Ram had brought horses. I collected myself, let him help me mount. We headed for the hills. As we left camp I saw Blade and Swan and Mather with their heads together, exercised about something. Narayan did not ride but he could lope along when he wanted.

He was right. Seeing was better than hearing. I might not have believed a verbal report.

The plain had flooded. At the north and south ends water roared out of the hills. The aqueducts had gone mad. I said, "Now we know where those work parties headed. They must have diverted both rivers. How deep is it?"

"At least ten feet already."

I tried guessing how high it could rise. The hills were deceptive. It was hard to tell. The plain was lower than the land beyond the hills but not much. The water should not get more than sixty feet deep. But that would be enough to flood the city.

Mogaba was in a fix. He had no way out—unless he built boats or rafts. Shadowspinner would not have to waste a man to keep him tied up.

"Good gods! Where did the Shadowlanders go?" I had a bad feeling I had one foot in a bear trap.

Narayan summoned a man on scout duty. He told us the Shadowlanders had pulled out in two forces, north and south, shortly after sunrise.

I consulted maps in my head, told Narayan, "We have to run. Fast. Or we'll be dead before noon. Get up here behind me. You. Soldier. Get up behind Ram and hang on. Are there other men out here?"

"A few, Mistress."

"They'll have to look out for themselves. Let's go!"

We were a sight, I'm sure, only one of us a competent rider and she so sick she had to stop twice to throw up. But we got back to camp before the hammer fell.

Blade had them ready to march. Now I knew what he'd been up to with Swan and Mather. He had heard about the water and had sensed its significance. He awaited orders.

"Send cavalry north and south to scout and harass."

"Done already. Two hundred men each direction."

"Good. You're a natural." I'd already recalled, rejected, and reexamined a trick that had been played on my armies in the north. Hurry was essential. I could see what might be dust north of us. "Move the infantry into the hills. I want every horseman to cut brush and drag it behind, headed due east. Get messengers off to the skirmishers. I want contact kept as long as possible. Draw them eastward and keep leading them as long as they'll follow."

The ruse would not work after dark—if it worked at all. Then Shadowspinners' pet shadows would tell him he'd been taken. But that would be time enough to elude him.

If he kept chasing me Mogaba's men would escape. He would not want that.

Blade wasted no time. Swan and Mather dashed around helping. Our differences would wait.

A new sense of confidence and discipline was apparent as the troops moved into the hills. They trusted me and Blade to get them through this. The horsemen headed out, raising enough dust for a horde on the march.

Blade, Swan, Mather, Narayan, and I watched from a low hill. "That will do it if he can be fooled at all,"

I said. "He'll see us just slipping out, get excited, try to nab us on the run."

Swan raised crossed fingers to the sky. Blade asked, "What's our next move?"

"Drift north through the hills."

"He's biting," Mather said.

Blade said, "It occurs to me that, for speed's sake, he would have left behind anyone not in top condition."

I told him, "You are learning. And you're turning nasty."

"Nasty business."

"Yes. The rest of you understand?"

Swan wanted it explained. "Spinner would leave his injured and second-line troops behind so they wouldn't slow him down. They should be up where the north road enters the hills. We can take them by surprise. Narayan, send some scouts ahead."

Narayan was pleased with me now. There was a lot of killing going on. There was promise of a real Year of the Skulls.

Chapter Forty-Nine

Smoke drifted into the darkness, glanced right and left, cursed softly. There they were again. Those men! He could not shake them. They knew where he was going before he went.

It was disheartening and frightening. The longer he delayed visiting his contacts the stronger Long-shadow's image grew within his mind and the more terrified he became on a level so deep it was a part of his soul. Something terrible had been done to him, something that had reached into him as deeply as a man could be reached. Somehow Longshadow had hidden a fragment of himself inside him, to drive him into executing the Shadowmaster's will.

The voice within had become a shriek. If he did not shake the watchers he would not be able to avoid betraying his contacts.

He pretended not to notice the men, though they did nothing to remain anonymous. Did she know and just want to scare him away from his contacts? Maybe. Maybe it did not matter if he betrayed them.

He started walking.

His shadows followed.

He tried to elude them, relying on a superior knowledge of the city. He had haunted the shadows and alleys and hidden ways all his life. As he knew the palace better than anyone living, so he knew Taglios. He gave it his best. And when he stepped out of a shanty warren where he got lost twice himself trying to get back out, one of his stalkers was waiting, leaning against a building.

The man grinned.

Longshadow filled Smoke's mind. The Shadowmaster was angry. His patience was failing.

Smoke stamped across the street. "How the hell do you keep track of me?"

The man spat to one side, smiled again. "You can't evade the eye of Kina, wizard."

"Kina!" Another terror to pile atop his fear of Longshadow.

"You can run but you can't hide. You can twist and wiggle but you can't get off the hook. You can skulk and whisper in locked rooms but you can't keep secrets. Each breath you draw is numbered."

The fear deepened.

"And always has been."

Smoke turned to run.

"There's a way out."

"What?"

"There's a way out. Look at you. Maintain your allegiance to the Shadowmaster and you're dead if your Taglian friends find out. If they don't kill you, he will when he's done with you. But you can get out. You can come home. You can shake the terror that's like a beast starving for your soul."

Smoke was too frightened to wonder why the thug did not talk like a street creature. "How?" He would try anything to get out from under the Shadowmaster's thumb.

"Come to Kina."

"Oh. No!" He nearly shrieked. The only escape was to yield himself to a greater horror? "No!"

"Up to you, wizard. But life isn't going to get any better."

This time Smoke did run. He did not care if he was followed. Exercise reduced panic. As he neared his destination he realized that he had not seen any bats since leaving the palace. That was new. Where were the Shadowmasters' messengers?

He bustled into a tall slum tenement, hurried upstairs, pounded on a door. A voice said, "Enter."

He froze two steps inside the doorway.

The man he had been talking to leaned against the opposite wall. There were eight corpses in the room, all strangled. The man said, "The goddess doesn't want your master to know her daughter is here."

Smoke squeaked like a stomped rat. He fled. The man laughed.

The man amongst the corpses shrank. He became the imp Frogface, who chuckled, then faded away.

Smoke calmed down before he reached the palace. His mind started working. He had one bolt left. It could bite him as easily as his enemies, but . . . Engulfed by the darkness he could but flee toward the only light he saw.

He would *not* yield to Kina.

Chapter Fifty

As dusk gathered I descended on Longshadow's stay-behinds and routed them completely. The slaughter was great. It failed being complete only because my cavalry was otherwise occupied. We had the field to ourselves before the last light left the sky.

"Old Spinner's going to know in a few minutes," Swan said. "I figure he'll have him a litter of kittens, then he'll get pissed. We ought to go somewhere where he can't catch us."

He was on the right track. Coming through the hills I had been considering going after the group left at the southern approach. Not till Swan spoke did I realize I would not be able to sneak up on that group. Night had come. Night belonged to Shadowspinner. He would know where we were and where we were headed. Unless that was away from him he would be waiting when we arrived.

Too, he might be desperate enough to appeal to Longshadow. Maybe Longshadow had help on the way already. Whatever lay between them, it would

not be as great as their enmity for the rest of the
world. Though premature, theirs was a squabble
over the spoils of conquest.

Blade asked, "Any way we could stay here and
masquerade as the Shadowmaster's men?"

"No. I don't have the skill. Our best bet is to go
back north till he stops chasing us, then just keep
him nervous while we decide what to do next."

Narayan had started worrying about missing his
delayed Festival. Though I had passed my first test
he was suspicious of my will to become the Daughter of Night. A move north would assuage him. And
the men needed time away from danger, to recuper-
ate and digest their successes.

Blade asked, "The men in the city?"

"They're safer than they were. Shadowspinner
can't get at them now."

Narayan grumbled. Sindhu was in there.

I said, "Mogaba will cope. He's good at coping."
Too good. We would have trouble down the road,
him and me.

Nobody liked heading back north, except Narayan.
But no one argued.

I had gained ground, definitely.

Chapter Fifty-One

Smoke was no earthshaker as a wizard but within his limitations, which he recognized, he was competent and effective. And forewarned, he was forearmed.

The woman knew his every move? Then she commanded some unsuspected agency for espionage. He needed blind that only a few minutes.

He scuttled through the palace, ducking his employers, who were looking for him. He dodged into one of his shielded rooms, barred the door.

Obviously his shielding had been penetrated because that man had implied she knew everything, meaning she had been peeking here, too. She was more than she pretended. *Much* more. She *was* the Daughter of Night. And that fool the prince had been blinded by her. Hadn't they been out to the gardens again tonight?

No one could stop her but him. Maybe he could shake loose from Longshadow later.

The Shadowmaster's face formed in his head. His

legs turned to jelly. He shook his head violently, forced the apparition away, hurriedly set about checking his defenses.

He found a pinhole through which some wicked spirit could have oozed. Or a shadow, for that matter.

He plugged it. Then he worked a spell that pressed his limits. It would conceal his whereabouts till he became the object of a very determined search. Secure, he filled a small silver bowl from a mercury flask, working as swiftly as he dared. Before he was finished he feared that he had been too slow.

Someone tried the door. He jumped but concentrated on opening the path to Overlook. It came. It came. More quickly than he expected, it came. The Shadowmaster had been thinking of him, too.

The racket at the door became pounding and shouting. He ignored it.

The dread face appeared on the surface of the mercury, amazed. It mouthed words. There was no sound. The Shadowmaster was too far, Smoke's power too feeble. The little wizard gestured violently, Pay attention! He was startled by his own temerity. But this was a desperate hour. Desperate measures were necessary.

Smoke grabbed paper and ink and scribbled. They were trying to break down the door. Damn, the woman had reacted quickly.

He held his message up for Longshadow. The Shadowmaster read. He reread. Then Longshadow looked him in the eye and nodded. He appeared bewildered. Carefully, he mouthed words so Smoke could read his lips.

The door began to give. And something else was trying to get in now, clawing and tearing at the plugged pinhole.

The door gave a little more.

Smoke got half the message before the pinhole plug broke. Dense smoke boiled into the room. A face glared out of it. Hideous and fanged and filled with grim purpose, it came for him. He squealed, jumped up, overturned table and bowl.

The door gave way as the demon caught him. He screamed and tumbled down into an abyss of terror.

The guards took one look, cursed, dropped the ram and fled. The prince stepped inside, saw the thing ripping at Smoke. The Radisha crowded up behind him. "What the hell is that?"

"I don't know. I don't think you ought to stay to find out." He looked for a weapon, recognized the absurdity of the impulse as he grabbed a swordlike sliver split from the doorframe.

The monster looked up, startled. It stared. Apparently this situation was beyond its instructions. It hung there, motionless.

The Prahbrindrah threw the sliver like a spear.

The thing shrank away into an upper corner of the room, swiftly and dramatically, leaving behind an odor like cinnamon and mustard and wine all mixed.

"What the hell was it?" the Radisha demanded again. She was petrified. The Prahbrindrah jumped over to the wizard. Smoke's blood was everywhere, along with shreds of clothing. The thing had driven him into a corner. What was left of him had drawn itself into a tight fetal ball.

The prince dropped to his knees. "He's alive. Get some help. Fast. Or he won't be for long." He started doing what he could.

Chapter Fifty-Two

Longshadow let out one long scream of rage that echoed throughout Overlook. It brought toadies running, bent with fear he would take it out on them. Whatever it was. "Get out! Get out and stay . . . Wait! Get in here!"

Calm returned suddenly. He'd always had a facility for gaining control when the crisis was tight. That was when he thought his best, responded most quickly. Maybe this was a blessing in disguise.

"Bring the big sending bowl. Bring mercury. Bring that fetish that belongs to my guest and ally. I must contact him."

They scurried around in terror. That was good to see. They held him in high fear. Fear was the power. What you feared ruled you. . . . He thought of shadows and a plain of glittering stone. The rage boiled up. He rejected it, as he rejected fear. One day, when the distractions were eliminated, that plain would bend to him. He would conquer it, end the fear of it forever.

They had everything set before he was ready himself. "Now get out. Stay out till I call."

He activated the bowl and reached for his man. He touched nothing. He tried again. Again. Four times. Five. The rage was about to break through again.

The Howler responded.

"Where have you been?"

"Aloft." Scant whisper, barely perceptible. "I had to set down first. Bad news. She's tricked our friend again. Slaughtered another several thousand men."

That went past Longshadow. Shadowspinner's travails were nothing. "Is she there? At all?"

"Of course she is."

"Are you positive? Have you *seen* her? My shadows can't find her. Last night they couldn't do more than suggest she *might* be in a given general area."

"Not with my own eyes," Howler admitted. "I'm tracking her forces, though, waiting for the chance to strike. Late tonight, I think."

"I've just had a report from the wizard in Taglios. A desperate effort on his part. All our agents there have been strangled. He says she's there. With her Shadar shadow. And she knows he's ours. Before he finished, something demonic burst in and tore him apart."

"That's impossible. She was here two days ago."

"Have you *seen* her? With your own eyes?"

"No."

"Recall. She always favored illusion and misdirection. There was evidence she was regaining her powers. Maybe much faster than she let on. Maybe she's tricked us into believing she was one place when she was another. The Taglian said our agents were killed to keep them from reporting her presence."

The Howler did not respond.

Both men thought. Longshadow finally said, "I can't fathom why she'd send an army to make us believe she was in our territories. But I know her. You know her. If it's that important to her that we believe her somewhere she isn't, then it's lethally important to us. There's something in Taglios she doesn't want us to discover. Perhaps she's on the track of the Lance. Someone carried it away from the battlefield. It hasn't been seen since."

"If I go we're liable to lose Dejagore and Spinner. His skills are impaired. His mind is as dull as a knife used to chop rock."

Longshadow cursed softly. Yes. Pray come the day when Shadowspinner was no longer needed. When there was no need for a bulwark against the north. But somebody had to bear the brunt now. "Do something. Then go." The runt could understand that. "Collect her quick. Hell will be a pleasure compared to what we'll face if she stays loose till all her powers are restored."

"Consider it done," the Howler whispered. "Consider her taken."

"I take nothing for granted where Senjak is concerned. Get her, dammit! Get her!" He slammed a fist into the mercury. That killed the connection.

He let the rage roar through him. He hurled things, broke things, till it was appeased. Then he went up into his tower and glowered his hatred at the night-hidden plain.

"Why must you torment me? Why? Turn away. Let me be." If that was not out there, ready to burst its bonds, he would be free to deal with these things himself. He would make short work of these problems if he could see to them himself. But he needs must rely on incompetents and agents with insufficient power to get the job done.

He thought of the Taglian wizard. That tool had not done the job for which it had been forged but it had served. Pity it had been destroyed so quickly.

A pity.

Chapter Fifty-Three

The cavalry rejoined us two days north of Dejagore, where I made camp. The general mood was positive. The men resented having been withdrawn. They did not want to believe they had just been lucky, not invincible. I wanted them to know their luck could turn. They did not believe me. Most people believe only what they want to believe.

Their confidence had infected Narayan and Blade. Those two would have turned south again without question had I ordered it. I was tempted. I considered myself lucky to be sick. It kept me thinking rationally.

They presented a plan for harassing Shadowspinner into another trap. I told them, "Spinner won't charge into traps. If we separate him from his men maybe we can trap them. But not him."

Narayan leaned close. "It wasn't luck, Mistress. It was Kina. Her spirit is loose. It is the time of foreshadowing. The Year of the Skulls approaches. She

passes her hand over the eyes of her enemies. She is
with us."

I wanted to tell him that the man who counts on
the aid of a god deserves the help he doesn't get but
I reconsidered. The Deceivers were true believers.
Whatever else, however bloodthirsty and criminal
their enterprises, they believed in their goddess and
mission. Kina was not just a convenient fiction ex-
cusing their crimes.

After months of dreams I had trouble not believing in Kina myself. Maybe not as Narayan's kind of
goddess but as a potent force that fed on death and
destruction.

Blade asked, "Why not take Shadowspinner out of
the picture?"

"Right. A stroke of genius, Blade. Maybe if we all
wish hard enough he'll come floating belly up."

He smiled. His smile was no fawning grin like Narayan's but it was powerful because he used it so
seldom. He offered me a hand up. "Take a walk with
me, please."

Right on the edge there, Blade. He was not sufficiently impressed, I feared. I reminded myself to remember he probably had his own agenda and I did
not have the foggiest what it might be.

We walked away from the others. Narayan and
Ram and Swan all watched, each with his particular
breed of jealousy.

"Well?"

"Shadowspinner is the main enemy. Kill him and
his army would collapse."

"Probably."

"I have eyes and ears. My brain works. When I'm
curious I ask questions. I know what Narayan is. I
know what you are to him. And I think I know what
they want you to become."

No great surprise, that. Probably half the army
had some notion, though they might not believe Ram
and Narayan deserved their legendary reputation.
"So?"

"I've seen Sindhu in action. I understand Narayan is better."

"True."

"Then point him at Shadowspinner. He could have the Shadowmaster dead before he knew what hit him."

Strangling a sorcerer is a good way of disposing of him. One of Spinner's magnitude relies heavily on voice spells and, secondarily, gesture spells. Stick him with a knife or sword or missile and he can still use both voice and hands unless you kill him instantly. A Narayan could take away the voice. Assuming he could break a neck as fast as he claimed, gestures would not matter.

"Stipulated. I think. Leaving one small problem. Moving Narayan near enough to use his rumel."

"Uhm."

"Narayan, of his kind, is what I used to be of mine. The pinnacle. The acme. I've watched him. He's death incarnate. But he lacks the skills needed to get close to Shadowspinner. He just never learned how to turn invisible."

Blade chuckled. "Bet that's a trick he'd love you to teach him."

"No doubt. You've thought this through. You've seen the difficulties. You think you've seen ways around them. So tell me how we do it. I don't think it's practical but I'll listen."

"There are distinct kinds of assassins. A lone crazy who doesn't care if he gets killed himself. A cabal grasping for power, ready to turn on itself when its target is eliminated. And the professional."

I saw no point. I said so.

"To be successful we have to avoid the weaknesses of various kinds of assassins. I've watched you. Your skills aren't what they were but you sell yourself short. You could disguise a strike team sneaking up on Shadowspinner. If we create the illusion that our goals are impersonal he won't guard against personal attack. Right?"

"To a point."

"To a point. Shadowspinner shouldn't know you have problems with Mogaba. So go after ways to relieve the city. While a handful work on killing Shadowspinner."

"Tell me how."

"Narayan should do the actual killing. You will have to disguise the attack group or make it invisible. Ram goes because he must. I go because no one else is better with a weapon. Swan goes because his presence implies the involvement of the Taglian state. Mather would be better because there's a personal involvement with the Woman, but Cordy needs to hold the reins here. He's steady. He thinks. Willow is all passion, action without thought. Add however many specialists Narayan needs."

"Two arm-holders." I said it in Stranglers' cant. Blade gave me a quick glance. He was surprised I was that far into that world. We walked in silence. Then I said, "You've just talked more than I've heard since I met you."

"I talk when I have something to say."

"Do you know card games?" I had seen none south of the equator. Here the well-to-do played dominoes or board games, the impoverished games with dice or sticks you shook in a canister and tossed.

"Some. Cordy and Mather had cards but they wore out."

"Know what a wild card is?"

He nodded.

I stopped, bent my head, closed my eyes, concentrated, conjured a ferocious illusion. It took form high above, a flying lizard twice the size of an eagle. It dove.

Crows have sharp eyes. They have brains, for birds, but they are not geniuses. They panicked. The panic would make their reports of the event incomprehensible.

Blade said, "You did something." He watched the crows flee.

"The birds are spies for one of the wild cards in our game." I told him what I had found in the grove and what I thought it meant.

"Mather and Swan have mentioned this Howler and Soulcatcher. They did not speak well of them. But they didn't speak well of you, either, as you were. What's their interest here?"

I talked about them till the crows returned. Blade had no trouble grasping the intricacies of scheming in the old empire. He must have had experience.

The crows reestablished their watch. I did not disturb it. Too often would generate suspicion. Blade wore a thin, pleased smile. As we approached the others, waiting silently, watching intently, each with his concerns too evident, Blade whispered, "For the first time I'm glad Cordy and Willow dragged me out."

I glanced at him quickly. Yes. He seemed completely alive for the first time since I'd met him.

Chapter Fifty-Four

The Prahbrindrah Drah turned slowly before a mirror, admiring himself. "What do you think?"

The Radisha eyed his tailored dress, bright silk, and jewels. He cut a handsome figure. "When did you turn into a peacock?"

He half drew a sword he'd had forged as a symbol of the state. "Nice?"

It was as fine a weapon as could be produced by Taglian craftsmen, hilt and pommel a work of art incorporating gold, silver, rubies, and emeralds in a symbolic intertwining of the emblems of Taglian faiths. The blade was strong, sharp, practical, but its hilt was overweight and clumsy. Still, it was not a combat weapon, just a trapping of office.

"Gorgeous. And you're trying to make a fool of yourself."

"Maybe. But I'm having fun doing it. And you'd be having fun making a fool of you if Mather was here. Eh?"

The Radisha eyed him narrowly. He was not as

open as he had been before Lady caught his eye. He was up to something and for the first time in their lives he was not sharing. That worried her. But she said only, "You're wasting your time. It's raining. Nobody goes to the gardens when it's raining."

"It won't last."

That was true. It was just a brief rain. They always were, this time of year. The real rains were more than a month away. But still . . . She felt he should avoid the gardens tonight, with no rational basis for her feeling.

"You're investing too much in it. Slow down. Make her work harder."

He grinned. Give the woman that. Murderess she might be but she did put a smile on his face. "Don't count me so smitten I'll give away the palace."

"I wasn't thinking that. But she's changed since she came back. It concerns me."

"I appreciate it. But I'm in control. Taglios is my first love. And hers is the Company. If she's up to anything it's trying to make sure we don't go back on our bargain."

"That could be enough." Regarding the Black Company she still hovered over the abyss between his position and Smoke's.

"How's Smoke?" he asked.

"Hasn't come to yet. They say he lacks the will to recover."

"Tell those leeches that for their sakes he'd better. I want to know what happened. I want to know what that thing was. I want to know why it wanted to kill him. Our Smoke has been up to something. It could get us destroyed."

They had discussed that again and again. There were implications in Smoke's behavior which boded evil. Till they learned the truth, they suspected, a sword hung over their heads.

"You haven't said what you think."

"I think everyone who sees you will think you look like a prince of the blood instead of a vegetable peddler someone threw ill-fitting clothing on and called a prince."

He chuckled. "You're right. In your sarcastic way. I never cared what I looked like. Wasn't anyone I wanted to impress. Time to go."

"Suppose I go along, this once?" A facetious suggestion, to see how he wriggled.

"Why not? Get ready. It ought to be amusing, seeing her response."

And instructive? The Radisha's estimate of her brother rose. He was not completely smitten. "I won't be long."

She was not. It took her longer to pass instructions to Smoke's attendants than to prepare to go out.

Chapter Fifty-Five

Croaker leaned on the lance supporting the Company standard, wearing his Shadar disguise. He was bored. He was not alert. He was depressed. He had begun to despair of escape. He was ready to say the hell with it and try walking first time a faint chance arose.

The Prahbrindrah Drah and Soulcatcher chattered and laughed beneath paper lanterns while garden staff came and went. They were oblivious to anything but one another. The surprise guest, the Radisha, was out in the cold, ignored.

Croaker had grumbled about spending so much time on the prince and not enough on preparing soldiers. Catcher had laughed, told him not to worry. She would be true to him forever. This was just politics.

He would not be able to resist her much longer. She had him on the run, desperate, on the brink of surrender. Once he did that she would have won everything.

Maybe he *should*. Maybe once she counted that final coup she would just go away, back north, where her prospects were so much finer. She talked about going north sometimes.

Being her companion was cruel. She had made of him something more than spoil. She talked about the Soulcatcher inside sometimes, when what she had chosen to be became too much to bear. In those moments, when she was human, he was most vulnerable. In those moments he wanted to comfort her. He was sure the moments were genuine, not tactical. Her approach to conquest was not subtle.

Brooding, it took him a while to notice that the Radisha was paying him more attention than a bodyguard deserved. She was not obvious but she was subjecting him to intense scrutiny. It startled him, disturbed him, then just left him curious. Why? Some flaw in his disguise? No way to tell. He'd never seen the man he was supposed to be.

He started thinking about what Lady might be doing, what relationships she might be forming. Was there yet another level to Catcher's vengeance? Did she not only want to seduce him and rape his heart but want Lady to find someone—so she could then let her know he was alive after all?

Weird people. All this for little pains. Relatively little pains. Maybe not so little to them, who in their ways were demigods. Maybe to them love was more significant than to mere mortals.

The Radisha was damned near staring at him. She frowned like someone trying to recall a face.

He had little to lose. He winked.

Her eyebrows rose, her only reaction. But she did not study him anymore. She pretended interest in her brother and the woman he thought was Lady.

Croaker resumed brooding. Lost in his own inner landscapes he did not notice the crows departing, one by one.

* * *

Though she had the greater capacity, Catcher did not show off the way Lady did. The coach was dull and quiet. Croaker, beside the driver, clutched his lance and wondered what they were talking about below. The prince and his sister had accepted a ride because the skies had begun to leak again.

The drizzle suited his mood perfectly.

The driver said, "Ho!"

Croaker glimpsed the sudden glow in an alleyway now drawing abreast. As he turned a blinding, fist-sized ball of pink fire shot out, smashed into the left-hand door of the coach. A second ripped out behind it, hit the front of the coach, flared brilliantly. The horses broke loose, leaving the vehicle. A third ball hit the coach, shattered a rear wheel. The coach heeled over almost to the point of toppling. Croaker jumped. The counter-momentum of his kickoff was just enough to stop the tipping. As the coach crashed back he hit the street on the side away from the alley.

Men charged out of that alley.

Croaker ripped open the coach door. Catcher and the Radisha were unconscious. The prince was dazed but awake. Croaker grabbed his pretty suit and yanked.

Up above, the driver cried out.

Croaker charged around the rear of the smoldering coach—smack into what looked like a floating bundle of rags. He stabbed with the lance he still clutched.

The bundle howled.

Croaker's blood stilled in his veins.

There were three men with the Howler. They turned on Croaker.

The prince stumbled around the front of the coach, dandy's sword drawn. He cut one of those men from behind.

The Howler screamed. He waved both hands wildly. Croaker stabbed him again. The whole street boomed and rocked. Croaker was flung back against the coach, thought he felt ribs give way. The boom seemed to echo endlessly up and down a deep canyon. His last clear thought was, not again. He'd just gotten over a serious injury.

People were scurrying around like panicky mice when Croaker recovered. The Radisha knelt over her brother. The more collected bystanders had dragged the attackers away. Two seemed to be dead, a third badly injured. Croaker got to his knees, pressed fingers against his ribs. Pain answered but it was not the pain of broken bones. He'd gotten through it with bruises. He pushed toward the Radisha, asked, "How bad is he?"

"Just unconscious, I think. I don't see any wounds." She did not look at him. There was shouting way up the street. Belated help was on its way.

Croaker looked into the coach.

Soulcatcher was gone.

Howler was gone.

"He took her?"

The Radisha looked up. Her eyes widened. "You! I thought there was something familiar . . ." Soulcatcher's spells had perished? He was himself now?

"Where is she?"

"That thing that attacked us . . ."

"A sorcerer called the Howler. As powerful and nasty as the Shadowmasters. Working for them now. Did he take her?"

"I think so."

"Damn!" He lowered himself gingerly, recovered the lance, used it to support himself. "You people! Get out of here! Go home. You're in the way. Wait! Did anyone see what happened?"

A few witnesses confessed. He demanded, "The thing that fled. Where did it go?"

The witnesses indicated the alley.

Using the lance as a crutch—he had a badly twisted ankle to go with the bruised ribs—he hobbled into the alleyway.

Nothing there. The Howler was gone and Catcher with him.

As he headed back he realized what the absence of Catcher's spells meant. He was free. For a while he was free.

The Prahbrindrah Drah was sitting up. The onlookers, realizing their prince had been attacked, were turning ugly, threatening the attacker who had survived. Croaker bellowed, "Back off! We need him alive. I said go home. That's an order."

Some recognized him now. A voice said, "It's the Liberator!" The title had been bestowed by public acclaim when he and the Company had undertaken to defend Taglios.

Some went. Some stayed. Those moved back.

The racket of help too late drew nearer.

The prince looked up at Croaker in amazement. Croaker offered him a hand. The prince accepted it. On his feet, he whispered, "Is the disguise part of some grand strategy?"

"Later." The prince must think he had masqueraded as Ram all along. "Can you walk? Let's get off the street before more trouble finds us."

Help arrived in the form of a half dozen palace guards. They had been summoned by someone with enough presence of mind to go for them.

The prince asked, "Someone snatched Lady?" Bemused, he muttered, "I guess that was the whole point, else we'd all be dead."

"That's my guess. Are they in for a surprise. Let's get moving." As they started walking, surrounded by the guards, Croaker asked, "Where was your pet wizard while all this was happening?"

"Why?" the Radisha demanded.

"That little shit has been on the Shadowmasters' payroll for weeks. Ask him about it."

The prince said, "I'd love to. But a demon tried to kill him and almost succeeded. He's in a coma. Won't come back."

Croaker glanced back. "Somebody ought to bring the prisoner. He might tell us something useful."

He would not. He had died while no one was looking.

Croaker was amazed at himself, taking charge the
way he was. Maybe it was pressure from so many
months of helplessness. Maybe it was urgency
brought on by the certainty that he would not have
long to grab hold of his destiny.

The prince had to be right. Lady had been the object of the attack. That meant the bad boys had lost
track of her somehow and had thought Catcher was
her. He smiled grimly. They would not be prepared
for the tiger they had caught.

How long would Catcher toy with them before revealing herself? Long enough?

Count on nothing. Hurry.

He by damned had to grab for all he could get
while the opportunity existed.

Croaker finished his story. The prince and his sister had listened agape. The Radisha recovered her
poise first. She'd always had the harder edge. "Way
back, Smoke cautioned us that there might be more
going on than met the eye. That there might be play-
ers in the game we didn't see."

All eyes turned to the unconscious wizard. Croaker
said, "Prince, you used that sticker pretty well tonight. Think you'd have trouble pricking him if he
asked for it?"

"No trouble at all. After what he's done the trouble I'll have is not sticking him before we get a story
out of him."

"He's not all bad. He walked into a trap trying to
do what he thought was right. His problem is, he
gets an idea in his head and he can't get it out if it's
wrong, no matter what evidence you hit him with.
He decided we were the bad guys come back for general mayhem and he just couldn't change his mind.
Probably never will. If you execute him he'll die
thinking he's a hero and martyr who tried to save
Taglios. I think I can waken him. When I do, you

stand by to stick him if he tries any tricks. Even a puny wizard is deadly when he wants."

Croaker took an hour but did tease the wizard out of life's twilight and got him to choke out his story.

Afterward, the prince asked, "What can we do? Even if he's as contrite as he says, the Shadowmasters have a hold we can't break. I don't *want* to kill him but he is a wizard. We couldn't keep him locked up."

"He can stay locked up in his mind. You'd have to force-feed him and clean him like a baby but I can put him back into the coma."

"Will he heal?"

"His body should. I can't do anything about what the devil did to his soul." Smoke's past cowardice looked like outrageous courage now.

"Do it. We'll deal with him when there's time."

Croaker did it.

Chapter Fifty-Six

Shadowspinner's shadows remained blind to my whereabouts. He did not seem able to adjust. And his bats were useless. Were in fact extinct in that part of the world where my band stole through the night.

I signalled a halt a mile from where my scouts said Spinner had established his camp. We had come a long way in a short time. We needed rest.

Narayan settled beside me. He plucked at his rumel, whispered, "Mistress, I'm of a divided mind. Most of me really believes the goddess wants me to do this, that it will be the greatest thing I've ever done for her."

"But?"

"I'm scared."

"You make that sound shameful."

"I haven't been this frightened since my first time."

"This isn't your ordinary victim. The stakes are higher than you're used to."

"I know. And knowing wakens doubts of my ability, of my worthiness ... even of my goddess." He seemed ashamed to admit that, too. "She is the greatest Deceiver of all, Mistress. It amuses her sometimes to mislead her own. And, while this is a great and necessary deed, even I, who was never a priest, notice that the omens have not been favorable."

"Oh?" I had noticed no omens, good or bad.

"The crows, Mistress. They haven't been with us tonight."

I had not noticed. I had grown that accustomed to them. I assumed they were there whether I saw them or not. He was right. There were no crows anywhere.

That meant something. Probably something important. I could not imagine their master allowing me freedom from observation for even a minute. And their absence was not my doing. And I doubted it was Shadowspinner's.

"I hadn't noticed, Narayan. That's interesting. Personally, it's the best omen I've seen in months."

He frowned at me.

"Worry not, my friend. You're Narayan, the living legend. The saint-to-be. You'll do fine." I shifted from cant to standard Taglian. "Blade. Swan. Ready?"

"Lead on, my lovely," Swan said. "I'll follow you anywhere." The more stressed he became the more flip he was.

I looked them over, Blade, Swan, Ram, Narayan, the two arm-holders. Seven of us. As Swan had observed, the obligatory number for a company on quest. A totally mixed bag. By his own standards each was a good person. By the standards of others everyone, excepting Swan, was a villain.

"Let's go, then." Before I grew too philosophical.

We did not have to talk about it. We had rehearsed farther away. There would be no chatter to alert Shadowspinner.

It was a slovenly encampment. It screamed demoralization. But for Spinner my ragbag army could have beaten those Shadowlanders. And they knew it. They were waiting for the hammer to fall.

We passed within yards of pickets who sat facing a fire and grumbling. Their language resembled Taglian. I could understand them when they were not excited.

They were demoralized, all right. They were discussing men they knew who had deserted. There seemed to be a lot of those and plenty of sentiment for following their example.

Narayan had the point. He trusted no one else to find his way. He came sliding into the hollow where we waited. In a whisper that did not carry three feet he told me, "There are prisoners in a pen to the left, there. Taglian. Several hundred."

I turned that over in my mind. How could I use them? There was potential for a diversion there. But I did not need one. "Did you talk to them?"

"No. They might have given us away."

"Yes. We'll stick to the mission."

Narayan went ahead. He found us another lurking place. I began to sense Shadowspinner's nearness. He did not radiate much energy for a power of his magnitude. Till then I had been sure only that he was in the camp. "Over there."

"The big tent?" Narayan asked.

"I think."

We moved closer. I saw that Shadowspinner felt no need for guards. Maybe he thought he was his own best guard. Maybe he did not want anyone that close while he was asleep.

We crouched in a pool of darkness, a dozen feet from the tent. One fire burned on its far side. No light came from within. I eased my blade out of its scabbard. "Blade, Swan, Ram, be ready to cover us if something goes wrong." Hell. If anything went wrong we were dead. And we all knew it.

"Mistress!" Ram protested. His voice threatened to rise.

"Stay put, Ram. And don't give me an argument."

We'd had the argument already. He did not give up. I moved forward. Narayan and his arm-holders drifted with me. So did the smell of fear.

I paused two feet from the tent, drew my blade down the canvas. It cut without a whisper. An arm-holder widened the slash enough for Narayan to slip through. The other followed, I went next, then the first arm-holder.

It was dark in there. Narayan held us in place with a touch. He was a patient hunter. More so than I could have been in his place, knowing the moon was about to rise and rape away the darkness. Its fore-glow had been visible as we'd approached the tent.

Narayan started moving, slowly, certainly, disturbing nothing. His arm-holders were as good as he. I could not hear their breathing.

I had to rely on extraordinary senses to keep from stumbling over things. I felt the Shadowmaster's presence but could not pin it down.

Narayan seemed to know where to go.

There had to be hangings ahead. No light from the fire outside reached us. How I wished for some light.

Light I got, unexpectedly. Just enough light to unveil the awful truth.

Shadowspinner was off to our left, seated in the lotus position, watching us through a grim beast mask. "Welcome," he said. His voice was like a snake's hiss. It was feeble. It barely carried. "I've been waiting."

So the shadows had not been fooled after all.

He guessed my thoughts. "Not the shadows, Dorotea Senjak. I know how you think. Soon I shall know all that is inside your head. You arrogant bitch! You thought you could take me with three unarmed men and a sword?"

I said nothing. There was nothing to say. Narayan started to move. I gestured slightly, a Strangler's signal. He froze. There was a chance if Shadowspinner truly believed these men unarmed.

Then I spoke. "If you think you know me, then you

don't know me at all." I wanted him closer. I wanted
him where Narayan could reach him. "Dark Mother,
Mother Kina, listen! Thy Daughter calls. My Mother,
attend me."

He did not move. He hit me with something invisible that knocked me back ten feet and tore a groan
out of me.

The discipline shown by Narayan and his arm-
holders astonished me. They did not rush Shadowspinner. They did not come to me and separate
themselves farther from their target. They moved
only slightly, so they were better balanced and disposed, their adjustment barely perceptible.

Shadowspinner rose slowly, a man in pain. He
slipped a crutch beneath one arm. "Yes. A cripple.
With no chance for repairs because my only ally
won't lend me help he might regret when he decides
I've outlived my usefulness. And I have you to
thank." He extended a hand. An almost invisible rope
of indigo fire snaked from his fingers to me. He made
a pulling gesture. The rope dragged me forward. The
pain was intense. I contained my scream, barely.

He wanted me to scream. He wanted me to waken
the camp so he could show his incompetents what
he had accomplished despite their inattention. He
wanted to play cat and mouse.

The wall of the tent behind him exploded inward.
Two blades ripped canvas and Ram came flying
through. Shadowspinner turned. Ram smashed into
him, sent him stumbling toward Narayan.

Narayan and his arm-holders moved like mon-
gooses striking. Narayan had his rumel around the
Shadowmaster's throat so fast my eyes insisted it
was witchcraft. The arm-holders had the Shadowmaster's limbs extended before he lost momentum.

The purple rope ripped away from me. It lashed
one of the arm-holders. The man's eyes grew huge.
He stifled a scream and tried to hang on but lost his
grip.

Shadowspinner whipped the rope at Narayan.

Narayan's eyes bugged. He lost his grip on his rumel. Shadowspinner turned on the other arm-holder.

Ram grabbed Shadowspinner from behind, by the neck and buttocks, and hoisted him overhead. Shadowspinner lashed at him. He did not seem able to feel pain. He dropped to one knee, smashed the Shadowmaster down on the other.

I heard bones break. The world would have heard an earth-shaking scream if Narayan had not been so good with a rumel. He looped Shadowspinner's neck on the fly, as Ram hurled him down. Falling with Spinner, he had a tight loop on when the cry tried to force its way out.

Ram and Narayan both hung on.

Blade stepped inside the tent, casually drove his blade through Shadowspinner's heart. "I know you people have your ways, but let's not take chances."

There is an incredible vitality in someone like Shadowspinner. Blade was right. Even stabbed several times and thoroughly strangled, back broken, Shadowspinner kept struggling. Ram, Narayan, and both arm-holders hung on. I stepped up and helped Blade cut and stab.

Swan stood outside the gap in the tent and gawked, so rattled he could do nothing but keep watch. Poor Swan. War and violence just were not his thing.

We carved Shadowspinner into a half dozen pieces before he stopped struggling. We stood around the results. All of us were covered with blood. Nobody seemed inclined to do anything but pant and wonder if we'd really succeeded. Narayan, who seldom showed any humor, broke the spell. "Am I a Strangler saint now, Mistress?"

"Three times over. You're immortal. We'd better get out of here. Everybody grab a piece."

Swan made a choked, questioning noise.

I told him, "The only way to make sure is burn him to ash and scatter the ashes. Someone like Longshadow could bring him back even now."

Swan dumped his last meal. Even so, he looked

shamed, as though he thought he had contributed nothing.

I picked up Spinner's head. As I passed I winked and gave Swan's hand a squeeze. That should take his mind off his troubles.

The moon was up. It was a day short of full. Barely over the horizon, it was an orange monster. I gestured for the others to hurry, while there were still shadows to mask our going.

We were halfway to the perimeter when a terrible howl rolled down out of the night. Something wobbled across the face of the moon. Another howl tore the night. There was deadly agony in it.

Ram shoved me. "Got to run, Mistress. Got to run."

All around us Shadowlander soldiers rose to see what the racket was.

Chapter Fifty-Seven

Croaker glanced at the moon as he entered the city barracks. Not four hours had passed since the attack but already all Taglios knew the Shadowmasters had struck at the Prahbrindrah Drah. The city was united in outrage.

Already the city knew that the Liberator was alive, that he had feigned death in order to lead their enemies into a fatal mistake. The military compound was swamped with men who wanted to rampage through the Shadowlands till not a blade of grass survived.

It would not last. He could do nothing with this ill-armed and untrained horde. But for their sakes he ordered them to assemble at the fortress Lady had begun, then move south in forces of five thousand. They could sort themselves out on the road.

He suspected most would change their minds before they reached Ghoja. However strong their rage they did not have the supporting resources to mount a vengeance campaign. But he knew they would not

listen, so told them what they wanted to hear and
stood aside.

The Prahbrindrah Drah accompanied him. The
prince was in a rage himself, but a rage channelled
by realism. Croaker discharged his duties to those
who wanted him to be larger than life, then found
the horses that had pulled the coach. While they
were being prepared he stamped around the barracks gathering equipment and supplies. Nobody
questioned him. Would-be soldiers stared at him like
he was a ghost.

He took a bow and black arrows from hiding.
Soulcatcher had brought them out of Dejagore with
his armor. "These were a gift a long time ago. Before
I was anything but a physician. They've served me
well. I save them for special times. Special times are
here."

An hour later the two left the city. The prince wondered aloud if he had made the right choice, out-
arguing his sister about joining Croaker. Croaker
told him, "Turn back if you want. We don't have time
to examine our hearts and dither over choices. Before you go, though, tell me where Lady sent those
archers."

"Which archers?"

"The ones who killed the priests. I know her. She
wouldn't have kept them with her. She would've sent
them somewhere out of the way."

"Vehdna-Bota. To guard the ford."

"Then we ride to Vehdna-Bota. Or I do, if you're
going home."

"I'm coming with you."

Chapter Fifty-Eight

There was no escape from the Shadowlander camp. We were trapped. And I did not know what to do.

Ram said, "Be Kina." Big, gentle, slow Ram. He thought faster than I did.

It was a task of illusion, only slightly more difficult than making witchfires run over armor. It took just a minute to transform both of us. Meantime, the Shadowlanders closed in, though not with the enthusiasm you would expect of men who had caught their enemies flatfooted.

I raised Shadowspinner's head high. They recognized it. I used an augmentation spell to make my voice carry. "The Shadowmaster is dead. I have no quarrel with you. But you can join him if you insist."

Swan had an impulse. He bellowed, "Kneel, you swine! Kneel to your mistress!"

They looked at him, a foot taller than the tallest of them, pale as snow, golden-maned. A demon in man's form? They looked at Blade, almost as exotic. They looked at me and at Shadowspinner's head.

Ram said, "Kneel to the Daughter of Night." He was so close I could feel him shaking. He was scared to death. "The Child of Kina is among you. Beg for her mercy."

Swan grabbed the nearest Shadowlander, forced him to his knees.

I still do not believe it. The bluff worked. One by one, they knelt. Narayan and his arm-holders started chanting. They chose something basic, repeated mantras, of a sort common in Gunni ceremonials and Shadar services. They differed mainly in including lines like, "Show mercy, O Kina. Bless Thy devoted child, who loves Thee," and, "Come to me, O Mother of Night, while blood is upon my tongue."

"Sing!" Swan bellowed. "Sing, you scum!" Typically Swan, he roared around forcing the slow to kneel and the mute to cry out. His actions were not sane. Sane men do not force enemies who outnumber them a thousand to one. They should have torn us apart. The thought never occurred to them.

"We are a feeble-minded species," Blade observed in wonder. "But you'll have to keep escalating or they'll start thinking."

"Get me water. Lots of water." I held the Shadowmaster's head high and shouted for silence. "The devil is dead! The Shadowmaster is cast down. You are free. You have won the countenance of the goddess. She has blessed you though you have turned your faces away for generations, though you have denied and reviled her. But your hearts know the truth and she blesses you." I raised the intensity of my witchfire showmanship, became a fire with a face. "She has given you freedom but no gift is free."

Blade brought a waterskin. "I need a goblet, too," I whispered. "Keep the water out of sight." I continued trying to generate a state of hysteria. That was less difficult than reason suggested it should be. The Shadowlanders were tired, terrified, hated the Shadowmasters. Narayan led another singalong. Blade brought me a goblet from Shadowspinner's tent. I prepared it. The spell was difficult but once again I achieved an unexpected success.

I knew the water in the goblet was water. It tasted like water when I took a drink. "I drink the blood of my enemy." To the Shadowlanders it looked like blood when Narayan and his arm-holders started using it to smear marks on Shadowlander foreheads. I invested those marks with the power to stick. Those men would bear the stain of blood as long as they lived.

They even put up with that. A lot of them. A lot decided to try their legs and headed for home.

After a few hundred had been marked I ordered the Shadowlander officers to join me. Several score did so, but most had chosen to stretch their legs. Their class was more committed to the Shadowmasters than were the rank and file.

I told the Shadowlander officers, "There is a price for freedom as there's a price for everything. You are mine now. You owe Kina. She asks one task of you."

They did not ask what. They wondered if they had been stupid to stay.

"Continue to beleaguer Dejagore. But don't fight the men trapped there. Take them prisoner when they try to escape, expecting only those called the Nar. They're enemies of the goddess."

That was what they had been doing anyway, I learned. The flooding had played havoc with what food stores remained in the city. Mogaba's rationing ignored the natives. Disease was rampant. The natives had revolted already. Mogaba had thrown hundreds from the wall to drown. The lake swarmed with corpses.

Such draconian measures had cost Mogaba the support of many of his soldiers. They had begun deserting. Thus the prisoners in the camp stockade.

There had been nothing but silence from that stockade. Maybe the prisoners did not know what was happening. Maybe they were scared to attract attention. I sent Blade to let them out and tell them where to find Mather.

If the Shadowlanders did not stop me I'd have to accept this absurd twist as real.

They did not raise a murmur. At dawn they marched off to take their posts in the hills.

Narayan sidled up wearing his biggest grin. "Have you doubts yet, Mistress?"

"Doubts? About what?"

"Kina. Have we her countenance or not?"

"We have somebody's. I'll take Kina. I haven't seen anything this unlikely since my husband ... I wouldn't believe it if I wasn't here."

"They have lived under the Shadowmasters for a generation. They've never been permitted to do anything but what they're told to do. Penalties for disobedience were terrible."

That was part of it. So was the will to defy oppression. And maybe Kina had something to do with it, too. I did not intend looking the gift horse in the mouth.

The majority of the prisoners had gone. I had had two held to interview. I told Narayan, "I'll see Sindhu and Murgen now."

They came. Sindhu remained Sindhu, wide and stolid and brief. He told me what he had seen. He told me we had friends there. They would stay in place, ready to serve their goddess. He told me Mogaba was a stubborn man who meant to hang on to the last man, who did not care that Dejagore had become a hell of disease and hunger.

Murgen told me, "Mogaba wants a place in the Annals. He's like Croaker was about throwing up times when the Company suffered worse."

Murgen was about thirty. He reminded me of Croaker. He was tall, lean, permanently sad. He had been the Company standardbearer and Croaker's understudy as Annalist. In the normal course twenty years down the road he might have become Captain. "Why did you desert?" It was not the sort of thing he would do, regardless of his opinion of his commander.

"I didn't. One-Eye and Goblin sent me to find you. They thought I could get through. They were wrong. They didn't give me enough help."

One-Eye and Goblin were minor sorcerers, old as sin, perpetually at loggerheads. Together with Murgen they were the last of the Black Company from the north, the last of those who had elected Croaker Captain and made me his Lieutenant.

We talked. He told me the men we had recruited coming south were disaffected with Mogaba. He said, "He's trying to make the Company over into crusaders. He doesn't see it as a warrior brotherhood of outcasts. He wants it to be a bunch of religious warriors."

Sindhu interjected, "They worship the goddess, Mistress. They think. But their heresies are revolting. They are worse than disbelief."

Why was he incensed? A prolonged exchange failed to illuminate me. No godless person can comprehend those minute distinctions in doctrine that provide true believers excuse for mayhem. It is hard enough to accept the fact that they really believe the nonsense of their faiths. I always wonder if they are pulling my leg with a straight face.

Those two gave me a lot to digest. I tried. But it was morning. Sleep or no sleep, it was time to be sick. I was sick.

Chapter Fifty-Nine

Longshadow's insubstantial messengers warned him
of Howler's return long before Howler appeared. He
went to Howler's landing place to wait. He waited.
And waited. And grew troubled. Had the little ragbag undertaken some treachery at the last instant?

No, shadows said. No. He was coming. He was
coming.

He was slow. He was in mortal agony. Never had
he endured such pain, never had he suffered so long.
Pain obliterated consciousness. All that remained
was will supported by immense talent. He knew only
that he had to go on, that if he yielded to the pain he
would tumble from the sky and end his life in the
wastes.

He screamed till his throat was raw, till he could
scream no more. And the poison continued spreading through his old flesh, eating him alive, raising
the level of pain.

He was lost. None could save him but one who wanted him destroyed.

The blazing, crystal-topped towers of Overlook rose above the horizon.

Howler was but a few leagues away, shadows said, barely able to keep moving. He had the woman but was otherwise alone.

It began to make sense. Howler had had to fight. Senjak had been stronger than anticipated. Let Howler get her here. Let Howler manage that. Once he had the woman he would have no more need of the Howler. The woman's knowledge would be enough.

Then shadows came from somewhere far away, frolicking in with news that had him cursing before he heard the half.

Shadowspinner slain! Killed by the devotees of that mad goddess Senjak had claimed.

Was there no end to the bad news? Could not two good things happen in succession? Must a triumph always presage a disaster?

Stormgard was lost. Shadowspinner's host would evaporate like the dew. Half the Shadow empire's armed strength would disappear before sunset. Those ragged remnants of the Black Company would come out of the city. That madman who led them would pursue his insane quest.

But he had Senjak. He had a living library of every power and evil ever conceived by the mind of man. Once he broached that cask nothing on earth could deny him. He would be more powerful than even she had been, the equal of her husband at his zenith. There were things locked in her head she would never use. There had been a core of softness to her at her hardest. He was not soft. He would not discard a tool. He would rule. His empire would dwarf the Domination and the Lady's successor empire. The world would be his. There was no one in it who could stand in his way. No one could match him

>ower for power now, with Howler crippled and un-
der sentence of death.

A random crow fluttered by, behaving as a normal
crow should, but its flight brought filth to his lips.
He had forgotten, if only for a moment. There *was*
one. *She* was loose out there somewhere.

The Howler's carpet came wobbling down, Howler's gurgling agony preceding it. It plunged the last
dozen feet, collapsed. Longshadow cursed again. Another tool broken. The woman, unconscious, tumbled off. She lay still, snoring. Howler tumbled, too,
and did not stop moving when he stopped rolling.
His body jerked convulsively. A whine poured from
him between attempts to scream.

A cold chill crept Longshadow's spine. Senjak
could not have done this. A poisonous sorcery of tre-
mendous potency was gnawing at the little wizard.
It was so powerful he could not defeat it alone.

There was something terrible loose in the world.

He knelt. He rested his hands on Howler, forcing
down his loathing. He reached inside and fought the
poison and pain. It retreated a little. He pushed himself. It retreated farther.

The respite gave Howler strength to join the struggle. Together they fought it till it receded far enough
for Howler to regain his reason. The little sorcerer
gasped, "The Lance. They have the Lance. I did not
sense it. Her bodyguard stabbed me twice."

Longshadow was too shocked to curse.

The Lance was not lost! The enemy had it! He
croaked, "Do they know what they have?" They had
not before. Only the mad captain in Stormgard knew
what it was. If they learned the truth . . .

"I don't know," Howler squeaked. He started
shaking again. "Don't let me die."

The Lance!

Take one weapon away and they found another.
Fate was a fickle bitch.

Longshadow said, "I won't let you die." He had
meant to until that moment. But they had the Lance.

He would need every tool he could find. He shouted at his servants. "Bring him inside. Hurry. Throw her into the keystone cell. Put shadows in there with her."

He cursed again. It would be a long time before he could tap that cask of knowledge. It would be a long battle saving Howler.

The poison eating Howler was the most potent in this world because it was not of this world, if legends were true.

He glanced southward, at the plain of glittering stone, shimmering in morning's light. Someday . . .

The Lance had come out of there in ancient times. It was a toy compared to what lay there still, ready to be take up by him who had the will to seize it.

Someday.

Chapter Sixty

I invested six days arranging my own investure of Dejagore. Fewer than six thousand men remained of the three great armies Shadowspinner had gathered. Half those men were substandard for various reasons. I strung them along the shores of the lake. My own men I posted behind them. Then I sent Murgen back to the city.

He did not want to go. I did not blame him. Mogaba might execute him. But somebody had to go to the survivors and let them know they could come out. He was to tell everyone but Mogaba's loyalists.

My own people did not understand. I did not explain. They had no need to know. They needed to carry out orders.

The night after Murgen left, several dozen Taglian soldiers deserted from the city. Their reports were not pleasant. Disease was worse. Mogaba had executed hundreds more natives and a dozen of his own troops. Only the Nar were not grumbling.

Mogaba knew Murgen was back, suspected he had

seen me, and was hunting him. He'd had a bitter confrontation with the Company wizards over the standardbearer.

Mutiny was in the offing—unless the desertions absorbed that energy. That would be a first. Nowhere in the Annals was there a record of a mutiny.

Narayan grew more nervous by the hour as he worried about his delayed Festival, frightened I would try to evade it. I kept reassuring him. "There's plenty of time. We have the horses. We'll go as soon as we have this set." Also, I wanted some idea what was happening south of us. I'd sent cavalry to see what effect news of Spinner's fate was having. Little information had come back yet.

The night before Narayan, Ram, and I headed north, six hundred men deserted Mogaba and swam or rafted out of Dejagore. I had them greeted as heroes, with promises of important positions in new formations.

Shadowspinner's head, with the brain removed and destroyed, greeted them at the entrance to my camp. It would be our totem in days to come, in lieu of the missing Company standard.

Six hundred in one night. Mogaba would be livid. His loyalists would make it difficult for that to happen again.

I gathered my captains, such as they were. "Blade, there's something I have to do up north. Narayan and Ram will go with me. I'd hoped to know more about the south before I left but we have to take what we get. I doubt Longshadow will do anything soon. Keep your patrols out and sit tight. I shouldn't be gone but two weeks. Three if I visit Taglios to report our success. You might reorganize now that we have some real veterans joining us. And consider integrating any Shadowlanders interested in enlisting. They could be helpful."

Blade nodded. He had few words to waste even now.

Swan looked at me with a sort of soulful longing. I winked, suggesting his time would come. I'm not sure why. I had no reason to lead him on. I did not mind him remaining attached to the Radisha. Maybe I was attracted. He was the best of the crop, in his way. But I did not want to stumble into that trap again.

The heart is a hostage, the old saw says. Better not to give it up.

Narayan was happier once we rode out. I was not thrilled but I needed his brotherhood. I had plans for them.

Shadowspinner might be dead but the struggle had just begun. Longshadow and Howler had to be faced, and all the armies they could call up. And if those failed at every confrontation in the field there was still Longshadow's fortress at Shadowcatch. Rumor had Overlook tougher than my own Tower at Charm had been and getting tougher every day.

I did not look forward to the struggle. Despite the luck I'd had, Taglios was not ready for that kind of fight.

Maybe luck had bought me time enough to raise my legions and train them, to mount leisurely expeditions, to find capable commanders, to retrain myself in the use of my lost skills.

My immediate goals had been attained. Taglios was in no immediate danger. I had my base. I was in undisputed command and unlikely to have more trouble with the priests or Mogaba. With care I could lock up the Stranglers as an adjunct to my will, an invisible arm able to dispense death anywhere someone defied me. My future looked rosy. The biggest potential nuisance was the wizard Smoke. And he could be handled.

Rosy. Positively rosy. Except for the dreams and the sickness, both of which were getting worse. Except for my beloved sister.

Will, Lady. The Will will reign triumphant. My husband had said that often, confident that nothing could resist his will.

He had believed that right up to the moment I killed him.

Chapter Sixty-One

Croaker trotted his mount into the garrison encampment above Vehdna-Bota ford, which was a minor crossing of the Main used mostly by locals and open only a few months each year. He dismounted, handed his reins to a gaping soldier who had recognized the Prahbrindrah Drah.

The prince needed help dismounting. The ride had been hell for him. Croaker had shown no mercy. The ride had been little better for him.

"You really do this for a living?" the prince groaned. His sense of humor had survived.

Croaker grunted. "Sometimes you can't waste time. It's not like this all the time."

"I'd rather be a farmer."

"Walk around. Work out the stiffness."

"That will irritate the sores."

"I'll put ointment on after we talk to whoever's in charge."

The soldier now held both horses. And stared. By now others had recognized them. Word flew around like swallows dipping and darting. An officer loped out of the only permanent structure in the compound, gathering his clothing around him. His eyes bugged. He dropped onto his face before his prince.

The Prahbrindrah Drah snapped, "Get up! I'm in no mood for that."

The officer rose murmuring honorifics.

The prince grumbled, "Forget me. I'm just following him. Talk to him."

The officer turned to Croaker. "I'm honored, Liberator. We thought you dead."

"I thought I was, too. For a while. And I need to get that way again. The prince and I are joining your company. We're not being watched now but we'll be hunted soon by a distant and wicked eye." He was sure the search had not yet begun because no crows had chased them during their ride. "When the search passes this way we want to be indistinguishable from your soldiers."

"You're in hiding?"

"More or less." Croaker explained some. He stretched the truth some, bent it some, made it clear that powerful enemies wanted to find him and that the fate of Taglios could hinge on their remaining anonymous till they joined Lady at Dejagore.

"First thing you do," he told the officer, "is make sure none of your men speak to anyone outside the camp. Our presence isn't to be discussed at all. Our enemies have spies everywhere. Most aren't human. A stray dog, a bird, a shadow could carry tales. Every man has to understand that. We can't be discussed. We'll take different names and become ordinary troopers."

"I don't quite understand, sir."

"I don't think I can explain. Take us being here as proof. I'm back, escaped from captivity, and I need to reach the main army. I can't alone, even disguised. Do you have men who know how to ride?"

"A few, possibly." Puzzled.

"These horses have to be returned to the new fortress. Hopefully before the hunt starts. They're a dead giveaway. Their riders should make no stops and should disguise themselves. We don't want them identified with this company."

Croaker had not discussed plans while travelling because someone might hear. But the prince got the drift quickly. "You're going to march this company down to Dejagore?"

"Yes. You and I will be archers in the ranks."

The prince groaned. "I have less experience walking than riding."

"And I have a tender ankle. We won't push." While Croaker talked his gaze darted, seeking the potential listener. He continued talking to the officer. Again and again he tried to drive home the need for the archers to keep quiet about their mission till they found Lady's army. One slip could kill them all. He made it sound like the Shadowmasters had all their men and demons out trying to destroy him and the prince and anyone with them.

True in theme, anyway.

The officer rounded up volunteers to return the stallions, impressed them with the need to deliver the animals rapidly, without telling anyone where Croaker and the prince had gone. He sent them off.

Croaker sighed. "I feel safer already. Get me a turban and some Shadar clothes and something to darken my hands and face. Prince, you look more Gunni."

Half an hour later they were ordinary archers except for accents. Croaker became Narayan Singh. Half the Shadar alive were Narayan Singh. The prince adopted the name Abu Lal Cadreskrah. He felt it would shield him from scrutiny because it suggested mixed Vehdna and Gunni parentage, which could only mean that his mother had been a Gunni prostitute. "No one in his right mind would think the Prahbrindrah Drah could demean himself that far."

Croaker chuckled. "Maybe so. Get some rest. Use

that horse liniment. We'll pull out as soon as we get stores and transport together."

A day and a half later, grimly silent, ready for anything, the archers crossed the river. Croaker grew more fearful and excited by the hour. How would Lady react when he turned up alive?

He was scared of the answer.

Chapter Sixty-Two

Longshadow did without sleep for six days while he fought the sorcery gnawing at Howler's flesh and soul. He triumphed, but barely. Then he collapsed.

Shadowcatch was an old, old city. Forever in the looming shadow of glittering stone, it was a repository for much ancient lore, much known nowhere else, much known only to Longshadow, who had plundered its libraries and had disposed of everyone who shared any knowledge he coveted.

Among the legends of the plain, which had been old when the city had been founded, was one about the Lances of Passion. It said their heads had been forged of metal taken from the sword of a demon king devoured by Kina during the great battle between Light and Shadow. That demon king's soul was imprisoned in the steel, fragmented amongst eight lance heads. He could not be restored while Kina slept.

The shafts of the lances, too, were the object of

legend. Two were supposed to have been formed from the thighbones of Kina herself, taken after she had been tricked into endless sleep. One was supposedly the penis of the Regent of Shadow, that Kina had hacked off during the great battle. The rest were supposed to be of wood from the tree in which the goddess of brotherly love, Rhavi-Lemna, had hidden her soul shortly before the Wolves of Shadow ran her down and devoured her, soon after Man was created. Kina had witnessed the concealment and had torn up the tree and had made it into arrows and lance shafts. If ever the Lords of Light did bring Rhavi-Lemna together again, out of the bellies of the hateful Wolves, she would have no soul. And they could not get that back for her while Kina lay sleeping.

Each of the outbound Free Companies of Khatovar had followed one of the Lances when they had broken into the world to bring on the Year of the Skulls. But who had sent them forth?

Longshadow could not be sure. The ghost-spirit of sleeping Kina? The Lords of Light, who would restore Rhavi-Lemna? The children of the demon king, who remained imprisoned in those lance heads while she slept? The Regent of Shadow, weary of being at a disadvantage in the lists of love?

The librarians of old recorded the return of all the Companies but one, the Black Company, which lost its own past and wandered aimlessly down the centuries, till it elected a Captain eager to seek out its roots.

Longshadow knew very little about the Lances but he did know more than anyone else alive. Howler and Catcher suspected some. No one else had a hint that the Black Company's standard was anything but an old artifact that had survived for centuries, till it vanished during the battle at Dejagore.

Only to resurface in Taglios, in the hands of a bodyguard.

Its recovery was high among Longshadow's priorities. He would send for it as soon as Howler recovered. He would devote his own time to harvesting the knowledge of his captive.

But first he slept, having conquered the Howler's wounds.

Chapter Sixty-Three

It took the imp Frogface five days to locate his mistress. Then he waited till the attention of Overlook's master lapsed before he made his way inside. He entered with trepidation. Longshadow was a powerful sorcerer, dreaded in the demon worlds.

His entry disturbed no one. Overlook's defenses were meant to stop shadows from the south. He found his mistress in a dark cell beneath the fortress's roots, her drugged mind in a cell of its own, deep inside her brain. He debated. He could forget her. He could help and maybe win his freedom. Freeing her was not within the specific orders she had given him.

He stretched out beside her, bit a hole in her throat, drank her blood. He cleansed it and returned it.

She wakened slowly, sensed what he was doing, let him finish. He closed the wound. She sat up in the darkness. "The Howler. Where am I?"

"Overlook."

"Why?"

"They mistook you for your sister."

She laughed bitterly. "My act was too good."

"Yes."

"Where is she?"

"Last seen near Dejagore. I hunted you for a week."

"And they couldn't see her? She's getting stronger. What about Croaker?"

"I've been hunting you."

"Find him. I want him back. I can't let him reach my sister. Do anything you have to to stop that."

"I'm forbidden to take life."

"Anything else, then, but keep them apart."

"You don't need help here?"

"I'll handle . . . You're free to roam here?"

"Pretty much. Parts are sealed behind spells only Longshadow can penetrate."

"Search the place. Tell me what everyone is doing. Then find Croaker and my sister."

The imp sighed. So much for gratitude.

She caught the sense of the sound. "Do it right and you're free. Forever."

"Right! I'm gone."

She waited for her captors to come receive their surprise. As she waited she heard the whispers of darkness carrying from the nearby plain. She caught some of what was said, began to taste the fear that plagued Longshadow.

She could not just sit there like a trapdoor spider, waiting. Longshadow and Howler were sleeping. She should go.

The very stones of Overlook had been hardened against sorcery. She melted her way out, for those stones would melt before they yielded.

The lower levels were dark. Surprising. Longshadow feared the dark. She climbed slowly, wary of ambushes, but she encountered no one. She grew nervous as she approached the light.

Nothing waited there, either. Apparently. Was the fortress deserted?

Something was wrong. She extended her senses, still detected nothing. Onward and upward. And more nothing. Where were the soldiers? There should be thousands, constantly scurrying like blood in the veins.

She spied a way out. She had to descend a stairway to reach it. She was halfway down when the attack came, a wave of little brown men carrying cruel halberds, wearing armor of wood and strange, ornate animal helmets.

She had a spell prepared, a summoning that taxed her limits. She struck a pose, loosed it. It broke a hole in the fabric of everything. Sparks of ten thousand colors flew. Something huge and ugly and hungry started through, tearing the hole wider. Steel left no mark upon its snout. Its snarls chilled the blood. It ripped itself out of the womb of elsewhere and flew after the garrison. Men screamed. It ran faster than they did.

Soulcatcher walked out into the night blanketing Overlook. "That will keep them busy." She looked north, angry. A long walk lay ahead of her.

Chapter Sixty-Four

The bridge I had wanted built was incomplete but we did cross on foot while soldiers brought our mounts across by the ford. My move was symbolic, meant to lend encouragement to the engineers.

Narayan was impressed and Ram was indifferent, except to say it was nice to cross the river without getting his feet wet. He did not see the implications of a bridge.

Because I was sick it took longer to reach Ghoja than I anticipated. We were pressed for time. Narayan rode the edge of panic but we reached the holy grove late the evening before the ceremonies. I was exhausted. I told Narayan, "You handle the arrangements. I can't do anything more."

He looked at me, concerned. Ram said, "You *must* see a physician, Mistress. Soon."

"I've decided to. When we're done here we head north. I can't take this much longer."

"The rains . . ."

The season would start soon. If we dallied in Tag-

ios we would return to the Main after it started ris-
ng. Already there were scattered showers every day.
'The bridge is there. We might have to leave our
mounts but we can get across."

Narayan nodded curtly. "I'll talk to the priests. See
that she rests, Ram. Initiation can be stressful."

That was the first I had heard it hinted that I was
expected to go through the same initiation ceremony
as everyone else. It irked me but I was too tired to
protest. I just lay there while Ram borrowed fire and
rice and prepared a meal. Several jamadars came to
pay their respects. Ram warned them off. No priests
came. By then I had sunk into a lassitude so deep I
did not bother to ask Ram if that was significant.

I caught movement from the corner of an eye, a
watcher where none should be. I turned, caught a
glimpse of a face.

That was no Deceiver. I had not seen that face
since before the fighting that had cost me Croaker.
Frogface, they called him. An imp. What was he doing here?

I could not catch him. I was way too weak. Nothing I could do but keep him in mind. I fell asleep as
soon as I'd eaten.

Drums wakened me. They were drums with deep
voices, the kind men sound by pounding with fists
or palms. Boom! Boom! Boom! No respite. Ram told
me they would not let up till next dawn. Other drums
with deeper voices joined them. I peered out of the
crude lean-to Ram had built for me. One was not far
away. The man pounding the drum used padded
mallets with handles four feet long. There was one
such drum at each of the wind's four quarters.

More drums throbbed within the temple. Ram as-
sured me it had been cleansed and sanctified.

I did not much care. I was as sick as ever I had
been. My night had been filled with the darkest
dreams yet, dreams in which the whole world suf-

fered from advanced leprosy. The smell lingered in my nostrils, worsening the sickness.

Ram had anticipated my condition. Maybe he had watched me in my sleep, predicting my sickness from how I rested. I don't know. But he put up a crude privacy screen so I would not become a public entertainment.

I was past the worst when Narayan came. "If you don't go see a physician after this I'll personally drag you to Taglios. Mistress. There's no reason not to take the time."

"I will. I will. You can count on it."

"I do. You're important to me. You're our future."

Chanting began in the temple. "Why is it different this time?"

"So much to crowd in. Ceremonial obligations and initiations. You won't have to do anything till tonight. Rest. And you'll rest again tomorrow if the ceremony wears you out."

Just lying around. Nothing to do. That was a strain itself. I could not recall a time when I'd had nothing to do but lie around. Once I got control of my nausea I tried to extend and stretch my talents.

They were coming back almost of their own accord. I was capable of more than I suspected. I was close to being a match for the wizard Smoke, now.

Good news must be balanced by bad, I suppose. My elation died when I looked up from cupped palms and found myself caught in a dream right there in broad daylight.

I could see both the horror of the worst dream and the grove around me. Neither seemed completely real. Neither was more substantial than the other.

I went from the caverns of death to a plain of death. I had gone there only rarely. I associated that plain with the battle during which Kina had devoured hordes of demons. A great black figure strode across the plain, her movements stylized, like Gunni dances. Each step shook the plain. I felt the shaking. It was as real as an earthquake.

She wore nothing. Her shape was not quite human. She had four arms and eight breasts. Each hand clutched something suggestive of death or warfare. She wore a necklace of baby skulls. From her girdle, like bunches of withered bananas, hung strings of what I first took to be severed thumbs but which, as she stamped closer, proved to be more singular and potent male appendages.

Her hairless head was shaped more like an egg than a human head. At first it impressed me as insectoid but she had a mouth like that of a carnivore. Blood dribbled down her chin. Her eyes were large and filled with fire.

The stench of old death preceded her.

That unexpected apparition shook me to the core.

And from some corner of memory Croaker stepped with his irreverent and sarcastic outlook. *Old Busybody smells ripe for her centennial bath. Might even be time for her to brush her teeth.*

The thought was so startling I looked around. Had someone spoken?

I was alone. It was just a thought in his style, loosened by the strain. When I looked forward again the apparition had faded. I shuddered.

The smell lingered. It was not imaginary. A man passing stopped, startled. He sniffed, looked odd, hurried off. I shuddered again.

Was that how it would be? Dreams awake and asleep, both?

I shuddered a third time, frightened. My will was not strong enough to resist *that*.

Several times during the day the stench came back. Mercifully, the apparition did not accompany it. I did not make myself vulnerable by opening channels of power again.

Narayan came when it was time. I had not seen him since morning. He had not seen me. He looked at me oddly. I asked, "What's the matter?"

"There's something . . . An aura? Yes. You feel like

the Daughter of Night should feel." He became embarrassed. "The initiations start in an hour. I talked to the priests. No woman has ever joined us before. There are no precedents. They decided you'll have to face it the way everyone does."

"I take it that's not . . ."

"The candidates stand naked before Kina while she judges their worthiness."

"I see." To say I was not thrilled would be an understatement, though, initially, my objection was a matter of vanity. I looked like hell. Like a famine victim, withering limbs and bloating belly. We'd seldom eaten well since we had fled from Dejagore.

I gave it some thought. It presented me with little choice, really. If I refused to disrobe, I suspected, I would not leave the grove alive. And I needed the Stranglers. I had plans for them. "I'll do what has to be done."

Narayan was relieved. "You won't have to expose yourself to everyone."

"No? Just to the priests and jamadars and other candidates and whoever is helping put on the show?"

"It's been arranged. There will be six candidates, the minimum permitted. There will be one high priest, his assistant, one jamadar as chief Strangler, with orders to strike down any chanter who raises his eyes from the floor. You may pick those three men yourself if you like."

Odd. "Why so thoughtful?"

Narayan whispered, "I shouldn't tell you. Opinion is divided about whether you're the true Daughter of Night. Those who do believe expect you to have the priest, his assistant, and the chief Strangler put to death after Kina bestows her favor. They want to risk the minimum number of men."

"What about the other candidates?"

"They won't remember."

"I see."

"I'll be among the chanters as your sponsor."

"I see." I wondered what would happen to him if

I failed. "I don't care who the priests and Strangler are."

He grinned. "Excellent, Mistress. You must prepare. Ram. Help me put the screen up again. Mistress, this is the robe you'll wear till you stand before the goddess." He handed me a white bundle. The robe looked like it had been used for generations without having been mended or cleaned.

I got ready.

Chapter Sixty-Five

The temple had changed inside. Fires burned, dull and red, around the perimeter. Their light sent shadows skulking over ugly carvings. A huge idol had materialized. It was a close representation of the thing from my vision, although equipped with an ornate headdress loaded with gold and silver and gemstones. The idol's eyes were cabochon rubies, each a nation's ransom. Its fangs were crystal.

Three heads lay under the idol's raised left foot. Priests were dragging a corpse away when my group of candidates entered. The dead man had been tortured before he had been beheaded.

Ten men lay on their faces to the right, ten more to the left. A four-foot aisle passed between groups. I recognized Narayan's back. The twenty chanted continuously, "Come O Kina unto the world and make Thy Children whole we beseech Thee Great Mother," so swiftly the words ran together. I was last in line. The chief Strangler stepped into the aisle behind me, black rumel in hand. I suspect his main function was to stop a candidate who developed cold feet, not to eliminate chanters who peeped.

Twenty feet of clear space lay between the chanters and the dais where the goddess stood. The three heads lay at eye level. Two appeared to watch our approach. The third stared at the sole of Kina's foot, clawed toes inches from its nose.

Two priests stood to my right, beside a tall stand supporting several golden vessels.

The ceremony started out basic. Each candidate reached a mark and dropped his robe, moved to another mark on a line, abased himself and murmured a ritual prayer. The prayer just petitioned Kina to accept the appellant: in the last case, me, as her daughter. But when I spoke the words a gust of wind blew through. A new presence filled the place. It was cold and hungry and carried the smell of carrion. The assistant priest jumped. This was not customary.

We candidates rose, knelt with our palms resting atop our thighs. The head priest ran through some extended rigamarole in a language neither Taglian nor Deceivers' cant. He presented us to the idol as though it were Kina herself. While he yammered, his assistant poured dark fluid from a tall spouted container into one like a gravy boat. Once he stopped chattering the head priest made holy passes over that smaller vessel, lifted it, presented it to the goddess, went to the far end of the line, placed the pouring end of the vessel to the candidate's lips and filled his mouth. The man had his eyes closed. He swallowed.

The next man took his with his eyes open. He choked. The priest showed no reaction, nor did he when two more men did the same.

My turn.

Narayan was a liar. He had prepared me but he had told me it was all illusion. This was no illusion. It was blood—with some drug added that gave it a slightly herby, bitter taste. Human blood? I do not know. Our seeing that body dragged away was no accident. We were supposed to think about it.

I got through it. I'd never endured anything like it but I'd been through terrible things before. I neither hesitated nor twitched. I told myself I was just minutes from taking control of the most terrible power in this end of the world.

That presence moved again.

It might take control of me.

The chief priest handed the vessel to his assistant, who returned it to the stand, began to chant.

The lights went out.

Absolute darkness engulfed the temple. I was startled, thinking something unusual had happened. When no one got excited I changed my mind. Must be part of the initiation.

That darkness lasted half a minute. Midway through, a scream rent the air, filled with despair and outrage.

Light returned as suddenly as it had gone.

I was stunned.

It was hard to take everything in.

There were only five candidates now. The idol had moved. Its raised foot had fallen, crushing one of the heads. Its other foot had risen. The body of the man who had been two to my left lay beneath it. His head, held by the hair, dangled from one of the idol's hands. Before the lights had gone out that hand had clutched a bunch of bones. Another hand that had clutched a sword still did so but now that blade glistened. There was blood on the idol's lips and chin and fangs. Its eyes gleamed.

How had they managed it? Was there some mechanical engine inside the idol? Had the priest and his assistant done the murder? They would have had to move fast. And I had not heard a sound but the scream.

The priests seemed startled, too.

The chief priest darted to the pile of robes, flung one my way, resumed his place, ran through one abbreviated chant, cried out, "She has come! She is among us! Praised be Kina, who has sent her Daughter to stand beside us."

I covered my nakedness.

The normal flow had been disrupted somehow. The results had the priests ecstatic and, at the same time, at a loss what to do next.

What *do* you do when old prophecies come true? I've never met a priest who honestly expected miracles in his own lifetime. For them miracles are like good wine, best when aged.

They decided to suspend normal business and go straight to the celebration. That meant candidates got initiated without standing before Kina's judgment. It meant human sacrifices forgotten. Quite unwittingly I saved the lives of twenty enemies of the Stranglers scheduled to be tortured and murdered during that night. The priests freed them to tell the world that the Deceivers were real and had found their messiah, that those who did not come to Kina soon would be devoured in the Year of the Skulls.

A fun bunch of guys, Croaker would say.

Narayan took me back to our fire, where he told Ram to drive off anyone with the temerity to bother me. He settled me with profuse apologies for not having prepared me better. He sat beside me and stared into the flames.

"It's come, eh?" I asked after a while.

He understood. "It's come. It's finally real. Now there's no doubt left."

"Uhm." I left him to his thoughts for a while before I asked, "How did they do that with the idol, Narayan?"

"What?"

"How did they make it move while it was dark?"

He shrugged, looked at me, grinned feebly, said, "I don't know. That's never happened before. I've seen at least twenty initiations. Always one of the candidates is chosen to die. But the idol never moves."

"Oh." I could think of nothing else till I asked, "Did you feel anything in there? Like something was with us?"

"Yes." He was shivering. The night was not cold. He said, "Try to sleep, Mistress. We have to get started early. I want to get you to that physician."

I lay me down, grimly reluctant to drift off into the land of nightmare, but I did not stay awake long. I was too exhausted, physically and emotionally. The last thing I saw was Narayan squatting there, staring into the flames.

Much to think on, Narayan. Much to think on, now.

There was no dreams that night. But there was sickness aplenty in the morning. I threw up till there was nothing left but bile.

Chapter Sixty-Six

The imp drifted away from the grove. The woman had not been hard to find, though that had taken longer than he had hoped. Now for the man.

Nothing. For a long, long time, not a trace.

He was not in Taglios. A frantic search produced nothing. Logic suggested he would search for his woman. He would not know her present whereabouts so he would head toward her last known location.

He was not at the ford. There was no sign he had visited Ghoja. Therefore, he had not. They would be talking about it still, as they were talking about him still in Taglios.

No Croaker. But a whole horde was headed for the ford, descending from the city. The woman had just missed meeting them headed north. A stroke of luck, that, but there was no way to keep her from learning he was alive. Not in the long run.

The prime mission was to keep them apart, anyway.

Was he amongst that mob? Couldn't be. Their talk would have pointed him out.

The imp resumed his quest. If the man had not crossed at Ghoja and was not amongst the horde, then he would cross the river elsewhere. Sneaking.

He visited Vehdna-Bota last because it seemed the least likely crossing. He expected to find nothing there. Nothing was what he found. But this was a significant nothing. A company of archers was supposed to be stationed there.

He tracked those archers and found his man.

He had to make a decision. Run to his mistress—which would take time because he would have to find her—or take steps on his own?

He chose the latter course. The rainy season was fast approaching. It might do his job for him. They could not get together if they could not cross the river.

Amidst a moonless night the growing Ghoja bridge collapsed. Most of its timberwork washed away. The engineers could not figure out what went wrong. They understood only that it was too late to rebuild this year.

Any Taglian forces not back across before the waters rose would spend half a year on the Shadowlander side.

Satisfied, the imp went looking for his mistress.

Chapter Sixty-Seven

The archers halted in sight of the Taglian main camp. "We're safe now," Croaker told the prince. "Let's make a proper entrance."

Cavalry had found them two days earlier, forty miles north. Horsemen had visited regularly since yesterday. The archers had kept their mouths shut admirably. Willow Swan had led one patrol. He had not recognized anyone.

Croaker had had the captain borrow horses. The archers' transport consisted only of mules enough to carry what the soldiers themselves could not. Two mounts had arrived an hour ago, saddled.

The prince dressed up as a prince. Croaker donned what he called his work clothes, a warlord's outfit given him back when he had been every Taglian's hero. He had not taken it along when he had gone south the first time.

He dug out the Company standard and reassembled it. "I'm ready. Prince?"

"Whenever." The march south had been hard on

the Prahbrindrah Drah but he had endured the hardships without complaint. The soldiers were pleased.

They mounted up and led the archers toward the camp. The first crows arrived during that passage. Croaker laughed at them. " 'Stone the crows!' People in Beryl used to say that when the Company was there. I never did figure out what it meant but it sounds like a damned good way to do business."

The prince chuckled and agreed, then faced the greetings of soldiers from the camp who could not decide which of their visitors was more unlikely.

Croaker spied familiar faces: Blade, Swan, Mather . . . Hell! That looked like Murgen. It *was* Murgen! But nowhere did he spy the face he wanted to see.

Murgen approached in little spurts, each halving the distance between himself and his Captain. Croaker dismounted, said, "It's me. I'm real."

"I saw you die."

"You saw me hit. I was still breathing when you took off."

"Oh. Yeah. But the shape you were in . . ."

"It's a long story. We'll sit around and talk about it all night. Get drunk if there's anything drinkable." He glanced at Swan. Where Swan lighted, beer usually appeared. "Here. You left this behind when you went off to play Widowmaker." He shoved the standard at Murgen.

The younger man took it like he expected it to bite. But once he had hold of it he ran his hands up and down the shaft of the lance. "It really is! I thought it was lost for sure. Then it's really you?"

"Alive and in a mood to do some serious asskicking. But I've got something else on my mind right now. Where's Lady?"

Blade made a perfunctory acknowledgment of the prince's presence, said, "Lady went north with Narayan and Ram. Eight, nine days ago. Said she had business that couldn't wait."

Croaker cursed.

Swan said, "Nine days ago. That really him? Not somebody fixed up to fool us?"

Mather said, "It's him. The Prahbrindrah Drah wouldn't lend himself to any deceit."

"Ain't that my luck. Ain't that the story of my life? Just when my future is so bright I have to wear blinders."

Croaker noted a broad, stubby man behind Blade. He did not know the man but recognized personal power. This was someone important. And someone not thrilled to see the Liberator alive. He would bear watching.

"Murgen. Stop making love to that thing. Fill me in on what's been happening. I've been out of touch for weeks." Or months, if filtered truths were considered. "Can somebody take this animal? So we can all go find some shade?"

There was more confusion in the camp than might have been if Longshadow had materialized there. The return of a dead man always complicates things.

Without appearing to take particular note Croaker noticed that the short, wide man stayed close, pretending insignificance beside Blade, Swan, and Mather. He never spoke.

Murgen talked about his experiences since the disastrous battle. Blade told his tale. Swan tossed in a few dozen anecdotes of his own.

"Shadowspinner himself, eh?" Croaker asked.

Swan said, "That's the old boy's head on the pole over yonder."

"The field gets narrower."

Murgen said, "Let's hear your story while it's still news."

"You going to put it in the Annals? You been keeping them up?"

Embarrassed, the younger man nodded. "Only I had to leave them in the city when I came out."

"I understand. I look forward to reading the Book of Murgen. If it's any good you've got the job for life."

Swan said, "Lady was doing one of them things herself."

Everyone looked at him.

He wilted some. "Well, what she really did was talk about writing one. When she got the time. I don't think she ever really put anything down. She just said how she had to keep some things straight in her head so she could get them down right. The obligation of history, she called it."

"Let me think a minute," Croaker said. He picked up a stone, threw it at a crow. The bird squawked and fluttered a few feet but did not take the hint. It was Catcher's, all right. She was back in circulation, free. Or in alliance with her captors.

After a while Croaker observed, "We have a lot of catching up to do. But I suspect the critical business is to end this problem with Mogaba. How many men does he have left in there?"

"Maybe a thousand, fifteen hundred," Murgen guessed.

"One-Eye and Goblin stayed when he's become their enemy?"

"They can protect themselves," Murgen said. "They don't want to come out here. They think there's something waiting to get them. They want to sit tight till Lady gets her powers back."

"Powers back? Is she? Nobody mentioned that." But he had suspected it for a long time.

"She is," Blade said. "Not as fast as she'd like."

"Nothing happens as fast as she'd like. What are they afraid of, Murgen?"

"Shifter's apprentice. Remember her? She was there when we got rid of Shifter and Stormshadow. She took off on us. They say she's locked into the forvalaka shape but still has her own mind. And she's out to get them for killing Shifter. Especially One-Eye." One-Eye had killed the wizard Shapeshifter because Shifter had killed his brother Tom-Tom long ago. "The wheel of vengeance turning." Croaker sighed. "She's maybe out to get everybody who was involved."

"That angle hasn't come up before."

"I think they're imagining it."

"You never know with those clowns." Croaker leaned back, closed his eyes. "Tell me more about Mogaba."

Murgen had a lot to say.

Croaker observed, "I always suspected there was more to him than he showed. But human sacrifices? That's a little much."

"They didn't just sacrifice them. They ate them."

"What?"

"Well, their hearts and livers. Some of them. There was only four or five guys really into that with Mogaba."

Croaker glanced at the wide man. The fellow was indignant to the point of explosion. Croaker said, "I guess that explains why Gea-Xle was such a peaceful town. If the city guard *eats* criminals and rebels . . ." He chuckled. But cannibalism was not humorous. "You, sir. We haven't been introduced. You seem to have strong feelings about Mogaba."

Murgen said, "That's Sindhu. One of Lady's special friends."

"Oh?" What did that mean?

Sindhu said, "They have abandoned themselves to Shadow. The true Deceiver seldom spills blood. He opens the golden path without tempting the goddess's thirst. Only the blood of an accursed enemy should be spilled. Only an accursed enemy should be tortured."

Croaker glanced around. "Anybody know what the hell he's talking about?"

Swan said, "Your girlfriend is running with some strange characters." He chose a northern dialect. "Maybe Cordy can explain. He's spent more time trying to figure it out."

Croaker nodded. "I suppose we ought to put an

end to this. Murgen. You game to go back again?
Take a message to Mogaba?"

"I don't want to sound like a slacker, Captain, but
not unless it's an order. He wants to kill me. Crazy
as he's gotten, he might try it with you standing right
there watching."

"I'll get somebody else."

"I'll do it," Swan said.

Mather jumped him. "It's not your no nevermind,
Willow."

"Yes, it is. I got to find out something about myself, Cordy. I wasn't no help when we went after
Shadowspinner. I froze up. I want to see if something's wrong with me. Mogaba is the guy to show
me. He's about as spooky as a Shadowmaster."

"Damned poor thinking, Willow."

"I never did have any sense. I'll go, Captain. When
you want to do it?"

Croaker glanced around. "Anything going on,
Blade? Any reason we shouldn't walk over and take
a look, send Swan?"

"No."

Chapter Sixty-Eight

Life is full of surprises. I don't mind the little ones. They add spice. It's the big ones that get me.

I stumbled into a parade of big ones at my new fortress.

The first thing they did was arrest all three of us and shove us into a cell. Nobody bothered to explain. Nobody said anything. They seemed surprised I did not go berserk.

We sat in gloom and waited. I was afraid Smoke had won his point at last and had turned the Prahbrindrah Drah against me. Narayan said maybe I'd missed a few priests and this was all their fault.

We did not talk much. We used only sign and cant when we did. No telling who was listening.

Three hours after we went into the cell the door opened. The Radisha Drah strode in, backed by a squad of her guards. It got crowded in there. She glared at me. "Who are you?"

"What kind of question is that? Lady. Captain of the Black Company. Who should I be?"

"She even takes a deep breath, kill her." The Radisha wheeled on Ram. "You. Stand up."

Faithful Ram might not have heard. He looked to me. I nodded. Then he stood. The Radisha grabbed a torch from a guard, held it close to Ram, circled him slowly. She sniffed and sniffed. After her third circuit she relaxed. "Sit. You're who you're supposed to be. But the woman. Who is she?"

That seemed a little too tough for Ram. He had to think about it. He looked at me again. I nodded. He said, "She told you."

She looked at me. "Can you prove you're Lady?"

"Can you prove you're the Radisha Drah?"

"I have no need. No one is masquerading as me."

I got it. "That bitch! She never was short on nerve. Walked in here and took over, eh? What did she do?"

The Radisha considered some more. "We have the right one this time. Guards. You may go." They went. The Radisha said, "She didn't do much. Mostly played up to my brother. She wasn't here that long. Then somebody called the Howler knocked her out and carried her off. Thinking she was you, Croaker said."

"Ha! Serves the bitch . . . Who said?"

"Croaker. Your Captain. She brought him with her, disguised as that one." She indicated Ram.

Some sort of impenetrable membrane lay between my ears and my heart. Very carefully, before it broke, I asked, "Did Howler take him, too? Where is he?"

"He and my brother went to find you. Disguised. He said she would look for him as soon as she got free of the Howler and Longshadow."

My mind slid away from the unbelievable, dwelt on crows. Now I knew why there had been none spying till shortly before we reached the fortress. She had been in unfriendly hands. "He went to Deja-gore?"

"That's my guess. My fool brother went with him."

"And I came here." I laughed, maybe crazily. That

membrane was giving. "I'd appreciate it if everyone would leave. I need some time alone."

The Radisha nodded. "I understand. You two come with me."

Narayan rose but Ram did not budge. I asked, "Will you wait outside, Ram? Just for a while?"

"Yes, Mistress." He went out with the others. I'd bet he did not go five feet past the door.

Before they left Narayan started telling the Radisha I needed a physician.

The anger and frustration faded. I calmed down, thought I understood.

Croaker had been struck down by a random arrow. In the confusion his corpse had disappeared. Only now I knew he had not been a corpse at all. And I thought I knew whence that arrow had come. My everloving sister. Just to get even with me for having thwarted her attempt to displace me when I'd been empress in the north.

I knew how her mind worked. I had evidence she was loose again. She would continue to keep us apart and punish me through him.

She was whole again. She had the power to do whatever she willed. She had been second only to me when I was at my peak.

I came as close to despair as I've ever come.

The Radisha invited herself in without knocking. A tiny woman in a pink sari accompanied her. The Radisha said, "This is Doctor Dahrhanahdahr. Her family are all physicians. She's my own physician. She's the best. Even her male colleagues admit she's marginally competent."

I told the woman what I had been suffering. She listened and nodded. When I was done, she told me, "You'll have to disrobe. I think I know what it is but I'll have to look."

The Radisha stepped to the cell door, used her own clothing to cover the viewport. "I'll turn my back if your modesty demands it."

"What modesty?" I stripped.

Actually, I was embarrassed. I did not want to be seen looking as bad as I did.

The physician spent a few minutes examining me. "I thought so."

"What is it?"

"You don't know?"

"If I did I would've done something about it. I don't like being sick." At least the dreams had let up since the initiation. I could sleep.

"You'll have to put up with it a while longer." Her eyes sparkled. That was a hell of an attitude for a physician. "You're pregnant."

Chapter Sixty-Nine

Croaker posted himself where he could be clearly seen from the city. Murgen stood beside him with the standard. Swan set off in a boat the cavalry had stolen off the banks of the river north of the hills.

Murgen asked, "You think he'll come?"

"Maybe not himself. But somebody will. He'll want to make sure, one way or the other."

Murgen indicated the Shadowlander soldiers along the shoreline. "You know what that's about?"

"I can guess. Mogaba and Lady both want to be Captain. She took care of Shadowspinner but thought it might be inconvenient if she told Mogaba. As long as he's trapped in Dejagore he's no problem."

"Right."

"Stupid. Nothing like this ever happened before, Murgen. Nowhere in the Annals can you find a squabble over the succession. Most Captains come in like me, kicking and screaming."

"Most don't have a holy mission. Lady and Mogaba both do."

"Lady?"

"She's decided she'll do anything to get even with the Shadowmasters for killing you."

"That's real sane. But it sounds like her. Looks like Swan's gotten some attention. Your eyes are better than mine."

"Somebody black is getting in the boat with him. Would Mogaba make up his mind that fast?"

"He's sending somebody."

Swan's passenger was Mogaba's lieutenant Sindawe, an officer good enough to have commanded a legion. Croaker saluted. "Sindawe."

The black man returned the salute tentatively. "Is it you indeed?"

"In the flesh."

"But you're dead."

"Nope. Just a story spread by our enemies. It's a long tale. Maybe we don't have time for it all. I hear things aren't good over there."

Sindawe guided Croaker out of sight of the city, settled on a rock. "I'm caught on the horns of a dilemma."

Croaker settled facing him, winced. His ankle had taken a lot of abuse coming south. "How so?"

"My honor is sworn to Mogaba as first lord of the Nar. I must obey. But he's gone mad."

"So I gather. What happened? He was the ideal soldier even when he didn't agree with the way I ran things."

"Ambition. He's a driven man. He became first lord because he's driven." Among the Nar, chieftainship was determined by a sort of soldierly athletic contest. The all-round best man at physical skills became commander. "He joined your expedition thinking you weak, likely to perish quickly. He saw no obstacle to his replacing you, whereupon he would become one of the immortal stars of the chronicles. He's still a good soldier. But he does everything for Mogaba's sake, not that of the Company or its commission."

"Most organizations have mechanisms for handling such problems."

"The mechanism among the Nar is challenge. Combat or contest. Which is no good here. He's still the quickest, fastest, strongest amongst us. He's still the best tactician, begging your pardon."

"I never claimed to be a genius. I got to be Captain 'cause everybody voted against me. I didn't want it but I didn't not want it as badly as everybody else didn't want it. But I won't abdicate so Mogaba can rack himself up some glory."

"My conscience permits me to say no more. Even so, I feel like a traitor. He sent me because we've been like brothers since we were boys. I'm the only man left he trusts. I don't want to hurt him. But he's hurt us. He's blackened our honor and our oaths as guardians."

Sindawe's "guardians" was a Nar word for which there was no exact translation. It carried implications of an obligation to defend the weak and stand firm in the face of evil.

"I hear he's trying to stir up a religious crusade."

Sindawe seemed embarrassed. "Yes. From the beginning some have clung to the Dark Mother. I didn't realize he was one of them—though I should have guessed. His ancestors were priests."

"What's he going to do now? I can't see him getting excited about me turning up."

"I don't know. I'm afraid he'll claim you're not you. He may even believe you're a trick of the Shadowmasters. A lot of men thought they saw you killed. Even your standardbearer."

"A lot of men saw me hit. If anyone questioned Murgen closely they know I was alive when he left me."

Sindawe nodded. "I remain on the horns."

Croaker did not ask what would happen if he tried

to eliminate Mogaba. The Nar would fight, Sindawe included. That was not his style, anyway. He did not eliminate a man because he was a nuisance.

"I'll come over and confront him, then. He'll either accept me or he won't. It'll be interesting seeing where the Nar stand if he chooses mutiny."

"You'll exact the penalty?"

"I won't kill him. I respect him. He's a great soldier. Maybe he can continue to be a great soldier. Maybe not. If not, he'll have to give up his part in our quest."

Sindawe smiled. "You're a wise man, Captain. I'll go tell him. And everyone else. I'll pray the gods remind him of his oaths and honor."

"Fine. Don't dawdle. Since I don't want anything to do with this I'll be over as soon as I can."

"Eh?"

"If I put off doing something unpleasant I never get around to dealing with it. Go. I'll be right behind you."

Chapter Seventy

Longshadow consulted the shadows he had left in the cell with the missing woman. Then he visited the bedridden Howler. "You idiot. You grabbed the wrong woman."

Howler did not respond.

"That was Soulcatcher." *Her*. And *whole*. How had she managed that?

In a voice little more than a whisper, Howler reminded, "*You* sent me there. *You* insisted Senjak was in Taglios."

And what did that have to do with the result? "You couldn't scout the situation well enough to find out we'd been deceived?"

Contempt, poorly veiled, flashed across Howler's face. He did not argue. There was no point. Longshadow never made a mistake. Whatever dismayed him, it was always another's fault.

Longshadow pitched a tantrum. Then he went coldly calm. "Error, no error, fault, no fault, the fact is we've made an enemy. *She* won't bear it. She was just playing with her sister before. Now she won't be playing."

Howler smiled. He and Soulcatcher were not beloved of one another. He rasped out, "She's walking."

Longshadow grunted. "Yes. There is that. She's in my territories. Afoot." He paced. "She'll hide from my shadow eyes. But she'll want to watch the rest of the world. I won't look for her, then. I'll look for her spies. The crows will lead me to her. And then I shall test us both."

Howler caught the timbre of daring in Longshadow's voice. He was going to try something dangerous.

Disasters had knocked the daring out of Howler. His inclinations were toward the quiet and safe. That was why he had chosen to build his own empire in the swamps. They had been enough. And nothing anyone wanted to take away. But he had succumbed to seduction when Longshadow's emissaries had come to him. So here he was easing back from the brink of death, alive only because Longshadow still thought him useful. He was not interested in more risks. He would return to his sloughs and mangroves happily. But till he fashioned some means of flight he would have to pretend interest in Longshadow's plans. "Nothing dangerous," he whispered.

"Not at all," Longshadow lied. "Once I find out where she is the rest is easy."

Chapter Seventy-One

Volunteers willing to cross the lake with Croaker were few. He accepted Swan and Sindhu, rejected Blade and Mather. "You two have plenty to do here."

Three of them in a boat. Croaker rowed. The others did not know how. Sindhu sat in the stern, Swan in the bow. Croaker did not want the wide man behind him. That might not be wise. The man had a sinister air and did not act friendly. He was biding his time while he made up his mind about something. Croaker did not want to be looking the wrong way when that happened.

Halfway across Swan asked, "It serious between you and Lady?" He chose Rosean, the language of his youth. Croaker spoke the tongue, though he had not used it for years.

"It is on my side. I can't say for her. Why?"

"I don't want to stick my hand in where I'm going to get it bit off."

"I don't bite. And I don't tell her what to do."

"Yeah. It was nice to dream about. I figure she'll forget I'm alive as soon as she hears you still are."

Croaker smiled, pleased. "Can you tell me anything about this human stump back here? I don't like his looks."

Swan talked for the rest of their passage, evolving complex circumlocutions to get around non-Rosean words Sindhu would recognize.

"Worse than I thought," Croaker said as the boat reached the city wall where part had collapsed and left a gap through which the lake poked a finger. Swan tossed the painter to a Taglian soldier who looked like he had not eaten for a week. He left the boat. Croaker followed. Sindhu followed him. Croaker noted that Swan placed himself so he could watch Sindhu. The soldier tied the boat up, beckoned. They followed him.

He led them to the top of the west wall, which was wide and unbroken. Croaker stared at the city. It was nothing like it had been. It had become a thousand drunken islands. A big island marked its heart: the citadel, where they had dispatched Stormshadow and Shapeshifter. The nearer islands sprouted spectators. He recognized faces, waved.

Ragged at first, beginning with the surviving non-Nar he had brought to Taglios, a cheer spread rapidly. The Taglian troops raised their "Liberator!" hail. Swan said, "I think they're glad to see you."

"From the looks of the place they'd cheer anybody who might get them out."

Streets had become deep canals. The survivors had adapted by building rafts. Croaker doubted anyone travelled much, though. The canals were choked with corpses. The smell of death was oppressive. Plague and a madman tormented the city and there was nowhere to dispose of bodies.

Mogaba and his Nar came marching around the curve of the wall, clad in all their finery. "Here we go," Croaker said. The cheering continued. One raft, almost awash under the weight of old comrades, began laboring toward the wall.

Mogaba halted forty feet away. He stared, his face and eyes smoldering ice. "Say me a prayer, Swan." Croaker moved to meet the man who wanted so badly to be his successor. He wondered if he would have to play this out again with Lady. Assuming he survived this round.

Mogaba moved to meet him, taking stride for stride. They stopped a yard apart. "You've done wonders with nothing," Croaker said. He rested his right hand upon Mogaba's left shoulder.

Sudden silence gripped the city. Ten thousand eyes watched, native and soldier alike, knowing how much hung on Mogaba's response to that gesture of comradery.

Croaker waited quietly. It was a time when almost anything said would be too much said. Nothing needed to be discussed or explained. Everything hinged on Mogaba's reaction. If he reciprocated, all was well. If not . . .

The men looked one another in the eye. Hot fires burned within Mogaba. Nothing showed on his face but Croaker sensed the battle within him, his ambition against a lifetime of training and the obvious will of the soldiers. Their cheers made their sentiments clear.

Mogaba's struggle went on. Twice his right hand rose, fell back. Twice he opened his mouth to speak, then bit down on ambition's tongue.

Croaker broke eye contact long enough to examine the Nar. He tried to send an appeal, Help your chieftain.

Sindawe understood. He fought his own conscience a moment, started walking. He passed the two, joined the old members of the Company forming up behind Croaker. One by one, a dozen Nar followed.

Mogaba's hand started up a third time. Men held their breaths. Then Mogaba looked at his feet. "I can't, Captain. There is a shadow within me. I can't. Kill me.''

"And I can't do that. I promised your men I wouldn't harm you no matter your choice."

"Kill me, Captain. Before this thing in me turns to hatred."

"I couldn't even if I hadn't promised."

"I'll never understand you." Mogaba's hand fell. "You're strong enough to come face me when for all you knew you'd be killed. But you're not strong enough to save the trouble sparing me will cost."

"I can't snuff the light I sense in you. It may yet become the light of greatness."

"Not a light, Captain. A wind out of nowhere, born in darkness. For both our sakes I hope I'm wrong, but I fear you'll regret your mercy." Mogaba took a step backward. Croaker's arm fell. Everyone watching sighed, dismayed, though they had had little hope of rapprochement. Mogaba saluted, wheeled, marched away followed by three Nar who had not crossed over with Sindawe.

"Hey!" Swan yelled a moment later, breaking the silence. "Them bastards is stealing our boat!"

"Let them go." Croaker faced friends he had not seen for months. "From the Book of Cloete: 'In those days the Company was in service to the Syndarchs of Dai Khomena, and they were delivered . . .' " His friends all grinned and roared approval. He grinned back. "Hey! We've got work to do here. We've got a city to evacuate. Let's hit it."

From one eye he watched the boat cross the lake, from the other he kept watch on Sindhu.

It felt good to be back.

Thus was Dejagore delivered and the true Company set free.

Chapter Seventy-Two

The Howler perched atop a tall stool, out of the way while Longshadow prepared. He was impressed by the array of mystical and thaumaturgic gewgaws Longshadow had assembled during one short generation. Such had remained scarce while they had been in thrall to the Lady and nonexistent under the rule of her husband before her. They had wanted no one getting independent. Howler had very little though he was free now. He had little need to possess.

Not so Longshadow. He wanted to own at least one of everything. He wanted to own the world.

Not much of Longshadow's collection was in use now. Not much would be ever, Howler suspected. Most had been gathered mainly to keep anyone else from having it. That was the way Longshadow thought.

The room was brightly lighted, partly because it was approaching noon beyond the crystal walls, partly because Longshadow had packed a score of brilliant light sources into the room, no two of which used the same fuel. Against an ambush of shadows he left no precaution untaken.

He would not admit it but he was terrified.

Longshadow checked the altitude of the sun. "Noon coming up. Time to start."

"Why now?"

"They're least active under a noonday sun."

"Oh." Howler did not approve. Longshadow meant to catch one of the hungry big ones to train and send after Soulcatcher. Howler thought that a stupid plan. He thought it unnecessary and overly complicated. They knew where she was. It made more sense just to hit her with more soldiers than she could handle. But Longshadow wanted drama.

This was too risky. He could loose something nothing in this world could control. He did not want to be part of this but Longshadow left him no choice. Longshadow was a master of leaving one no choice.

Several hundred men climbed the old road to the plain, dragging a closed black wagon ordinarily drawn by elephants. But no animal would go near the shadowtraps, however much it was beaten. Only Longshadow's men feared him more than they feared what might befall them up there. Longshadow was the devil they knew.

Those men backed the wagon against the main shadowtrap.

Longshadow said, "Now we begin." He giggled. "And tonight, in the witching hour, your old comrade will cease to be a threat to anyone."

Howler was skeptical.

Chapter Seventy-Three

Soulcatcher sat in the middle of a field, disguised as a stump. Crows circled, their shadows scooting over wheat stubble. An unknown city loomed in the distance.

The imp Frogface materialized. "They're up to something."

"I've known that since they started blocking the crows. *What* they're up to is what I want to know."

The imp grinned, described what he had seen.

"Either they've forgotten to take you into account or they're counting on you feeding me incorrect information." She started moving toward the city. "But if they wanted to feed me false information they would confuse the crows, too. Wouldn't they?"

The imp said nothing. No answer was expected.

"Why do this during the daytime?"

"Longshadow is scared to death of what might break out if he tried during the night."

"Ah. Yes. But they won't move till nightfall. They'll want their sending at full strength."

Frogface muttered something about just how much did he have to do to earn his freedom?

Soulcatcher laughed, a merry little girl's laugh. "Tonight, I think, you'll have done with me. If you can do a creditable illusion of me."

"What?"

"Let's have a look around this city first. What's its name?"

"Dhar. New Dhar, really. Old Dhar was levelled by the Shadowmasters for resisting too strongly back when they first conquered this country."

"Interesting. What do they think of the Shadowmasters?"

"Not much."

"And a new generation is at hand. This could be amusing."

When darkness fell the great public square at the heart of New Dhar was strangely empty and silent, except for the cawing and fluttering of crows. All who approached developed chills and dreads and decided to come another time.

A woman sat on the edge of a fountain paddling her fingers through the water. Crows swarmed around her, coming and going. From the shadows at the square's edge another figure watched. This one seemed to be a gnarled old crone, folded up against a wall, her rags clutched tightly against the evening cool. Both women seemed content to stay where they were indefinitely.

They were patient, those two.

Patience was rewarded.

The shadow came at midnight, a big, dreadful thing, a terrible juggernaut of darkness that could be sensed while still miles away. Even the untalented of New Dhar felt it. Children cried. Mothers shushed them. Fathers barred their doors and looked for places to hide their babies and wives.

The shadow roared into the city and swept toward the square. Crows squawked and dipped around it.

It bore straight down on the woman at the fountain, dreadful and implacable.

The woman laughed at it. And vanished as it sprang upon her.

Crows mocked.

The woman laughed from the far side of the square.

The shadow surged, struck. But the woman was not there. She laughed from behind it.

Frogface, pretending to be Soulcatcher, led the shadow around the city for an hour, took it into places where it would destroy and kill and be recognized and fire hatreds long and carefully banked. The shadow was tireless and persistent but not very bright. It just kept coming, indifferent to what effect it had on the population, waiting for its quarry to make a mistake.

The crone on the edge of the square rose slowly, hobbled to the palace of Longshadow's local governor, entered past soldiers and sentries apparently blind. She hobbled down to the strongroom where the governor stored the treasures he wrested from the peoples in his charge, opened a massive door none but the governor supposedly could open. Once inside she became not a crone but Soulcatcher in a merry mood.

She had studied the shadow carefully while Frogface led it about. That shadow had to travel all the distance between two points. Frogface did not. He could stay ahead forever as long as he remained alert.

Her studies had shown her how she might contain it.

She spent an hour preparing the vault so it would keep the shadow in, then another arranging a peck of little spells that should distract it so that, by the time someone released it, it would have forgotten why it had come to New Dhar.

She stepped outside, closed the door till it stood open only a crack, arranged an illusion that made her look like one of the governor's soldiers. Then she sent a thought spinning toward Frogface.

The imp came prancing, enjoying himself, taunting his hunter into the trap. Soulcatcher shoved the door shut behind it, sealed it up. Frogface popped into existence beside her, grinning. "That was almost fun. If I didn't have business in my own world I'd almost want to hang around another hundred years. Never a dull moment with you."

"Is that a hint?"

"You bet it is, sweetie. I'm going to miss you all, you and the Captain and all your friends. Maybe I'll come back and visit. But I got business elsewhere."

Soulcatcher giggled her little girl's giggle. "All right. Stay with me till I'm out of the city. Then you're free to go. Wow! I bet this place blows up! I wish I could see Longshadow's face when he gets the news." She laughed. "He isn't half as bright as he thinks. You have any friends over there who might want to work for me?"

"Maybe one or two with the right sense of mischief. I'll see."

They walked on laughing like children who had pulled a prank.

Chapter Seventy-Four

Pregnant.

No doubt about it. Everything fell into place once the physician gave me that word. Everything made sense. And nonsense.

One time. One night. It never occurred to me that that could happen to me. But here I am swollen up like a gourd on toothpicks, sitting in my fortress south of Taglios, writing these Annals, watching the rains fall for the fifth month running, wishing it was possible to sleep on my stomach or side, or to be able to walk without waddling.

The Radisha has provided me with a whole crew of women. They find me amusing. I come back from trying to teach their menfolk something about soldiering and they point at me and tell me this is why women don't become generals and whatnot; it is hard to be light on your feet when you can't see them for your belly.

The baby is an active little thing, whatever it will be. Maybe it is practicing to be a long distance runner or a professional wrestler, the way it hops around in there.

My timing seems to be good. I have gotten almost everything I have to record written. If, as the women promise me, all my fears and doubts come to nothing and I survive this, I will have five or six weeks to get into shape before the rivers go down and the new campaign season begins.

Regular messages come from Croaker at Dejagore, thrown across the river by catapult. It is quiet down there. He wishes he could be here. I wish he could be here. That would make it easier. I know the day that the Main is down enough to cross I will be on the north bank and he will be there on the south.

I am feeling very positive these days, like not even my sister can ruin things now. She knows about this. Her crows have been watching. I have let them, hoping it irks the devil out of her.

Here is Ram, back from his bath. I swear, the closer I get to my date the worse he gets. You would think it was his child.

He is scared to death that what happened to his wife and baby will happen to me and mine. I think. He has grown a little strange, almost haunted. He is terrified of something. He jumps at every little sound. He searches the corners and shadows every time he enters a room.

Chapter Seventy-Five

Ram was scared with good reason. He had learned something he should not have. He knew something he was not supposed to know.

Ram is dead.

Ram died fighting his Strangler brothers when they came to take my daughter.

Narayan is a dead man. He is walking around somewhere out there, maybe grinning that grin, but he will not wear it long. He will be found, if not by soldiers hunting men with indelible red stains on their palms, then by me. He has no idea how strongly my powers have returned. I will find him and he will become a sainted Strangler much earlier than he would like.

I should have been more wary. I knew he had his own agenda. I have been around treacherous men all my life. But never, ever, did it occur to me that, from the beginning, he and his ranking cronies were interested in the child developing within me instead of in me myself. He was a consummate actor.

Grinning bastard. He was a true Deceiver.

I never even chose a name before they collected their Daughter of Night.

I should have suspected when the dreams went away so suddenly. As soon as I had been through that ceremony. *I* was not the one consecrated there. *I* did not change. *I* could not be marked that easily.

Ram was only a yellow rumel man but he knew they were coming. He killed four of them. Then Narayan killed him, according to the women. Then Narayan and his band fought their way out of the fortress. All while I still lay unconscious.

Narayan will pay. I will tear his heart out and use it to choke his goddess. They do not know what they have awakened. My strength has returned. They will pay. Longshadow, my sister, the Deceivers, Kina herself if she gets in my way.

Their Year of the Skulls is upon them.

I close the Book of Lady.

Envoi: Down There

Incessant wind sweeps the plain of stone. It murmurs across pale grey paving that sprawls from horizon to horizon. It sings around scattered pillars. It tumbles leaves and dust come from afar and stirs the long black hair of a corpse that has lain undisturbed for generations, desiccating. Playfully, the wind tosses a leaf into the corpse's silently screaming mouth, tugs it out again.

The pillars might be thought the remnants of a fallen city. They are not. They are too sparsely and randomly placed. Nor are any of them toppled or broken, though some have been etched deeply by gnawing ages of wind.

And some seem nearly new. A century old at most.

In the dawn, and at the setting of the sun, parts of those columns catch the light and gleam golden. For a few minutes each day auric characters burn forth from their faces.

For those remembered it is immortality of a sort.

In the night the winds die and silence rules the place of glittering stone.

To Be Continued in *Glittering Stone*